KU-616-631

ALL FALL DOWN

ITA DALY

BLOOMSBURY

First published in Great Britain 1992
Copyright © 1992 by Ita Daly

This paperback edition published 1993

The moral right of the author
has been asserted

Bloomsbury Publishing Ltd,
2 Soho Square, London W1V 5DE

A CIP catalogue record for this book
is available from the British Library

ISBN 0 7475 1627 8

Printed in Great Britain by
Cox and Wyman, Reading, Berkshire

Without limiting the rights under copyright
reserved above, no part of this publication may
be reproduced, stored in or introduced into a
retrieval system, or transmitted, in any form, or
by any means (electronic, mechanical, photocopying,
recording or otherwise), without the prior written
permission of both the copyright owner and the
above publisher of this book.

1

'Calm down, P.J. – just calm down.' Noreen pulled the sheet taut, then raised it, a snowy yashmak, to hide her smiles. As usual most of the bedclothes were on the floor by morning, blankets and bedspread having listed during the night, slipping inch by inch over the edge on P.J.'s side.

Duvets had been forbidden the master bedroom at Villierstown House. In some of the guest rooms they lurked and in Annabel's pretty room two doors away a plump and pink specimen awaited her return, but P.J. would not countenance them.

'I'm not a bloody Alpine farmer, I don't need to cower under one of them yokes. We live in a temperate climate, thank God. Sometimes it gets a bit nippy and then we put on an extra blanket. I don't want to be found some morning suffocated under a load of duck feathers.'

Noreen watched her husband now as he struggled to insert a cuff-link. He caught her eye.

'I'm perfectly calm.'

'You're not. Think of your blood pressure.'

'There's nothing wrong with my blood pressure – never was. I've the blood pressure of a man half my age. I'm fit and healthy because I *don't* worry about every fiddle faddle, because I don't stop to think of my blood pressure or my heart beat or my cholesterol level every time I take a bite to eat.'

'P.J. –'

'And I wouldn't be getting so excited now – '

'Ha!'

' – if tailors and shirt-makers didn't make it so difficult to get on the inside of their bloody garments.'

1

'P.J. – admit it. You just hate getting dressed.'

'And does that really surprise you – really now? Look at me, Noreen.' He took a flying leap on to the bed and began to tear open the buttons on his shirt. 'You can see that in my case it is clearly a question of gilding the lily.'

She began, ineffectually, to push at him. 'I thought you said you have a breakfast meeting.'

'Begod, you're right. Here, help me to button up these damn things.'

As their fingers met she slapped his away and, catching both her hands, engulfing them in his, he kissed her mouth. 'I can't stay here – you're a source of temptation to me. I'll finish dressing downstairs.'

She watched the room settle after his exit. Door and window frames ceased to tremble, billowing curtains deflated into prim folds; even the pile on the carpet seemed to flatten.

She recognized the phenomenon, feeling its echo within her. Life without P.J. *was* flatter. Perhaps that was why she had wasted so many years, hanging round waiting for him to return. Time passed slowly in those circumstances, getting stuck in chunks. And then you woke up one morning and found that you were fifty.

Noreen had been fifty last Tuesday. P.J. had woken her at midnight with champagne and kisses and as she lay beside him afterwards she vowed that she would waste no more of her life. It was too valuable, too fleeting for that, and the only way to eke it out, to tend it, was to fill it with incident. From now on she would be busy, purposeful – she would find herself a job.

It was a revolutionary concept but she had tried the alternatives, failing to hit balls, both golf and tennis, falling asleep at good-cause committee meetings, watching as seeds refused to germinate and flowers refused to bloom. These were the prescribed remedies for boredom in the middle-aged wives of the wealthy, but Noreen was not so much bored as guilty and fearful: guilty that she took so much and returned so little, fearful as she watched her life with P.J. galloping past. So, as she had no aptitude for leisure pursuits and she had once enjoyed a job, she determined to find one again. But what would P.J. say?

Noreen jumped out of bed as she heard the skittering of gravel under the wheels of a car. The staff had arrived.

This was her little joke and she told it to herself every morning, hoping that it would make her feel more relaxed about the entry of Mrs Donovan and her daughter June, but she still liked to be safely installed in the bathroom before Mrs Donovan's key turned in the side door. Once inside, she could stay as long as she liked; in fact, Mrs Donovan expected her to linger. And she wasn't forced to run like a hen before June and her trundling vacuum cleaner.

She sometimes thought that all this prolonged bathing couldn't be good for her skin, that it must dry out the natural oils which could not be replenished by slashing Yves Saint Laurent bath oil into the water. But she had never got used to the idea of other women cleaning her house; she could not lie in bed or sit with her feet up while they got on with the work, so she lingered in the bathroom instead.

P.J. told her how foolish was this attitude and how well he was paying Mrs Donovan and her daughter, and P.J. was right and she was a wimp. Perhaps she should take an assertiveness training course . . .

Yah! She stuck out her tongue then smiled at herself in the bathroom mirror. She knew herself to be the envy of many women, with a phenomenally successful husband, who, even after he had made his first million showed no inclination to trade in his wife for a smarter model.

And she lived in a beautiful house and had two wonderful children. Yes, *two*. For Aubrey, whatever else you said about him, was undoubtedly a bit of a genius. And then there was her own darling Annabel.

When Noreen began to think of Annabel her face lost some of its rigidity and allowed you to see its prettiness. Even at fifty and with a jawline which had begun to sag, she still gave an impression of girlishness, the blue eyes wide with hope and surprise, the mouth not quite formed, vulnerable. When she saw her reflection, which it was difficult to avoid doing in this house, she could not herself evaluate her overly familiar features and it was left to Annabel to offer a soft reassurance: 'You look so pretty tonight, Mummy.' Or, 'You should always wear blue – see how it brings out your eyes.'

P.J.'s compliments coming as precursors could never be taken at face value.

Annabel would soon be home from school, and home for good this time. Noreen intended to make this a wonderful summer for

3

her, one that she would remember for the rest of her life. Maybe by this time next year she would have left home, but this summer would be hers, Annabel's summer.

Noreen slipped out of her robe and into the scented bath water. The skin on her face was covered by a pale, green, slimy substance which would harden to a dirty grey and which promised to cause the blood vessels to dilate and thus increase the flow of oxygen to the epidermis. This enhanced oxygen flow would fight off the free radicals and retard the onward rush of time. (Tarrying in other corners of her life, Time made a bee-line for her face.) The young woman who had sold her this face pack – for that is what we are speaking of – had seemed more like a doctor than a beautician, with her gravitas, her white coat and her large spectacles. She had spoken at such length and used so many terms which Noreen didn't understand that the efficacy of the product did not seem in doubt.

The shelves of Noreen's bathroom were filled with creams and lotions and ampoules, for the face, for the hands, for the throat. From this clutter she now plucked two small circles of lint impregnated with witch-hazel and these she pressed gently on to her eyelids. She sighed and lay back.

She was not a narcissist but she had to do something, stuck in this bathroom for hours every day. She should have been born rich or poor, then she would have known how to handle leisure. As it was, she had been born to thrifty small farmers, encouraged to make her own bed, polish her own shoes and earn her own living. In her provincial boarding school tennis of a sort was offered as an extra-curricular activity but the nuns had made it quite clear that fripperies such as this were not for girls such as she, girls who with a lot of coaching, hard work and luck might one day sit for the Junior Ex. examination and, if they passed, secure for themselves a career in the Civil Service.

She had surprised the nuns and herself by coming fifteenth in Ireland in the examination but her career had been short-lived. At nineteen she had met P.J. McGuckian and a year later they were married.

She had known from the start that he was an extraordinary man, hairy, vital and vibrant. On their second date he had told her, 'I'm going to marry you,' and for the next nine months he had courted her, pursuing her with boxes of chocolates, bunches of flowers and declarations of love. He also told her from time to time that as he respected women, he had no intention of laying a finger on her until they were married. And he had kept his word. On the wedding night, however, he made up for lost time.

Not being a complete innocent, she had been prepared for the willy, even in its puffed up and angry-looking state, but when P.J. started clothing it in a sheet of diaphanous rubber she had almost fainted. This was Sin, this was what the nuns had warned her about.

P.J. had shown great delicacy. Shoving the willy inside his striped pyjama bottom, he had slid out of bed and moments later was standing in front of her, a figure of substance and dignity decently covered by his Foxford wool dressing gown.

Concern for his discomfiture had overcome Noreen's embarrassment and she had suggested timidly that he might be cooler without the dressing gown. (Neither of them had realized that Tenerife was going to be this hot in December.) But P.J. had not flinched, and as sweat trickled down from his black curls he had flicked it away with a careless hand and set about convincing her that he was no moral slouch.

'No one has greater respect for the Church than me, pet.' P.J. had taken her hand. 'Of course I believe in the infallibility of the Pope, but there are some things that I have to make up my own mind about. In the personal area that is.'

Over the years Noreen was to grow familiar with such views but in the early 1960s they were revolutionary – to her, at any rate.

'I'm a sinner, pet, I confess it,' said P.J. McGuckian, 'and I confess that I've slept with plenty of women in my time. Clean ones mind you – you need have no fear on that score. But – '. He leaned over her and gently pinched her cheek. 'Did I sleep with you? Did I lay a finger on you? No, because I respected you, I made you my wife. I gave you my name and I've chosen you to be the mother of my children.'

Noreen's innocent heart had leaped with joy. What a relief! A lifetime of sheathed willies would have meant not only sin, it would have spelled out bleakly a childless marriage.

'Eventually.'

'What, P.J.?'

'I'm going places, pet, and you're coming with me. You know that I'm only in a small way now – '

'Oh no.' A building contractor who stamped other men's cards did not seem particularly small to her. (P.J. did not in fact stamp anybody's cards but Noreen was not to know this.)

' – but I work like a nigger every hour that God sends. I'm not above mixing cement or lugging bricks or digging foundations. If one of my lads is out, I'll jump in and get on with the job.'

Noreen's eyes shone at this picture of a heroic and versatile husband.

'This is a great little country and it's just getting off the ground. I'm going to devote the next five years to building up my business and then I'll have the time to think about raising a family.'

'But P.J. – '

'Sure you're only a child and I'm not much more, we've plenty of time. I want to be able to provide for you and for my children. I don't want these little hands,' he paused to kiss them, 'red and chapped from washing nappies. I married you to give you a better life, not a worse one.' He took off his dressing gown, got into bed and turned off the light.

Noreen snuggled up to him. 'But, P.J. – what about, you know, natural methods?' She had only a hazy notion of what this actually meant for the nuns had been discreet to the point of obfuscation.

'Pet, listen to me, put that right out of your mind. It's all a load of rubbish. Anyway . . . didn't I tell you I respected you?'

'Yes.'

'Well then.' He was silent for a few seconds. 'There are certain things about the female person which are, I believe, private and personal. Unto themselves, so to speak. All that so-called natural stuff. I don't want to have to start asking you about whether you've had your – pardon me for mentioning it – your period or not.'

Noreen felt herself blush in the darkness.

'It's best for you not to worry about these things, pet. Leave all that to me. You promised to love, honour and obey – didn't you?'

'Yes, P.J.'

'Well then. The priest can hardly blame you for doing what your husband tells you – can he now?'

That night Noreen fell in love with P.J. McGuckian all over again. He was the hero of all the romances she had ever read, so considerate yet so accomplished. She stretched out tentative fingers to stroke the hair on his back, sniffing the strange, beguiling male smell. And her instinct told her that the nuns had been wrong on one count anyway. If P.J. had come to their wedding bed a virgin as she was it would have been a much less pleasurable occasion.

Noreen suddenly shivered in the cooling bath water. As usual, she had lost herself once she had started to think about P.J. She turned on the hot tap and switched on a transistor radio which stood on a marbled alcove beside the bath. She had already missed fifteen minutes of the Al Brown show and she liked to listen every morning.

Yesterday he had been lecturing the nation on its lack of backbone and today he would get telephone calls from every county; he would be lambasted and praised, given advice and told what to do with himself. His radio show went out five mornings a week and on Sunday night he had a two-hour television show – 'Brown Sunday'.

Everyone listened to him. In council estates and rural villas, on car radios and in corner shops, people tuned in and listened. Infant children lisped Al Brown before they learned to say Dada; husbands grew apopleptic, then worried when informed that Al did not approve of some less-than-pleasant personal habit. He was an opinion former, a mould breaker, a bloody old woman. He told the people what they thought before they themselves had become aware of it. He was the Id of the nation, disapproved of only by some university graduates and staunch Republicans who thought him above himself and a sleeveen, respectively.

This morning he was listening to a desperate woman from Galway who had reached the end of her tether and the point of exhaustion through her husband's insistence on always having sex standing up. He was a cyclist and he maintained that any other position was injurious to his knees. What was she to do?

Noreen smiled and closed her eyes.

In the kitchen, Mrs Donovan took a swipe at June and tried to grab her ear-phones. Her daughter sat at the kitchen table, idle and dreamy eyed. She was not listening to Al Brown.

'Get them things off and go up and start on the bedrooms

and don't take all day. I want you back here to help with the veg.'

Mrs Donovan had a tough time with June, who seemed to have missed out completely on her mother's work ethic. Lazy, spoilt and devious, she grew more like her father every day.

Mrs Donovan was conscious of her luck in having such a good position and she had respect for her employers – especially the boss. One of God's own gentlemen, that man. No airs and graces, always considerate and not above cracking a joke in the kitchen. She had worked for him for fifteen years now and eventually, when she retired, June could take over, if she minded her Ps and Qs . . . or her P.J.s.

Mrs Donovan tittered at her joke.

She would have a pension when she retired, the boss had said so. Not that she intended to retire for many a year, if God spared her. She enjoyed her work, keeping so many nice things in tip-top condition: cleaning the silver, polishing the Waterford glass, starching the damask table-cloths. Most of all though, she enjoyed the cooking. The boss had introduced her one day as 'our cook housekeeper' and she had liked the sound of that.

Of course, when they had big dos they got the caterers in. Not that Mrs Donovan thought much of the muck they served up – everything covered in shiny sauces and the orifices of fish and fowl obscenely stuffed with fruit and vegetables.

She knew for a fact that the boss didn't like it either – she knew what he liked and he got it from her. A nice bit of haddock now, with parsley sauce and floury potatoes; a well-done roast of beef; a chicken roasted and stuffed with a mixture of breadcrumbs, onions, sage and thyme. No mucking about, just plain, wholesome, well-cooked food.

Mrs Donovan's mouth began to water as she thought of such delicious fare. She got out her Maura Laverty cookery book and began to thumb through the well-worn pages. Mrs Donovan was not influenced by culinary fashions and fads, and over the years she had remained faithful to Maura Laverty. She swore by the woman, a woman who never messed you about and who knew moreover that rice was something that you cooked with sugar and milk and perhaps cinnamon, but never – God save the mark – with anchovies.

Vicious little brutes, Mrs Donovan wouldn't have them in

her kitchen under any circumstances; although she *had* been a late convert to garlic. And if you chewed the stalks of parsley afterwards, not a hint of a smell would linger on your breath. Not that it made much difference to her: the only flesh Mr Donovan had shown any interest in this past ten years was horse flesh.

All the more reason to be grateful for a good job. Mrs Donovan, a valiant woman and an artist, began to hum to herself as she thought how the boss's eyes would light up tonight as he saw what she would set before him.

2

Cars were backed up the entire length of Harcourt Street. It was always the same on a wet morning when, it seemed to Aubrey, every idle housewife in Dublin decided to drive into town and thus make a bad situation worse.

He turned now and glared at an example of the species who sat placidly buffing her nails, innocent of Aubrey's mounting irritation. Sighing, he turned on his radio. Al Brown welcomed him back and inquired if Breda was still there.

Breda was clearly certifiable, raving on about fish oils and energy levels, but Al might have been conversing with a Monsignor, making arrangements for his father's funeral, so serious and civil were his retorts and interjections.

Aubrey had very little time for Al, but he had to give it to him – the man was a pro. He had the women of Ireland eating out of his hand, and the more he chastised them the more they loved it.

Aubrey himself was pretty cheesed off with women at this point in time. They seemed to come only in two varieties – does and vixens. Initially, the does were fine: they listened to a man, laughed at his jokes and were usually pliant in matters of sex; but my God, how wearisome were their protestations of everlasting love after the second date. A fellow didn't know where he was with one of them. You picked up a siren in a night-club, all slinky dressing and come-hither eyes, and before the semen was dry she had become all soft and sappy. Just as you were thinking that it was time to move on, she began to clutch pathetically at your arm, stumbling after you like a Muslim wife. You could almost see the milk leaking from her boobs, and those eyes no longer shone with lust but at the expectation of a cosy semi and Horlicks in front of the natural

10

gas fire. (Dubliners, like other city dwellers, had become worried about pollution.)

The vixen, on the other hand, had been badly affected by a virulent strain of Hiberno-feminism. She downed pint after pint of Guinness, dressed in ugly tracksuits and dirty trainers and argued incessantly. She offered little in the way of reassurance or even friendship, the dirtiest word in her vocabulary being tenderness. Aubrey was partial to a little tenderness, particularly as dawn broke over the Dublin skyline and man (even such as Aubrey) was forced to face his own mortality.

Aubrey McGuckian was a more refined, less hirsute version of his old man. He spoke with tight, south Dublin vowels, slightly prissy but cultured. His laugh was light, musical and insincere, and his face in repose tended towards petulance.

At twenty-six he had made an impression on his native town for he had already established himself as one of its more controversial architects. He had always known he would be an architect, for he had grown up with buildings, watching from his high chair his father's empire expand. At school his drawings had all been of buildings – plans and elevations and more plans; no matter what *objet* was placed in front of him he would doggedly plough on his own geometric way, knowing that this was what would please his daddy.

On leaving university he had joined the family firm and thrown himself with delight into the task of designing office blocks and shopping malls – houses were not being built much in these days for the Irish had at last got their fertility under control. He moved out from home and into a flat, the better to meet P.J. on a man-to-man basis, and he set about injecting a bit of style into P. J. McGuckian plc.

Aubrey was a devout modernist; it was an article of faith with him; he would have no truck with the creeping revisionism he saw all round him, the softening of attitudes which was becoming endemic. By the mid-1980s modernism in Dublin, as in other cities throughout the world, was in crisis. Architects suddenly seemed to lose their nerve and hear, for the first time, the anguished cry going up from the man in the street: 'We don't like what you are building.'

It must be said that the man in the street was an uncultured clod who knew nothing about architecture but who was most

11

vociferously in touch with his own likes and it was uncertain why the architectural world should now hear him. Architects, after all, were people who knew about these things, who could talk with aplomb of brutalism and organic buildings. Why else would we have subsidized their long years in colleges here and there if it were not so that they could tell the rest of us what we liked?

Suddenly, none of this seemed to matter. An unbecoming humility began to make its appearance among the ranks of this once arrogant professional class. What you want you will get, became the new motto. Curtain walls were disguised and tricked out in an assortment of Edwardian and Victorian flourishes; all over the city there spread a rash of red-brick campaniles. Cognizance was taken of the height of existing buildings so that the only possible word to apply to these late twentieth-century in-fills was squat.

Dullsville, said Aubrey McGuckian, turning back to the drawing board. Ersatz rubbish. He did not defend the architecture which had gone up in Dublin over the past twenty years, an era which had managed to combine offensiveness with timidity. Like the supporters of Christianity and Communism, his war cry was 'It has not yet been tried.' Meaning, in this case, modern architecture . . . in Dublin, at any rate.

Aubrey was a disciple of Pei and other Harvard-trained architects who had suffered under the suppressive teachings of Gropius and who wanted to rebel against conformity, claiming the right to spontaneous expression. Buildings, Aubrey believed, should be exuberant not safe, joyous not mundane.

He set up his office on the top floor of P.J.'s building, innocently believing that he could teach his grandmother to suck eggs.

P.J. roared his disapproval, crunching the plans inside his huge paw and throwing them on to the floor.

'I asked you to design a shopping centre, for Christ's sake, not a cathedral. This is where the unemployed are going to come for their few slices of bacon. It'd be nice for them if they could find their way about, if we didn't have to issue road maps to them. Jesus – what do you think you're at?'

Aubrey cleared his throat. 'That's just it, P.J.' He had dropped the juvenile 'Dad' since coming to work here but had not been pleased either with the ring of 'Father'. 'I mean, that's what I mean – it's deliberate. It's supposed to have ecclesiastical overtones. These shopping malls, these *are* the cathedrals of the late twentieth century, these are where consumers come to worship. *This* is your modern world. You may not like it, I may not like it, but I am an architect, nonjudgmental. My role is to enhance these people's experience, to uplift them, not to patronize them, which, if you'll forgive me, is what you are doing, talking about their few rashers. They have a right to set the parameters of their own lives.'

He gave his head a little nod after this speech and stared boldly across at P.J.

P.J. shook his head in disbelief. A fool. He had fathered a fool.

'Listen, son,' he put an arm round his shoulder. 'It's like this. Sponduliks. Cost. I'm a businessman, not a patron of the arts. I'd like to be a patron of the arts, mind you, and I give value for money but I can't afford to be building glass staircases leading nowhere – '

'They aren't – '

'So cop on, son. Remember, I have to pay your salary.'

It was some ten months later that Aubrey had his dream of Palladio – nay, more a vision than a dream.

The uncharitable were later heard to say that the dream had been of P.J. telling him to wise up or else find himself out of a job. This was untrue. He *did* have a dream of Palladio.

The great man had taken him by the hand and walked with him through his Palazzo Chiericato, pointing out certain details to the dazzled Aubrey: the light airiness of the two-storey colonnade, the harmony of the rooms, the elegance of the entire structure. Then, turning aside, he had offered him a *cappuccino* and advised him to read again his *Le Antichità di Roma*.

Aubrey had awoken still in the grip of aesthetic pleasure. Pulling on a tracksuit, he had headed, not for the office but for a walk through Dublin, a voyage of discovery.

Where had his eyes been, he had asked himself, that he had until this moment failed to see the beauty all around him?

He stood in front of the Bank of Ireland and looked across at the façade of Trinity College; he stood in front of Trinity and looked back at the columns of the Bank of Ireland. He perched on a traffic island and surveyed them both from equidistance, oblivious of the fumes and noise, deeply moved by the beauty of stone. He sighed with pleasure, aware that his eyes were no longer smarting and gritty, mysteriously refreshed by the harmony upon which they now gazed. They had grown red and sore at a drawing

13

board where one foolish plan followed another, foetal deformities, aborted not by nature but by the will of P.J. McGuckian.

Who was not to blame, Aubrey now saw. Who was a victim, like his son, of a time lacking seriousness, where the architect was called on to design candle shops and hairdressing salons. Blaming the poor architect was like shooting the messenger. The invention of cavity walls surely foreshadowed the hollowness of lives played out against a backdrop of frivolity and emptiness?

As Aubrey trotted around the great eighteenth-century squares and terraces, he felt pleasure leaking away to be replaced by depression. Not much fun being an architect at such a time, born two hundred years too late, what was he to do? Give it all up and turn to making money like his father?

No – never that. Aubrey's face puckered at the thought of such humiliation, at the image of the smug gleam in P.J.'s calm grey eye. Never. Never. He would emigrate. He would stick with it. He would –

His father's image faded to be replaced by that of Andrea Palladio. In truth, this image had quite a look of P.J. about it, but cast with a more benign mien.

So that was the meaning of the dream, that was what Palladio had been trying to tell him. Build, Aubrey, build. Don't turn your back on your inheritance. You are my successor.

Pastiche. Aubrey took the word between his teeth, chewed it into its constituent parts and spat it out with contempt.

So Palladio's work was pastiche, as was the work of Inigo Jones and Lord Burlington; of Knobelsdorff in Germany, of Lovett Pearce, Gandon and Castle in Ireland. And who could deny the influence of the Parthenon on Le Corbusier?

One must work with the past, with respect for the past and recognition of the past. Andrea Palladio had pointed the way.

With this authorization, Aubrey now saw that his life's work would be in restoring his native city to its eighteenth-century splendour. It was a perfect size for such an undertaking, small in scale and yet undeniably a city, unlike Bath which could never be other than a town. And whereas much damage had been done, enough of the inner city remained intact to allow him to fulfil his vision. He called a press conference.

Now, overworked press people are not that easily summoned, and certainly the promise of more architectural babblings and

14

pronouncements hardly seemed like news. However, with a judicious word here and there, Aubrey let it be known that he would tell all. He would name names, spell out corruption, point the finger at fellow architects. He didn't even have to offer booze.

Aubrey did not deliver. He was too much his father's son to be indifferent to libel laws, but he did say sufficient nasty and malicious things about his fellow architects to keep the press people happy. When it came to accusing someone of lack of talent, he named names; he made no vague accusations, he was specific. He castigated his teachers one by one; he reeled off twenty mediocre buildings which had gone up in Dublin over the past fifteen years, analysing, with the aid of a projector and slides, the nature of their mediocrity. He wondered if the architects of the city were blind or wilful in their indifference to all the beauty which lay before them. And their general, overwhelming sin he found to be timidity, building half-skyscrapers, hybrid grotesqueries modern in skeleton but with unacknowledged nods in the direction of tradition.

A degree of truth and a greater degree of nastiness secured him the publicity he was seeking and an interview on the Al Brown show conferred on him a reputation for daring, a suggestion of the louche.

Although he had never been on radio before he was a natural for the medium.

'It seems to me, Mr McGuckian,' began the slimy Brown, cocky as ever and showing little respect for the professional classes, 'it seems to me that what you are advocating is a sort of regionalism. Would I be right there?'

Aubrey, quite sure that he had read more books on the subject than Brown, disposed of the interviewer with ease. And Brown, the professional, knew when not to argue back.

'I'm afraid, Mr Brown,' nobody called Al Mr Brown except when they wanted to make a point, 'I'm afraid that you don't understand the term if you accuse me of regionalism. I see nothing wrong with acknowledging Gandon and Castle. Or the Norman castle. Or the round tower for that matter. I'm Irish, I'm informed by my past – what's wrong with that? Because I acknowledge my heritage, because I don't shit on it, my buildings will be more truly international than those of the fuckers who are going around behaving like Frank Lloyd Wright's country cousins.'

This naughty language, coming over the airwaves, sent a frisson of delight down the collective spine of the listening public. Not that it was unfamiliar with such words; not that such words were not spoken nonchalantly in school playgrounds throughout the land. But it was a bit like picking one's nose in view of others, disgusting, shocking and rather daring.

The strange thing was that Aubrey, the private Aubrey, religiously eschewed such foul language. His public utterance had been deliberate, a stratagem to shock his audience into a state of attention. He had always despised P.J.'s casual swearing, seeing it as boggish, and now he had shocked himself a little by his ability to utter in public what he had never done in private.

He had finished the interview by declaring that he intended to set up his own firm and do his bit to protect the architectural heritage of his country. P.J., admiring his spunk, gave him his blessing and twenty thousand quid. And clients came tumbling over themselves to offer business. P.J. smiled and rubbed his hands: at long last his son was developing a nose. He decided that there must be something of himself in this mewling offspring, after all.

And there was, there was. The genes of destruction were strong. His idea of protecting Ireland's heritage did not encompass a lifetime spent patching up existing buildings. He would leave that to the timid and the talentless. He intended to put up spanking new replicas, true to the originals in every detail but better, because made with twentieth-century know-how.

In his humbler moments he compared himself to a modern dentist, viewing a Georgian streetscape as a dentist did the human mouth; identifying decay, eradicating it and filling the resultant gaps with perfectly matched crowns. He would crown the streets of Dublin, he would take from antiquity but build anew. He would raze and raise, elegant, ordered streetscapes so that in a hundred years' time people would talk about the neo-Palladianism; comparisons would be made between his work and the work of Richard Castle; theses would be written about him and his place in the architectural history of his country.

And who would sing of P.J. McGuckian? Who would remember him?

Sponduliks had been P.J.'s own tune and sponduliks now

16

became the undoing of his son. Aubrey found that there was a huge and ever-increasing gap between his vision and its execution, an enormous mouth that opened ever wider shouting 'Money, gimme more money.' Awestruck clients, losing some of their awe, became restive and began to talk of cash flow and budgets.

He had wanted to build real houses, red-bricked and stone-quoined. He had wanted, in the words of Inigo Jones, an architecture that was 'sollid, proporsionable according to the rulles, masculine and unaffected'. If his latching on to Palladio smacked of opportunism, a development of that nose which P.J. had celebrated, it was no less true to say that this style of architecture suited his personality, which sought reassurance in order, rules, structure. His puritanism responded to the restraint of the classical, and despite all the intervening flim-flam, the attitudinizing, the egomania, the resentment, in embracing it he was at some level being true to himself. His love affair with modernism had been no more than an adolescent infatuation, passionately felt but unsoundly based – it could not have lasted. And Palladio had rescued him from his folly and he would be true to the master for the rest of his life.

His clients, like himself, were men of culture. Reading about Aubrey, hearing him speak on radio they had sought him out. Aubrey was clearly a rising star and these men knew the benefits of reflected starlight shining into their lives.

They were of a kind, youngish, well dressed, well spoken. Aubrey identified them as the new Irishman – among whom he numbered himself – civilized, outward looking, a different breed from P.J. He felt at ease in their company, believing that they understood and shared his vision, that the proper restoration of Dublin was as important to them as it was to him.

It was a blow then to see them begin to shed their skins, to watch them emerge, mutant P.J.s, greedy, ignorant, telling him to cut the cackle and keep to the budget: they were not Medici princes.

Only in their clothing and their metaphors were they superior to his father apparently. Aubrey was so discouraged, so totally disillusioned, that he gave in without a fight. He was not therefore too surprised to find that his first project, a fine, sweeping terrace on the banks of the Grand Canal, was publicly ridiculed in the pages of the *Irish Times*. The article appeared under the heading, 'Looking for a job-lot in break-front pediments?' and was accompanied by a series of malicious photographs, each one highlighting some incongruity in the terrace, minor details which would not be visible to the passer by.

The writer had drawn attention to each one of Aubrey's modifications: the push-out P.V.C. windows, the pre-cast concrete used instead of granite for lintel and sill, the twin, kennel-like entrances hidden behind each fine Georgian door.

Although Aubrey didn't agree that these invalidated his original plan he did see them as aberrations, but surely the writer could tell that this wasn't his fault? That commercial demands, not lack of integrity, had forced these modifications upon him? Couldn't he tell the difference between Aubrey and the rest of them, who didn't know or didn't care?

Apparently not. Aubrey found himself lumped with the talentless, differentiated from them only by the extra malice with which he was treated in recognition of his status as a former star.

His clients became even ruder and more demanding and he was not mollified when Dublin Corporation slapped a preservation order on his terrace: Dublin Corporation was neither on the side of the angels nor the aesthetes.

He still had plenty of work but his lustre had dimmed. It was over a year now since anyone from a newspaper or radio had rung him up to ask for a quote or an interview. He felt he had been cheated in some way – given bad advice, been taken advantage of, and he didn't know whether to blame Andrea Palladio or P.J. McGuckian. In fact, of late the two had begun, alarmingly, to merge into one. Aubrey felt it was time he took a holiday.

The fug inside the car brought him out of his gloom and opening the window he saw a chance to extricate himself from the traffic jam. Flicking on his hazard lights, he put his gearshift in reverse and shot backwards up the momentarily empty outside lane. This was not strictly speaking legal, but nobody said boo to him, much less beeped a rude horn. Perhaps they admired his skill as they seethed damply behind their wheels. And it was too wet for a traffic warden or garda to be abroad.

He would take his mother out to lunch, if he could persuade her. Aubrey loved his mother, even if at times he lost patience with her. She was sweet and beautiful but it was difficult to forgive her for having had the bad taste to marry P.J.

He felt sorry for her. What did she do all day long in that big house, on her own most of the time, with P.J. out busy making his next million? Poor, sweet lady, was her son's reaction when he came upon her sitting idly in some corner of her mansion, twiddling her thumbs. And when there was company, she seemed annihilated, invisible in the bright reflection of her husband's glow.

She was too much of a wife and mother to win the approval of Aubrey, the egalitarian, the new man. Everybody had a career nowadays, even rich men's wives. And she was bright, she could find something to do. Aubrey didn't like feeling responsible for her but he knew that nobody else would. P.J. thought that it was enough to throw banknotes in her direction, expecting her to sit up and beg prettily when she wanted more. And she did.

By now Aubrey had worked himself into a state of exasperation with both his parents. Swinging on to a stretch of dual carriage-way, he put his foot on the accelerator and felt the Lamborghini move in shuddering response. He was beginning to wonder if she deserved being taken out to lunch.

As he swung into the avenue of Villierstown House, he started to feel more cheerful. The house always had this effect on him, its beauty soothing him and surprising him every time he turned off the avenue and on to the gravel sweep.

Despite the greyness of its cut-stone façade it gave an impression of lightness, for it had a trick of presenting itself as floating rather than resting solidly on its foundations. Two storeyed in front and three behind where the ground fell away, its many windows looked out slyly, deflecting the curious gaze, their panes of thin, eighteenth-century glass absorbing the light and returning to the world outside a gilded or smoky opacity.

The true glory of the house lay in the entrance hall, lovely, airy and full of light streaming down from the cupola above to fall on the black and white lozenges of stone which formed the floor. All the doors were of pale oak, more delicate than the usual dark mahogany of the period, and towards the back of the oval room a staircase curved upwards to the first-floor gallery. Ascending the staircase one was accompanied by pot-bellied, roistering cherubs and languid nymphs, gazing out through garlands of trailing flowers. Aubrey did not approve of the manner in which this stucco work had been painted by P.J., the main colours fighting for dominance, but he was in no doubt about the quality of the original work. Here was a stuccador whose spirit, anarchical and joyful, was still breathing forth after two hundred years.

The rooms to the front of the house, the saloon, dining room and morning room, were high ceilinged and long windowed and in these the plasterwork was restrained. The biggest room, the saloon, had a fine Bossi fireplace of inlaid marble and three windows reaching to the ground. All the rooms gave a sense of light and space, though this was mitigated by the clutter of furniture which filled each of them.

Shortly after moving into Villierstown P.J. had developed an interest in antique furniture. This interest had been prompted by the unease he had felt sitting in the vast, underfurnished rooms, thinking nostalgically of the cosier dimensions of his previous home. He had begun to poke around auction rooms, seeking out big, solid pieces that would put a dent in those empty spaces. Soon he found he was enjoying himself, travelling from auction to auction, finding bargains, outbidding or outsmarting the dealers. Each acquisition was borne home like a trophy, carefully positioned and then never moved.

The resultant jumble had turned the main downstairs rooms into obstacle courses, so that one moved around with caution. Even P.J., who moved like a dancer, occasionally found himself bumping into something and then he would roar for Mrs Donovan or June and order them to remove some innocent clock or vase that had been sitting harmlessly on a mantelpiece well out of harm's way. P.J.'s enthusiasm did not extend to ornaments.

Aubrey revved then cut the engine and let himself in through the white-painted double doors.

'Mother,' he called, dawdling on the staircase, letting a hand stray over a nymph's pointed bosom. 'Where are you?'

'Up here, in the bedroom.'

The double curve of the staircase and the height of the gallery off which they opened gave the bedrooms a feeling of remoteness, a sense of being cut off from the lower part of the house. Silence enveloped the first floor and Aubrey could feel it soothing him as he walked along the gallery and gazed down at the distant black and white of the floor below. He knocked at his mother's door, then bounded in.

'How's my favourite girl?' He kissed her fastidiously on both cheeks.

'Aube! How good to see you.'

Aubrey had forbidden the use of his baptismal name which he considered pretentious and ridiculous when coupled with McGuckian. From eighteen onwards he had decreed that he was to be known as Aube, and Aube he had remained despite the occasional confusion in foreign hotels where he found the most expensive suites assigned to him – the reception clerk expecting Awb Ma-guk-een to walk forth in Arab robes.

'You're having lunch with me – get into something indecent.' This sort of drollery did not come easily to Aube but he worked on it.

'Darling . . . I really don't know if I can. There's so much to be seen to . . .' The truth was that such occasions embarrassed her. She had been eating in expensive restaurants for over twenty years, she was known in many of them and in P.J.'s company she had always found eating out a pleasure. She liked wine and fancy food and the feeling of being pampered. She liked looking around at the other diners, at the style of the women and the comportment of the men. P.J. liked to take her out. He would walk into a room, slap the head waiter on the back and be shown to the best table. When the wine waiter approached he would tell him to bring 'Whatever you recommend, son, you're the expert.'

Everybody loved P.J., and not just because of his legendary tipping. He made people relax, cheered them up, bringing in with him from the street a whiff of excitement. Life was being lived wherever P.J. McGuckian sauntered.

With his son, eating out was an altogether more serious business. There was much careful studying of *cartes*, lengthy consultations with the wine waiter and referrals to a little black book on vintages which he carried in his breast pocket. And when the wine did arrive there was all that embarrassing sniffing and slurping.

She didn't feel up to that this morning. 'I really don't think I will today, Aube, if you don't mind.'

'I do mind.'

'But Aube – '

'But me no buts. I've got a table booked at Leo's.' He hadn't of course but Leo would not turn away Aube McGuckian. 'Come on, mother – I really need cheering up. It's raining and I've had a hard week. How can you turn me down?'

She couldn't.

'I'm going down to have a chat with Ma Donovan. I'll see you when I see you but don't take all morning.'

Noreen, who had never kept anybody waiting in her life, rushed now to the wardrobe to see what she would wear. Her new Paul Costello, cream linen, pleated, almost to her ankles. He'd like her in that. He was fussy about her appearance, disapproving of some outfits, making suggestions about others. She suspected that he didn't like her in anything too glamorous, preferring her to look restrained with a hint of county. Now P.J. on the other hand –

She laughed. P.J. never noticed what she wore. 'A fine looking woman like you – everything suits you.'

Guiltily she began to dress. There she was again, making comparisons. It wasn't fair to any son to have to live in the shadow of such a father. She should try to remember that when he irritated her. She remembered how fiercely as a small boy he had fought for independence; how furious he would become with her if she tried to help him tie a shoe-lace or peel an apple. He would struggle and struggle, red in the face from effort, before he would admit defeat . . . so different from Annabel who to this day would sit placidly and allow anyone to do anything for her.

She had never had to prove herself though, never had to compete for her father's attention. Had he loved her more than his son? Noreen thought it was rather that he had taken her less for granted.

When he had decided that it was time to start a family and she had got pregnant almost straight away, he had merely said, 'Good, it's time I had a son to take over – I'm beginning to feel tired.'

And perhaps there was more truth in that than the lightness of the remark suggested. The business had been going through a rough patch, he had been working late at night and every weekend. Perhaps he didn't have the energy to fuss over her pregnancy; perhaps his measured approval on being presented with his son, 'A fine big fellow', had denoted no more than exhaustion.

By the time Annabel was in her mother's womb the business was on a safer footing, expanding, and with a good foreman running things. P.J. began to read baby books, to take an interest in Noreen's pre-natal classes. 'Naturally I won't be in there when she's being born, I don't approve of that carry on. But you can be sure I'll be in to welcome her as soon as she arrives.' (As with Aubrey, he had correctly predicted her sex.)

He was as good as his word. He had stretched out a hand to the tiny creature, then withdrew it. 'But she's so small, so frail – I'm almost afraid to touch her. Ah, look at her hair, Noreen, and her little nose.' He gently stroked the nose. 'You're a jewel, that's what you are, a perfect little jewel.'

He had looked down at the tiny baby with an expression of awe on his face, and as far as Noreen knew, he had retained that feeling towards his daughter ever since.

The favoured offspring, the precious one; whereas Aubrey was something he flicked aside, as one would an irritating fly at a summer picnic.

And how poor Aubrey buzzed, constantly looking for attention, constantly dancing in and out of one's line of vision, by turns petulant and cajoling. If only he would learn to relax more, tone down his abrasiveness. Even Noreen could see how difficult it was to like him, so how must he appear to less partial eyes?

He had missed out completely on P.J.'s charm, P.J., the universally loved. 'A sound man', 'a decent skin', 'big hearted', was how the world perceived him, each phrase silently acknowledging the dodgy element in his make-up. P.J. had been on the fiddle for thirty years – dodging the tax man, cutting corners, seeking political preferment wherever he could.

Bribery and corruption was the name of the game, but it would be a poor-spirited creature who would complain when the man could not be judged by ordinary human standards and when he had such an abundance of virtue besides.

Literally he was larger than life, standing six foot six, with a broad, though perfectly proportioned body. His head was perhaps a shade too small but this, together with tight, black curls and dimpled chin had cast him in an antique mould. Ozymandias, King of Kings, came to mind as one looked up at P.J. McGuckian.

He was a man of the people, never losing the common touch. Effortlessly he fitted in, in the bookie's office, the snooker hall, the local pub. When he went to see his home county, Cavan, play Gaelic football he was there without condescension.

His largesse, although bestowed with discretion, was widely spoken of. He never endowed anything, leaving that to the publicity-seeking ex-Jesuit boys, but he helped many a widow, many an orphan, many a poor sod down on his luck.

Scandal could not touch him. A lesser man would have been destroyed by the Greendale affair but P.J. emerged from it, if anything, with an enhanced reputation. That was in the early days when he had been building new suburbs, rehousing, as he saw it, Dublin's poor, amidst green fields. Aubrey referred to these housing schemes as 'Los Angelesque sprawl' but P.J. had been proud of what he was doing. Money was tight however, and everybody – bank managers, planners, Civil Servants – everybody was on his back. His houses, even when new, could only be described as shoddy.

It was in one such house, on the new Greendale estate, that the tragedy had occurred. There had been a small explosion from some sort of bottled gas heater and the kitchen wall had collapsed, killing a five-year-old child. At the public inquiry afterwards, it was affirmed that the explosion should not have caused the collapse if the houses had been built to the designated standards and men with pale faces and pinched mouths turned accusatory eyes on P.J. These were the faces that made the laws, that met in the law library and club, whose features were familiar to one another since schooldays.

P.J. had stood up and stared back at them, passion glinting in his clear, grey eyes. 'What standards are you talking about?' he had inquired in ringing Cavan tones. 'The only standards I know is to build houses for the people. The only standards I know is that I had a leaky roof over my head and no arse in my pants until I was sixteen years old. The only standard I know is that I want something better for my people now.'

Nobody thought of this as *lèse-majesté*, for standing up there P.J. had become a sort of monarch, a republican, a tricoloured one – and if that sounded like a contradiction, well, who said there was anything simple about nationhood?

'Have I done wrong in maybe rushing things, in not wanting these poor people out in the street for another cold and bitter night? Then I'm sorry I've done wrong. I apologize to you and to the people of Ireland.'

Later, he had appeared at the funeral. Weeping and going over to embrace the sorrowing parents, he had sworn that it was all his fault, that he would blame no poor brickie or foreman, but that it would never happen again, God's truth.

The people of Ireland had taken him to their heart and even congratulated themselves that such human qualities, a thing of the past in England and America, still flourished so vigorously in their own little country. God be praised.

And his sorrow had been genuine, Noreen knew that. She had seen him disconsolate for weeks, not eating, sleeping badly.

'Imagine, Noreen,' he had said, 'those poor parents. Imagine if it had been Annabel.'

He didn't, however, seem to make any connection between the tragedy and his part in it. He seemed to view it as an act of God. Uniquely for one raised in such a Catholic country he had no sense of guilt.

He belonged to the tiny minority of the truly amoral.

Blaming P.J. was like blaming a tidal wave or hurricane. He had laid waste huge tracts of his native city; he was responsible for the ugliest shopping malls, the meanest office buildings, the shoddiest housing estates, and still he was universally and perenially popular. He attended weddings and funerals, he was a minister of the Eucharist at his local church, he had never lost his Cavan accent. So he had made himself a millionaire along the way – well, good luck to him. He was, after all, a credit to us.

How could the son of such a father grow straight and strong? Aubrey had spent his life darting here and there, trying to emerge from the paternal shadow. As a result he seemed chameleon, without substance. Noreen sometimes wished tht he would get out, leave Ireland, seek a life for himself where P.J. McGuckian was unknown. For though she could not really like him, her heart went out to him. Every time he trotted out a new achievement, every time his abrasiveness was condemned, every time his pomposity was sniggered at, she was overcome by pity for him and his plight. He worked so hard and so gracelessly at everything he undertook that even his achievements seemed belittled. He had been the youngest architect ever to qualify from University College Dublin, but P.J. hadn't seemed to notice.

It wasn't that he was unkind to his son. He had beaten him only once – on that occasion he had been found smoking cannabis at school (anybody else would have been expelled but the monks made an exception because of P.J.). It was just that P.J. didn't seem very interested. He never bothered to disguise that with him Annabel was the one who rated. Sweet, manipulative Annabel was the centre of his world.

Poor Aubrey! And now here was his own mother, reluctant to have lunch with him. Noreen changed her earrings for a more discreet pair and with a final spray of perfume on her wrist she fixed a smile on her face and determined to be a good mother, a smart companion, an awed audience for the next couple of hours.

In the kitchen Mrs Donovan was suffering Aubrey none too kindly, as he sat at her table asking her inane questions and stealing bits of carrot from her chopping board. Aubrey munched on, unaware of Mrs Donovan's displeasure as he gazed at June with thoughtful lust. And June didn't even see him there. Languidly she rubbed a little cloth across a silver sugar bowl, listening to Queen on her headphones, allowing the beat to swamp her. She dreamed of chocolate skin with a sheen to it and white, white teeth that bit you cruelly as passion rose.

Aubrey's teeth were tinged a faint yellow.

3

P.J. patted his stomach. 'Well lads,' he said, 'that was a good day's work.' His eyes swept the table, noting with satisfaction the empty toast-racks, the cleared breakfast plates with only a smear of bacon grease here and there. P.J. believed that the most successful business deals were always concluded on full stomachs. 'Anyone for more tea or coffee?'

'No thanks, P.J.' Raymond Clark smiled too, knowing for certain that he hadn't ended up with the thin end of the wedge. He had just secured nine acres of prime commercial land with outline planning permission for a shopping mall from P.J., and he had secured them, moreover, at slightly less than their market value. He had never done business in Ireland before but he had come over forewarned by knowledge of the crooked charm of the race and he would have been suspicious of P.J.'s generosity if it were not for his own feasibility study – this tallied with everything that P.J. had told him: the Irish economy was strong, unaffected apparently by the recession which had hit the UK. Interest rates were low, inflation was low, unemployment was falling. Dublin had a large population of young singles with plenty of money to spend; the land in question was in a vibrant part of the city with a healthy throughput of shoppers per day. There was no reason why the proposed development of shops, restaurants and possibly a leisure centre would not succeed. P.J. was obviously speaking the truth when he said that he hadn't wanted to sell but that over-expansion resulting in a hiccough in the cash-flow situation was forcing his hand.

'It's been a pleasure doing business with you, P.J., a real pleasure.' Raymond Clark had begun to stow papers neatly inside his smart black leather case. 'This is my first visit to Eire but it won't be my last, I can assure you of that. And do you know,' he glanced up to share the joke with P.J., 'I was nervous as a kitten coming over – can you believe that? And now I'm quite reluctant to be returning so soon to the mainland.'

P.J. didn't even wince, just nodded and smiled. He was quite prepared to ignore English obtuseness, especially in the circumstances. For fifteen years he had been putting together that nine-acre site which he had unloaded this morning. He had got his outline planning permission and had been about to apply for the full permission when he began to get a whiff of something off those city streets. Unease, disease, a loss of confidence which many shopkeepers were experiencing without yet having identified it to themselves. The fabric of the city could not support another shopping mall, for the heart of the city was dying, its arteries clogged up and furred with cars. P.J. would not put it like this but that is what he had begun to smell.

His nose had never let him down yet and he knew now that it was time to turn his attention to the new towns on the outskirts of the city, to start expanding there. He was delighted that he had rid himself of a site which would turn out to be a liability and not displeased that he had unloaded it on an Englishman. Not that he was a racist or a man of prejudice, it was just that the Brits sometimes got up his nose.

'I'm coming back,' Raymond Clark shouted from the taxi. 'And next time I'll bring Marilyn with me. She'd just love it over here.'

P.J. stood waving until the taxi disappeared round a corner and then he walked back into the hotel. It was one of the first hotels he had built and he often used it for business deals transacted away from the office. He sometimes had a drink there or a coffee, liking its modesty and unostentatious comfort.

He strode through the lobby and over to the reception desk. 'How do, Sharon.' Sharon, an old pal, smiled at him.

'Now remember, all Mr Clark's expenses come to me. Don't be sending any bills after that poor man.'

'Mr McGuckian – you should know us better than that.'

He was about to turn away when a poster over Sharon's blonde curls caught his attention. 'Tea dances. Begod. When did you start holding them?'

'Actually this afternoon's is our first, it starts at four o'clock.'

P.J. examined the poster. A woman in a long dress, her head thrown back, her body encircled by her partner's arms.

'And they're going to do proper dancing, Mr McGuckian – you know – quicksteps and fox-trots and tangoes.'

'My sort of dancing, girl.'

'Listen.' Sharon stood up. 'Can you hear the band? They're rehearsing in the ballroom now.' They both turned their heads. 'Would you like to have a look, Mr McGuckian? I'm finished here for the day, I'll show you if you like.'

They stood inside the door, leaning against the wall. On a platform a band was playing 'Jealousy' and strobe lighting moved swathes of colour across the pale, wooden floor. Sharon found herself moving to the music, conscious of P.J.'s body at her side. She had long had an eye for P.J. and she moved closer to him now, brushing his hand to hers, prepared to throw caution to the winds as the high, sweet notes of a tenor saxophone snagged her fancy. Following the lighting with her eyes she whispered, 'Would you care for a cup of coffee, Mr McGuckian? In my flat, like, just across the road.'

P.J. blinked, then stared at her. What had brought this on? She had never shown any inclination before. However, he had not achieved greatness by his indifference to gift horses so, 'Sound,' he said. 'But I think you need something more sustaining than coffee after your morning's shift. I'll just go and pick up a bottle of champagne in the bar.' Lassies like this one, he knew, liked a bit of flash.

He was an absent-minded lover, running abstracted fingers through Sharon's curls, his mind still focused on that poster.

He had spent his youth dancing, travelling ten miles to his first dance stuffed into the back of a Volkswagen beetle with five other boys. He had borrowed a suit, doused down his curls and taken five bob from underneath the china dog on the mantelpiece. He had never danced before but he had soon got the hang of it and by the end of the night he felt like a veteran.

Everyone had been dancing mad in those days. Every Sunday night you would find yourself travelling, sometimes up to forty miles, to a dance hall where the girls were beautiful or the floor was exceptional or the band was out of this world.

Dancing was the fount of pleasure of P.J.'s adolescent years.

For four years, during the Christmas holidays and all through the summer months, he had danced the length and breadth of three counties, keeping assignations, seeking out the talent, meeting up with his school pal and dancing companion, Canice O'Keeffe.

Together, hands in pockets, Canice slightly behind P.J., they would swagger into the hall, take up a position, start the old foot tapping and eye up the talent. The dance hall was where he had put the gloss on himself, learning how to chat up a girl, order a lemonade, light two cigarettes at once.

By the time he had met Noreen, he was a sophisticate of the dance halls, although she was the better dancer, he had to admit. And they had danced their way through the early days of their marriage until changing fashions had forced them to stop. Neither of them had ever fancied rock and roll.

'Do you know what it is, Sharon,' said P.J., sitting up in the narrow bed and banging his head against the plasterboard partition, 'I think I'll try one of those tea dances. I used to be a great dancer in my day.'

Sharon held her head and groaned. She was not used to drinking a half bottle of champagne before dinnertime. She managed gingerly to nod and tried to look interested.

'Where I was a youngster we didn't go in much for things like tennis or golf but, by God, could we dance. We often went forty miles to a dance and thought nothing of it. We used to – '

But Sharon didn't wait any longer, fearful if she did that she would get sick all over the only millionaire she had ever been to bed with. However, she was a well brought up girl and, clamping one hand over her mouth, she stretched out the other and turned on the television set before rushing out of the door.

P.J. yawned and turned indifferently to the television set, which was wedged in at the foot of the bed. He was looking to see how he could turn it off when life threw up one of those coincidences that no novelist would ever dare use. For there, staring out at him in lurid colour was the face of Canice O'Keeffe, Minister for the Arts in the current government and erstwhile dancing companion of P.J. McGuckian.

P.J. turned the knob marked volume. Canice was frowning, always a sign that he was exercising his intelligence. ' – and of course I was proud. But it brought home something else to me, and that is the unbroken European dimension of Irish life.' From

30

the concentrated set of his features, P.J. guessed that Canice was reading from a teleprompter.

'My sojourn in Trieste, the honour which was bestowed on me by the Italian government in inviting me to open the James Joyce House, made me aware all over again of Ireland's crucial role in European culture. From the time that we sent out our monks to Christianize Europe in the Dark Ages, to the time when James Joyce went to spread his wings and share his genius with, among others, the Italians, to today, when our well-educated young people travel abroad as guest workers, we, despite our island status, have been a most outward-looking, continental country.'

P.J. found the off button. Canice's feet had always been more impressive than his brain. He had excelled particularly in the fox-trot, bringing to it his own original repertoire of steps.

'What do you think, Sharon?' P.J. beamed at her as she lowered herself carefully on to the bed. 'Did I tell you that Canice O'Keeffe was my great dancing buddy in the old days? And who do you think I've just seen on the television – this minute? Canice O'Keeffe! What do you say to that?'

Sharon had combed her hair, washed her face in cold water and repainted her lips. She still felt rough. Seeing P.J. begin to manoeuvre himself out of bed she made an effort. 'P.J., stay where you are and I'll run you a bath. I could scrub your back for you and we could play this little piggy.'

P.J. shuddered. 'No time, love, I'll just have a quick rub down. You're a lovely girl, Sharon, but *tempus fugit.*' P.J. liked to keep his rudimentary Latin polished up.

Tomorrow Sharon would get a large bunch of florist shop flowers with a note enclosed saying, 'Thanks. We must do that again sometime.'

And they might, depending on fate and the exigencies of P.J. McGuckian's life.

Back in the hotel nobody sniggered as he walked up to the reception desk. Ireland had grown sophisticated and knew how to treat its millionaires. The manager, leaving a tourist, came over to him. 'Your bike, is it, Mr McGuckian?'

'Yes, someone said they'd keep an eye on it.'

'Yes, Liam. He'll get it straight away.'

'Good lad.'

Cycling through the lunchtime traffic, P.J. pondered on life and love and good fortune and dancing. They had done well, Canice and himself, despite their inauspicious start in life. Not many silver spoons in Cavan where they had both been brought up but plenty of guts and determination and that mattered more in the long run.

Had Raymond Clark been born with a silver spoon? P.J. doubted it; self-made was embedded in the callouses on his hands and in the creases around his eyes; but P.J. had no regrets in pulling the wool over those creases.

All's fair. And it might teach him that Ireland was not an island off the mainland.

P.J. could feel irritation begin to gather as he thought of the Brits and their superiority. He could feel at home in most places – he had wined in Rome, dined in Paris, had a quick fuck in New York and all with tremendous pleasure, but there was something about London that he couldn't warm to. He had seen himself walk out of the Connaught Hotel with porters bowing and scraping and the minute he had opened his mouth to ask for a taxi, he might as well have been a bloody nigger.

It was always with a sigh of relief that he left that city and stepped on to an Aer Lingus plane, to be greeted by a smile and a soft word. He could understand British hostility given the carry on up in the North but – did he look like a Provo? They didn't use their heads, that's what was wrong with the Brits. Just let them hear an Irish accent and off went the alarm bells.

He scooted through a red light and began freewheeling down the hill to his office. In the front plaza the fountain had been turned off and little landlocked fishes rolled bronzed eyes towards heaven. Things began to wind down around this time on a Friday as P.J. allowed people to trickle home early, knowing that by doing so he would get more out of them the following Monday. He might go home early himself today. He wanted to talk to Noreen, to tell her about the tea dances. Perhaps they would start attending them – he had liked that big-band sound.

Waiting for the lift P.J. did a discreet shuffle. He smiled. Twinkle-toes McGuckian would grace the halls again.

In a small office near the British Museum in London, Irishmen in general and Canice O'Keeffe in particular were exercising the mind of Jack Buchanan.

Despite his name he could neither dance nor sing and perhaps a parent's momentary playfulness at the time of his baptism was responsible for his lifelong misanthropy. Whatever the cause he had grown up despising the human race, and now, aged seventy, he saw no reason to revise his opinions.

He seldom thought about the Irish for there were too many irritants closer to home. When they did come to mind he dismissed them as violent primitives on a lower rung of the evolutionary ladder who should be secured in their boggy fastnesses where they might murder one another as they pleased. He felt the same way about Arabs and about the entire population of the African continent.

Today he was being forced to think of Irishmen because he had been weak enough to give in to Cassandra's wishes. Cassandra was his wife, the daughter of an earl and twenty years his junior.

She was a social animal who liked to spend her time roaming through crowded rooms as deer do through forests. There she would munch an olive, sip a glass of white wine, exchange a bright word and a brittle smile. Though her restlessness was acute she was a perfectly good-humoured woman provided she didn't have to spend two consecutive nights in her own home. She had never heard of the board game Monopoly, let alone played it.

In London she went out quite happily on her own but when they went to stay at their villa outside Trieste she liked Jack by her side, for though she adored Italy she didn't quite trust the Italians.

Thus it was that she had commanded Jack as consort when she went to the opening of the James Joyce House in Trieste. She didn't know who James Joyce was but a party was a party, especially in Trieste where the citizens were becoming downright stingy. Jack did know who James Joyce was – an enemy of the English language – but Cassandra had only told him that they were going to an itty-bitty party, home by ten, before bundling him into the car.

Jack had only one real enthusiasm in life and that was for the English language. He loved it passionately and every night he thanked God that he had been born an Englishman, given such an inestimable birthright. He was jealous of its purity and yet constantly amazed by its vigour, its extraordinary ability to survive. Even today in the mouths of the illiterate, the ill-educated, even amongst West Indians, its grace and beauty were apparent. Its richness, its flexibility, its accuracy were all sources of wonder

33

to him. It was to protect it that he had founded *The Champion*, a newspaper which would be a watchdog and standard bearer for the language. He had only extended its brief when he had come to realize that bad grammar and sloppy syntax were outward signs of moral degeneracy. Self-abuse, one could be sure, was paralleled by abuse of the language. Jack was not in the least surprised to learn that a junior Tory minister who started every other sentence with the phrase, 'Well, between you and I,' was also responsible for impregnating half the female research assistants in the House of Commons.

In his crusade Jack recognized neither class nor club: Church of England bishops, Radio Four announcers, trade union officials, city gents and *Guardian* journalists had all felt the lash of his pen. People bought the newspaper less to find out about the salacious behaviour of the famous than for the novelty of reading about this behaviour in restrained and mellifluous, slightly archaic, prose.

He believed that much damage had been done to the language because of the licence granted to the writers of prose fiction, particularly those writing in this century. And among these he considered that James Joyce gave the most offence. He thought him a humbug whose fondness for coprology and schoolboy puns, together with his ill-mannered showing off, his place of birth and his cavalier attitude to someone else's language, gave him pride of place among the linguistic deviants.

When Jack had realized that he was standing in the very house where that moral degenerate and charlatan had lived with his concubine, he had shot up off his chair, refusing all further offers of refreshment. He had folded his arms and backed towards the door, but there was no escape and he was forced to endure the lengthy rantings of Canice O'Keeffe.

Inevitably the man had misused 'hopefully' and had twice said 'oblivious to', but on this occasion Jack was more outraged by the content of the speech than by the manner in which it was expressed.

The best English in the world, he was informed, was spoken in Dublin; *Ulysses* was probably the greatest novel ever written. The Irish had rescued the English language in the twentieth century by injecting new life and wit into it. Without the contribution of Irish writers over the past three hundred years, English literature would have been a paltry thing.

As a final insult, Jack had been forced to meet O'Keeffe. Some smiling, venal Italian had clamped them together in a corner where Jack had stared at O'Keeffe with bulging eyes and constricted throat for rage had struck him dumb and paralysed him. But he could still hear and what he had heard was the audacious sound of O'Keeffe trying to put him, Jack Buchanan, at his ease.

Jack's rage had turned to pain and he had grunted at Cassandra who, seeing his empurpled face, had taken him by the elbow and helped him to withdraw, smiling her goodbyes with honeyed and practised charm.

In the car he thought he was having a stroke but Cassandra had found his flask and poured some whisky down his throat. This had revived him.

And today, a week later, he was sitting in his office, planning his revenge. He pondered which of the young louts in his employ he would send over to Ireland – someone with a head for hard drink. They were all qualified in that respect and their degree of literacy didn't matter for Jack subbed all copy.

A good digger – Thorpe, perhaps. The reputed religiosity of the race might mean that he would have to dig deep but Jack was sure that he would come up with something. Anyone with such a cavalier attitude towards the English language must be morally unsound. And that sort of puffiness around the eyes always denoted raging lust. Jack would not be at all surprised to find that he was not only voracious but deviant as well.

Pigs in the parlour, that's what the Irish went in for . . . in other rooms too, perhaps.

For the first time in a week, Jack began to smile. He lifted a phone. 'Get me Thorpe.'

4

Aubrey shot down his shirt cuffs, stretched his legs under the table and stared at his mother. 'I'm thinking of going to the States. I've been mulling it over and I've decided that it's time I went to check it out.'

Noreen smiled and squeezed his hand. Isn't this what she had been hoping for him, wondering about just this morning?

'Aube – that's terrific news. I've always felt you should travel while you're young and America's the right place for you. Remember that's where your father was born, in Chicago. I can see you being a big success in – '

'Mother – I already *am* a big success.'

'I know that, darling – '

'And I'm not talking about emigrating. I'm thinking of a holiday, for God's sake.'

'Oh.' She had put her foot in it again, as she so often did with Aubrey. He was looking hurt, concentrating on removing some invisible substance from his tie.

'Of course you're a success. It's just – Ireland is so small and you've done it all and still in your twenties. I mean – '

'No need to explain. Maybe I will look round when I'm over there.' He snapped his fingers at a passing waiter, causing his mother to wince. 'OK. Finish that off and we'll go.'

She pushed the glass of *creme de menthe* from her. 'I'm ready, Aube.'

In the car she tried to make amends. 'I wonder if you could give me some advice, Aube.'

'I can try.'

She waited until they had stopped at a red light. 'I'm thinking of going back to work.'

'You?'

'Well I'm not completely over the hill – or am I?'

He smiled at her, his good humour restored. 'Far from it.'

'The lights.'

'I can't imagine that the old man will be overjoyed.'

'No, but I think I can win him round.'

'Well congratulations, Mother. I didn't think you had it in you – '

'Thanks very much.'

'But – what are you goind to do? You're not thinking of going into competition with Mrs Donovan and the lovely June?'

'Aube – I'm serious. I was a very good Civil Servant until I married your father and I don't see why I shouldn't be able to find something if I put my mind to it. I decided on my fiftieth birthday that I had wasted enough of my life – '

'Wasted your life – my God, my own mother talking like Simone de Beauvoir.'

'And I like being busy and as Mrs Donovan won't let me lift a finger I'll have to find something to do. I am going to look for gainful employment.'

Aubrey began to whistle the first notes of 'Buddy Can You Spare a Dime?'

'So – what do you think Aube? Do you think I'm mad?'

'*Au contraire.*'

She had to be content with that until he drew up outside Villierstown. He turned to her and took her hand. 'I'm really glad, Mother. This has been no life for you, not since we've grown up at any rate.'

'It's been a wonderful life Aube and I've loved every minute of it. I'm not complaining, I just want to do something. Now, do you think I can?'

'Can you type?'

'I never learned, I didn't need it for the Civil Service.'

'That's the first thing you must do then – learn to type. Keyboard skills and computer literacy and you will be any employer's dream.'

'Aube!'

'I mean it. You are intelligent, diligent, loyal and good-looking

37

and what's more, I'm proud of you. I really didn't think you'd have the spunk.'

'Thanks, Aube.'

'And don't worry about the old man. If he doesn't like it he'll have to lump it. Anyway, I'm rooting for you.'

'Thanks for the lunch.'

'Be good.'

Mrs Donovan had the double doors open before Noreen had found her keys. She glared after the Lamborghini then turned disapproving eyes on her mistress. 'The boss rang, Madam. Twice.'

'Oh dear. The lunch did go on a long time. Did he leave any message?'

'No, Madam. Just that he'd see you soon.'

In the bedroom Noreen flung off her lunching-out suit and thought how much she would enjoy being away from Mrs Donovan's rigidity. Years ago Noreen had offered to help with little things, maybe make the beds in the mornings, but Mrs Donovan had been scandalized. As she had by Noreen's suggestion that they adopt first-name terms. She had explained to Noreen that it was her own status as cook-housekeeper that was at stake. Formality needed to be observed in order to emphasize the difference between her position and that of those women who flung on a nylon housecoat and went off to clean the brasses for some so-called career woman.

What would she say if Noreen now joined their ranks, becoming a so-called career woman herself?

Noreen could see a grand coalition between P.J. and Mrs D. They both seemed to have much clearer ideas on Noreen's role in life than she did herself. Standing up to their combined disapproval would be difficult but Aubrey was on her side and Mrs Donovan disapproved of her anyway and P.J. could be won round. It was all a question of tactics.

The problem was that she was not used to defying P.J., she was out of practice. Over the years she had fallen in with his wishes, not out of fear but because she had wanted to. People said that P.J. was a bully but he had never tried to bully her. The last serious disagreement they had had was almost twenty years ago, before Annabel was born. Noreen found herself smiling when she remembered the occasion – the time. A lost era.

How innocent we were then, Noreen smiled at her reflection in the dressing-table mirror. What an innocent world, striving so hard to be *demi-monde*.

P.J. and Noreen had sold their first house and moved to a bigger one on a housing estate in south County Dublin. It was a select estate of detached houses occupied by young families – wives who stayed at home with the children and successful husbands who went out to run their pubs and butchers' shops or to sell insurance or expensive motor cars. None of them was as successful as P.J. McGuckian.

Those were heady days in Ireland, particularly in suburban Dublin where the new middle class was putting a toe in the water and finding it pleasantly warm. When the fiftieth anniversary of the 1916 Rising came around, it really seemed worth celebrating. Ireland had justified its independence at long last.

After the disillusion of the twenties, the poverty of the thirties, the long, grey years of the Second World War with Ireland hermetically sealed in neutral isolation, after the depression and the mass emigration of the fifties, the sixties broke in sunshine and hope.

It was a worldwide phenomenon, but it caused more dislocation in Ireland, a country unused to change, unprepared for the displacement of certainties and moral codes. An English poet was to declare ironically that sex had been invented by the Beatles in 1963, but when an Irish politician stated that there had been no sex in Ireland before the advent of television he spoke without irony and many people agreed with him.

What television managed to do was to vulgarize sex, as it vulgarized many other aspects of people's lives. As images of other worlds were beamed into kitchens and living rooms every night, a wave of self-consciousness swept the country followed by something very like shame. Everything about Ireland seemed suddenly old fashioned and dull, but behold, we now had the means of changing this. All we had to do was imitate as best we could what we saw on our television screens and life would be changed for ever.

Science and the Catholic church also held out the possibility of earthly happiness. As men began to grow their hair and women to shorten their skirts, as the Latin Mass disappeared, priests in confession gave husbands permission not only to indulge in sex, which they had always given grudgingly, but to take pleasure in it. And their wives were told that they might use the contraceptive pill.

From being a cross to bear life became a pleasure to enjoy. With more money around, people began to furnish their houses with cheap and cheerful stuff that they would throw out and replace in a few years' time. Motor cars became a commonplace and alcohol was what you were offered when you paid a visit – even at four o'clock in the afternoon, even though Christmas was months away. Package holidays became popular, tea was renamed dinner and people began to smile more. Couples became the social norm as wives began to accompany their husbands to the pub.

A great, grey cloud had momentarily lifted off the island and the Irish gazed at the sun, dazzled. There was a feeling of daring and excitement about, an innocent assumption that life had suddenly become permanently sweet. Even elderly parents who had missed the boat smiled now at their children's frolics.

On the estate where P.J. and Noreen lived and where people thought themselves a cut above the *hoi polloi*, there was a reckless determination to get rid of the baby with the bath water. Husbands and wives stared in disbelief at the black and white photographs from their youth, noting the ill-fitting clothes and anxious expressions of their parents, noting their own childish bashfulness in the face of the camera, the timidity with which they clung to their mothers' skirts.

Their children would not grow up thus. They would be nurtured by frankness and liberty. Parents owed it to their children to be happy and fulfilled, not to live their lives as *their* parents had, through them. Unshackled by the weight and gloom of the past, these people would possess the present. They would live life, they would reject guilt, above all they would embrace the modern.

Happiness seemed suddenly attainable and in the resultant stampede to grab it common sense was swept away. Foolishness became endemic as a hardy, peasant race found itself adrift on a pleasure cruiser.

The mild hysteria was exacerbated by a run of hot summers in the early 1970s. In the constant sunshine, the sense of unreality was reinforced so that Dublin seemed like California, a mirror image of the world that appeared nightly on television screens.

Noreen and P.J. bought a barbecue, then a neighbour followed suit. Soon Saturday evenings were full of the sounds of the emerging middle classes at play and the smell of charred beef.

Children grew tanned and tractable, wine and beer were spilt on otherwise parched grass, exposed flesh grew silky under the repeated applications of Ambre Solaire and Noreen started to shave her legs.

The carry-on started in the McHughs' house; Noreen remembered precisely the night of its initiation.

The friends and neighbours had got into the habit of adjourning to the McHughs after the barbecues had been put away and the children tucked up in bed. The McHughs had no children and lived in the biggest, corner house on the estate. It seemed a good idea to keep the party going in their house and so safe did the parents feel that most nights they didn't even bother getting a babysitter. Every twenty minutes or so one of them would scoot around all the houses to see that everything was OK.

'Right,' said James McHugh on that fateful night, when they had all drunk a bit too much and when Noreen was beginning to yawn. 'Now we're going to play a game of musical chairs, two teams – girls and boys.'

And so it had begun. The first night as each couple dropped out they had stayed around the house or garden, finding some quiet corner for a snogging session. Noreen had ended up with Gerry Higgins, a limp and sloppy kisser who was inclined to belch. By going-home time she had decided that the whole thing was silly but harmless. She thought no more about it until the following Saturday night as they were setting out for the McHughs when P.J. had inquired, almost *en passant*, 'Have you changed the sheets?'

She stared at him, puzzled. 'I changed them on Wednesday, you know that's my day for changing the sheets.'

'Oh, I think fresh ones. Come on, we'll do it together.'

She caught at his jacket as he bounded up the stairs. 'P.J., what are we changing the sheets for? I made the bed this morning, there's nothing wrong with – '

'Now, pet,' he turned to her, placing a hand on her shoulder, 'you know what this is about as well as I do.'

'I do not.'

'Come on, Noreen – a bit of fun. Last Saturday could be described as a practice run.'

Fun? She remembered Gerry's slack, wet lips fumbling around

her face; and Jim Ryan had bad teeth. 'You mean – further than last week? Go to bed with them?'

'A bit of fun.'

'No. I won't do it.'

'Ah, come on, pet. We're living in the nineteen seventies and it's only a bit of sport. What do you say – for the crack?'

'What about the others, the wives, what do they think?'

'I've told you – a bit of sport. There's no need to make such heavy weather out of it, pet.'

She remembered how her feet had dragged along the rough cement of the pavement as they had walked the few yards to the McHughs' house. She had drunk more wine than usual but had only succeeded in giving herself a headache while remaining uneasily sober. Finally, when partners were being sorted out she had been given one of the nicer men, a quiet, gentle fellow, the father of twin daughters.

Without even bothering to see whom P.J. had ended up with, she had led her partner home, up the stairs to her bedroom with its waiting bed, counterpane folded back, sheets with their harsh, just-ironed outlines.

She had turned her back on him and began to fumble with the buttons on her dress when her eye had caught the statue of the Blessed Virgin, looking reproachfully at her from the top of the chest of drawers, religious images not yet having been banished from the bedrooms of the bourgeoisie.

Noreen sat heavily on the bed, crushing the sheets. 'I'm sorry, I can't do it, I can't go through with it. My son is lying next door, asleep. I can't. I just can't.'

She made tea for them and brought it into the front room where she left the curtains undrawn. Noreen wanted everyone to know how she had spent her time.

There had followed a curiously unembarrassing interlude when they had sat together talking about their children and drinking tea. On leaving, the man had taken her hand and squeezed it. 'You're a great girl, Noreen,' he had said.

She had stayed up to confront P.J. 'Nothing happened here tonight, P.J., and it won't, ever.'

P.J., taking one look at her hectic cheeks and glassy eyes, had closed the curtains and pushed her gently on to a seat. 'All right Noreen, all right pet.'

'No – I mean it. I don't care if I am old fashioned, I don't care if everybody else does it. Never again.'

He had said nothing, sitting down opposite her, staring, with bowed head, at the carpet in front of his feet. She had waited, fearful of his reaction but determined to stand her ground.

Then she saw, unbelievingly, that he had begun to laugh, his whole body shaking. 'Noreen – do you know what it is – you're the only one of us with a titter of wit. We're fools, the lot of us, only I was lucky enough to marry an intelligent woman. Never again, I promise, Noreen. Never again.'

That was it. They stopped visiting the McHughs and within weeks they had begun to look for a new house.

And now would he think her desire to find a job was prompted by her intelligence? Probably not – except with P.J. you could never tell. And that was one of the reasons why she was in love with him still.

5

By now everybody else had gone home and P.J. locked himself into the empty building and took the lift down to the underground garage.

Checking that his bike was secure in the boot, he got into the Mercedes but stopped the car as it cleared the garage. He had made a decision.

He picked up the phone. 'Home at last? Good. I thought you might have run away and I've a surprise for you. Pet, pack us a few things, we're going away for the weekend. Don't start asking me questions, it's a surprise.'

He had intended the surprise for next weekend when Annabel would be home but seeing Canice on the television had set him thinking about his youth and about Cavan and he wanted now to go down straight away.

If they left after grabbing a bite to eat, they would be there in two hours and they could spend tonight in their new house. Everything was ready, beds made up, heat coming on as instructed. He was sure Noreen hadn't guessed; she had been with him when he had bought the lake and three acres of woodland two years ago but he had never mentioned anything about building a house there, wanting to keep it as a surprise.

During the past twenty years P.J. had acquired a flat in Cannes and a bungalow in Kerry but neither of them aroused much interest in him. He hated Cannes and he couldn't stand the cute Kerry hoors, but the idea of a house in Cavan appealed to him, giving him a sense of completing something. He wondered why he hadn't thought of it before now.

The lake was a childhood haunt, only five miles from the

townland where he had been reared and two and a half miles from the school and church he had attended as a lad. His first idea had been to build a traditional Irish cottage, but when he had told Aubrey this and Aubrey had lectured him on the rightness of his decision, P.J. had changed his mind.

Aubrey had grown severe. 'You have responsibilities to this area, P.J. Look at the ghastly haciendas going up all around. You can be an example to others by building a small, unpretentious cottage that will not offend the landscape.'

'I don't give a shite about the landscape. And it's my house so will you cop yourself on and stop telling me what I can and can't do. In fact I've decided that what I'm going to build is a Swedish-style wooden chalet with a sauna.'

He had only said this to annoy Aubrey, but the more he thought about it the more he liked the idea.

He put his best workers on the job and oversaw every step of the building, and a wooden chalet now stood, right on the shores of Lough Eannach, with a picture window looking on to the lake and with the woods forming a backdrop. P.J. looked forward to swimming in the lake, to casting his line as he had learnt to do on these same waters when he was ten. And there would be no parties, no grand entertaining, just himself and Noreen. And Annabel, of course, when she came home.

P.J. was a man who never touched wood, who never thought superstitiously of having to pay some day for so much good fortune. No problem, the youngsters nowadays said – the phrase might have been invented for P.J. Was it his Chicago birthplace, an American optimism drawn into his mother's bloodstream that made him so certain that happiness was his due?

It was only when he thought of Annabel that he felt a hiccough of fear, that his world became shadowed. She would soon be finished school and then what? University? P.J. distrusted universities, seeing them as dens filled with young louts lying in wait to pounce on his daughter. And if some man should cause her pain . . . His knuckles whitened on the steering wheel.

Perhaps, though, it didn't have to come to that. Annabel wasn't one for the book-learning, chip off the old block there. She mightn't want to go to any university. She could stay at home with them, for a few years at any rate. She was only eighteen, there was no need for her to start making decisions, rushing on to another stage of her life.

With a sigh of happiness P.J. realized that eighteen was just a step beyond babyhood.

The Mercedes knew its way home. P.J. listened to the well-bred, docile purr of its engine, its lack of fuss at the constant stopping and starting demanded of it in the heavy traffic. The city was looking well and P.J. acknowledged its chic as a tribute to himself. Twenty years ago these streets had told a different story. Then rows of tenement houses had been interspersed with empty sites; every corner had been defaced by ugly little shops selling their goods in unhygienic confusion. Children had congregated outside them, snot-nosed and noisy, while their blowsy mothers had screamed at them to 'Mind the cars, for Christ's sake!'

Now these children's children were housed in orderly suburbs with neat front gardens and rural views, and the city had been returned to the motor car and the moguls of industry and commerce. How smart the office blocks looked, particularly those built by P.J. McGuckian with their severity of line and general air of righteous economy. How Dublin bustled with self-confidence and purpose. How God smiled down on His children as He watched them so gainfully employed.

'Your tiny hand is frozen,' sang P.J. McGuckian, a recent convert to opera as he waited benevolently while a spruce little Japanese car inserted itself neatly into the traffic flow. Good little cars, useful little cars, just the ticket for Annabel to whizz her round and give her independence from the drunken young louts who were lying in wait at the door of every disco in town. It was a source of wonder to P.J. how young girls ever managed to survive the hazards of growing up and emerge into lovely womanhood, as his Noreen had. But then she had the fortune to meet P.J. McGuckian along the way.

As P.J. was driving home, planning his weekend ahead, Canice O'Keeffe, Minister for the Arts, took a quick dekko at his visage then seated himself once more behind his desk.

This interview would see him running late, eating into his weekend as so many of them were nibbled at. Canice didn't resent this for he took his position seriously and he had known, on receiving his seal of office, that sacrifices would be in order.

Giving his hair a final pat he bent forward and spoke through the intercom. 'Rosaleen, please show the gentleman from *The Champion* in now.'

He didn't know whether to feel disappointed or relieved to see a lone man walk into the room. No photographer then. Maybe that was just as well: with his Canaries tan fading and not having had the time for a sunbed top-up, he might not do himself justice, even in a black and white photograph.

And it would be black and white. *The Champion* was a small weekly – small but prestigious. Rosaleen had checked it out. Right for him, right for his image. Although Canice had a secret yearning to make the tabloids he realized that this did not accord with the dignity of his office.

'Welcome. Sit yourself down.'

'Larry Thorpe.' The man winced at Canice's hearty handshake.

'I had the pleasure of meeting your proprietor – and Lady Cassandra – when I opened the James Joyce House in Trieste.' Canice gave the town its full, three syllables, rolling them lovingly round his tongue. 'I was delighted to be able to offer them both some true, Irish hospitality. I suppose that's why you're here today – because of our meeting?'

Larry Thorpe leered, pulling down his lower lip to display long, pointed teeth. 'You could say that.'

'I didn't really have much of a chat with Mr Buchanan but Lady Cassandra told me how devoted he is to all the arts, especially to literature.'

'Yeah. Jack's a great reader.'

'Well then. You just fire ahead, I'm at your service.'

The reporter produced a small cassette recorder which he placed on Canice's desk. 'OK if I – ?'

'Of course.' Canice liked tape recorders. Elaboration on matters artistic often had to be couched in difficult language and Canice knew the risk of being misquoted. 'But before you start, some coffee?'

Canice's wish was Rosaleen's command. The coffee tray arrived almost as the Minister switched off his intercom.

Thorpe took a sip, looked around the room, then back at the Minister. He cleared his throat. 'I believe, Minister, that you have two very talented kids – right?'

Canice blinked, unprepared for this line of questioning. Perhaps the fellow wanted to start off with some background colour. 'My children. Yes. Two.'

'Your lad fancies his chances to make the next Olympic swimming squad?'

Paternal pride took over. 'More than fancies. He came third in Helsinki last year in the under-eighteen fifty metres freestyle.'

Thorpe seemed to receive this news with indifference, merely nodding his head. 'And your girl – Cliodna – ' he looked down at his notebook, mispronouncing her name, 'she's already had a small part in an Irish movie?'

'Well now – her mother and I were not overjoyed by that. It was an excellent film, very well made, but young people's heads can be easily turned and we want Cliodna to continue her education.'

'Yeah, right. So tell me then, Minister – what do they think of their Daddy's bit on the side?'

Canice stared at him, puzzled. 'Bit on the side? What are you talking about?'

'Now, now, Minister, I hope we are not going to be difficult. Your bit on the side, your piece of fluff – the ex-queen of country music, Honey Fitz.'

Canice choked on his coffee, spewing beige drops on to his pearl-grey lapels. With a look of concern the reporter plucked a tissue from a box on the desk and handed it to him. 'Take your time.'

Canice dabbed at his mouth, wiped his eyes. As he began to gather his wits, his puzzlement returned. He couldn't imagine where Thorpe had dug up this story, but why should he want to anyway? Why should something which hadn't even been written about when it had happened nearly twenty years ago, now be of interest to an English journalist?

From behind a wad of tissues, he took a look at Thorpe. Cheap suit. Going bald. And he was a government minister and an intellectual to boot. He straightened his shoulders.

'I know that *The Champion* has a fine reputation, Mr Thorpe. I can't imagine that its readers would be interested in your innuendoes. And I don't imagine Mr Buchanan would be pleased if – '

'Jack's orders. Never do anything without the say so from Jack.'

'I find that hard to believe. When I met your employer, we discussed things of a cultural nature. I was under the impression that *The Champion* was that sort of paper. At the James Joyce – '

'Yeah, Minister, we'll talk about James Joyce and all, if you like, but first things first. Now, you and Honey Fitz.'

Losing his temper, Canice banged the desk. 'Would you listen – there is no me and Honey Fitz. What you're referring to, not that it's any business of yours, is history. It all happened twenty years ago. Ancient history, for God's sake.'

'I see. Am I mistaken then in my information that you still see the lady on a regular basis?'

'I – who told you that? Look – it's not like that. It's not at all what it seems.'

'Really? Then could you explain to me please, how come, if it's not at all like that, how come that you, Minister, pay the mortgage? Ms Honey Fitz doesn't pay the mortgage, you do – right?'

Canice closed his eyes. This was dreadful, much worse than he had at first realized. The fellow had done his homework well and had come up with a completely false conclusion, but wasn't it an inevitable conclusion when the whole story wasn't told?

'So, Minister – what are you then? A benefactor? A good Samaritan?'

'Yes,' snapped Canice. Then, 'No.'

Worse and worse. Every time he opened his mouth he was making things worse. He still had no idea why Buchanan would be interested in all of this but that was of no importance now. If this got into print and the Chief read it, he was destroyed. The Chief – oh God. There was only one thing he could do.

Canice cleared his throat then stared manfully across the desk. 'Listen – ah – Larry, I'm going to be completely frank with you. Completely. Tell you the whole story. It'll take a little longer but I'm sure you have the time.'

'All the time in the world.'

'A grand county, Cavan,' Canice began, sitting well back in his chair the better to tell his tale. 'Did you ever hear tell of it?'

The reporter shook his head.

'Poor land but full of talent. I mean, look at us, Honey and myself, neighbours' children, and the millionaire, P.J. McGuckian – he was born in the next townland. That's something though, isn't it? All that talent coming from the same small county.' For a moment, Canice forgot his perilous state, caught in a wonder of admiration at the achievements of himself and his childhood

49

companions. The reporter's face brought him back sharply. Its expression reminded Canice – who abhorred all blood sports – of the mean, ferocious concentration of the greyhound as it closed on the hare. A noble animal, the hare, whose blood was too often spilled to provide amusement for the ignorant masses. Canice's attention began to wander again as he paused to admire the appositeness of his parallel.

'You were saying?'

'Yes, well, you see, when I met Honey again, I mean, when it all started, she was already famous and I was just beginning to make my way in the world. I'd only been in the Dáil a few years and we were in Opposition then, so I didn't cut the sort of figure I do today. No real power, so to speak. Anyway, I was asked down to open a new laboratory at my old school and Honey was there too, singing in the cabaret that the priests had put on. And do you know something? I didn't even recognize her.'

He had seen photographs of her of course, but these had not prepared him for the glory of Honey Fitz, *née* Marie Lydon, in the flesh. She had sashayed into the school hall, resplendent in high-heeled cowboy boots and a shocking pink pants suit. Her nails were long and scarlet, curling round the microphone like the petals of some exotic flower; her peroxided hair seemed impossibly spun, suspended perkily like candy floss above her brightly enamelled face.

But it was her eyes that were Canice's undoing, these same eyes that had brought her stardom, that had thousands flocking to her wherever she made an appearance. They were hazel, large, green-flecked and full of pain. They gave her an air of fragility, despite the vulgar clothes and raunchy movements; they hinted at heartbreak, a tragic past perhaps, mirroring the themes of her songs.

With those eyes Honey could not fail; besides which she had a good, rough voice, the stamina of a plough horse and a belief in her own tragic destiny. Queen of Country she had to be.

Her career had really taken off when she had changed her name: President Kennedy had just visited Ireland and reading about him and his family, she had seized on the name of his maternal grandfather as having the right ring for a country singer. By the time she met Canice in the school hall, she was Ireland's most popular female singer, with an American tour lined up and the possibility of an appearance on the Grand Ole Opry in Nashville, Tennessee.

Despite her success, however, she was still a simple girl and she was flattered when Canice remembered her and shook her hand warmly, speaking of the old days. Among Honey's friends and relations, TDs were figures of immense, almost magical powers who could bestow pensions on widows and the blind, withhold grants from needy farmers, scupper the plans of the local creamery manager with one squiggle of a pen in Dublin.

'How're you, Can – Mr O'Keeffe,' she had said, looking at him with eyes that had suddenly turned green.

'Canice is fine,' replied Canice, holding on to her hand.

He had taken her for a drink afterwards, where they were ushered into a private room in the pub because she, not he, would have been mobbed if they had appeared in public.

'You never sing at all these days, Canice?' Honey inquired, taking a sip of her advocaat and white lemonade.

'I got sense, girl.'

'You were very good.'

Always ambitious, when Canice had gone to Dublin to work as an eighteen-year-old clerk in the county council offices, he had immediately begun to look round to see where he could make his mark. Deciding on a career in music, he had bought himself a guitar and a pair of black and white patent-leather boots. He might as well have saved his money. Gigs were hard to come by, the music profession was oversubscribed. It was with relief that he turned to politics, after slogging it out for eighteen months. And the rest, as he now informed Honey, was history.

'Of course what you're doing now is great,' Honey smiled shyly at him, 'but I still think that you had a grand voice.'

He had taken her home to her ancient mother, now living in a spanking new bungalow which Honey had paid for. After several cups of tea, much talk of the old days and promises to keep in touch, he had said good night to them both and set out for Dublin.

And he had not thought about Honey again. She was lovely and vulnerable but he had his Nuala and an infant son and a political career which needed a lot of nursing. His hands were full.

Poor Honey did not get off so lightly; she had been shafted by Cupid, right in the middle of her plump and blushing heart.

For the previous five years Honey had not even thought about men – there had been no time. She had travelled around the country from one engagement to the next, snatching sleep, having her hair done, signing autographs for her fans. But she had always travelled hopefully and now she was in love. The fact that he was married only reassured her, for she had always known that she would sooner or later suffer from a broken heart. Wasn't that what the songs told her? Wasn't that what she shared with her audience every single night?

It must be said that at this point it was she who did the pursuing: she phoned his office, she sent him tickets for her concerts. She had almost cancelled her American tour, but when her agent had persuaded her to go she had sent Canice a photograph of herself posing with Johnny and June Cash outside the Grand Ole Opry. She had signed this photograph: Love from . . .

For months there was no response from Canice, he might have been made of stone. But fate must have been in cahoots with Cupid, and one May evening, as the days were lengthening and the air softening, he threw the two of them together in the foyer of a Dublin hotel. Canice was coming from a late sitting of the Dáil and going home to an empty house. (Nuala had taken the baby down to Kerry to see its grandparents.) Honey was waiting for a taxi to take her home, exhausted after spending seven hours in a recording studio.

He saw her home – to her doorstep. Then those eyes began to haunt him; he began to listen to music programmes on the radio in the hope of hearing her voice. The next time she sent him tickets, he went to the concert, stuffing Nuala's into his shoe and hobbling round to the stage door after the performance.

Once he got over his initial guilt he began to enjoy himself. Unlike Nuala, who was ambitious for him, Honey made no demands. She was pathetically grateful for any attention. She warmed special angora slippers which she had made and had them ready for him when he called, together with a silk robe with his initials embroidered in gold thread on the pocket. She sprayed herself and the sheets with scent. She groaned in a most satisfactory fashion when they made love, unlike Nuala, whom Canice suspected of reciting Hail Marys under her breath at the crucial moment. She told him over and over again how wonderful he was, how lucky she was, how he was the one love of her life.

When she discovered that she was pregnant she was delighted.

'You should see your face,' she had said to him, sipping pure orange juice, for she had given up advocaat and white lemonade the minute she had heard the good news.

'But what are we to do?' Poor Canice tried manfully not to dwell on visions of his career going down the spout.

'Nothing, silly. This is a part of you that no one can take away from me, this is what I've wanted all along. No one will know who the father is, and God, Canice, I'm earning more than enough for the two of us.'

Over the months Canice grew reassured and Honey blossomed. She never suffered from morning sickness, she continued singing until three months before the birth. The shock was all the greater then when the baby was born hideously deformed and lived for only three days.

Canice's reaction was complex: he was sorry for Honey but he also experienced an overwhelming sense of relief. There would be no illegitimate child running round Dublin, proclaiming his paternity with every lift of his eyebrow, every turn of his head. This nightmare was over, only to be replaced by a sense of guilt – had he wished the child dead?

Honey's reaction, on the other hand, was quite simple – she felt herself destroyed. This was a sorrow from which she could not recover; her songs had not prepared her for this. She began to drink heavily, mixing whiskey with the tranquillizers which the doctor had prescribed for her. She cried incessantly, locking herself away and allowing no one but Canice to come near her. He thought she would get over it, that it was just a question of time. He could see her getting back to the singing, her career enhanced by her personal tragedy. Honey knew that she would never sing again.

Canice would not abandon her, although he knew that the affair was over. The dead child had been conceived in sin, its blighted and brief existence a judgment surely on its parents' acts of adultery. Canice went to confession and emerged shriven and determined not to sin again. He would devote himself to his family and to helping the poor woman he had wronged. He stuck by Honey, finding a little house where she could live, sitting with her, holding her hand while she cried, trying to persuade her to turn, as he had, to God.

Honey would have no truck with a God who had allowed a tiny hapless creature to suffer so terribly. It was only after eighteen months, when she had begun periodically to surface and see beyond her pain, that she agreed to go to confession, just to please Canice. She started going to Mass again for the same reason. At first she fought with God, hating Him, as she sat in the church, for what He had done to her baby. Then she grew bored with the whole business until eventually she found that she had begun to enjoy religion. She liked the visits to the church, the gloom, the silence, the heavy cold which hung over the building even on warm summer days. She particularly liked early Mass on winter mornings. She would get up in the dark and walk through derelict, deserted streets to a church which glowed, luminously beckoning her in from the cold. She started making the First Fridays, never missing one.

She didn't think too much about meanings or relevance, and unlike Canice she had no feelings of guilt. She threw herself into her churchgoing as she had into her singing, enjoying its sensory pleasures: the glow of candles, the smell of incense, the soothing rise and fall of mumbled prayers.

At this stage Honey was still supporting herself and it was she who put down the initial lump-sum payment on the house. Canice assured her, however, that if the need arose he would foot the bills. And he was prepared to do just this and eventually indeed did so, although when he made the offer he had been sure that Honey would soon meet someone else, someone more worthy than he, and fall in love again. He had discounted Honey when she had quoted from one of her hits, 'I'm a one-man woman.'

Honey had made no demands on him over the years. If he came to see her regularly once a fortnight, if he paid her bills and escorted her to confession once a month, it was because he wanted to and not because of blackmail, moral or otherwise. He was a free agent as far as Honey was concerned but she was still a one-man woman.

And so she clip-clopped round her little pink house in high-heeled fluffy slippers, rarely changing out of her negligées, of which she had some two dozen in varying shades of pink. She listened to her old hits, she looked at videos and old films on TV. She ate chocolates and drank tea and spent a long time on her nails and hair. She was content, staid and chaste, and she looked like anyone's stereotype of a kept woman.

Mistress was written in her eyes and in her heart and if it found no fleshly expression, this was a mere technicality. She lived for her man, and her man, though foresworn to another, would never run out.

Canice finished telling his story and wiped a tear from his lower lashes. There was silence in the room until Larry Thorpe emitted a sigh and shook his head either in admiration or disbelief. 'I'll tell you something, Minister – I believe you. I mean, this is just too weird – you couldn't have made it up. I've listened to some stories in my time, but this! There's only one possible explanation, Minister, you're either a complete fool or a total saint.'

A saint, a saint, cried Canice silently.

'But what's this with the – ah – first Fridays?'

'Devotions,' Canice offered, on firm ground. 'Devotional prayers and observances in the Catholic church. You go to Holy Communion on the first Friday of every month for nine months in a row and obviously confession on the Thursday beforehand. It's a good way to start each month you know, it marks it off.'

Thorpe was looking at him now with an expression approaching wonder.

'So there's no story really, for you, is there? I mean, your readers would hardly be interested when there's no – no sex, or anything of that nature?'

'Hold on a minute. Are you suggesting that our readers are only interested in sex?'

'Of course not – '

'There you are then. This is what's known as human interest. Thousands of people will be interested in this. They may not believe it, mind . . .'

Canice began to tear at his fringe, a nervous habit which he resorted to under stress. 'But – I don't understand. I mean, I thought *The Champion* was mainly a cultural sort of paper, interested in the arts – '

'Minister, to quote another fine newspaper, "All human life is here." We at *The Champion* are interested in the Whole Man. Do you know what my boss found out? Jack Buchanan discovered that after a night of fornication Leonardo da Vinci's pee was always a brighter colour, so when you see a lot of yellow in one of his paintings you know that he was on the razzle. He used the pee, see, mixed it to get a stronger colour. Jack never felt the same about da Vinci after that. It coloured his view, you might say.'

He stood up and with an insolent wave of his hand sauntered out of the office.

'Thanks for the coffee, darling,' Canice heard him say as he passed by Rosaleen's desk.

Canice flung open a window and stuck his head out, seeking unpolluted air.

What, *what* had possessed him to tell his story to Thorpe? He must have been mad. Nobody would believe it, not on the other side of the water anyway. His name, the dignity of his office would be dragged through the mud, and the Chief was big on the dignity of office.

When he thought of the Chief, Canice put his head down on his desk and moaned. He could imagine his voice thundering down the line, demanding an explanation. Demanding his head.

'I am a ruined man,' said Canice O'Keeffe, *sotto voce*. 'Ruined, finished, I might as well put the gun to my head now and get it over with.'

Except of course that he didn't own a gun, never having had a licence. And Canice O'Keeffe was as law-abiding as he was God-fearing.

At the realization of his own righteousness and the unfairness of life, two fat, glistening tears swelled over his eyelids and made their way gently down his yellow cheeks.

Twenty years without carnal knowledge but who would believe that once *The Champion* got going? They were the same, all English newspapers were the same – gutter press. Gutter souls, gutter people. They would misunderstand him of course, being unable to understand decency and kindness, qualities foreign to their own natures.

Wouldn't you think they would be satisfied with their eight hundred years of persecution and leave us alone? Weren't we equal partners now, in the EC? Weren't we doing our best to solve the troubles with them, co-operating with them at every turn?

But no, they were still there ready to pounce, waiting to put the boot in at every opportunity.

He could imagine the headlines and the joy with which they

would be seized upon across the water: 'Eire Minister's Love Nest Discovered', 'Love Irish Style: Government Minister Confesses All'.

He had told them that himself, given it to them on a plate, thinking that even an Englishman would realize that he would never tell a lie involving the sacraments.

An Irishman would understand that, but then an Irishman would not have gone poking around in his private life. Canice had had many a grilling from the Irish press but always on questions relating to the public good. They acknowledged, had acknowledged twenty years ago, that a man's personal life was his own business. The English, on the other hand, were obsessed by sex – his mother used to always say that, warning him against the dangers of ever emigrating over there. But –

Canice got up and began to pace around his office. There was something here that didn't add up.

He had met Jack Buchanan at a party, a party at which he was more or less – give or take the Italians – host. Jack Buchanan owned a newspaper which, according to Rosaleen, was interested in the arts. Why then should Jack Buchanan send a journalist over to Ireland deliberately to dig up something which had happened twenty years ago? Jack Buchanan was out to get him and he didn't know why.

He had taken him on face value; he had welcomed him to the party – on behalf of the Irish government he had welcomed him and his wife. With his own hand he had refilled their glasses, wanting to make them feel at home, worried that they might feel out of it amidst all the Irish and Italian *bonhomie*. He had suffered Jack's brusqueness, seeing it as no more than the usual English stiffness, feeling sorry for the man because he had been finding it so difficult to relax.

Had that brusqueness then signified something else? Dislike? But of what? Of whom?

Perhaps Jack Buchanan had a pathological dislike of all Irishmen; or of all government ministers; maybe even of all James Joyce devotees, although this seemed less likely given that the man was supposed to be a lover of literature. Whatever the reason, he had sought out Canice O'Keeffe to destroy him.

How right Nuala was. Every time she saw him off on one of his jaunts she would straighten his tie, give his cheek a wifely peck and admonish him: 'Be careful now. You know what an innocent abroad you are, Canice.'

But what sort of defence was that to offer the Chief? He might as well resign right now, before the story broke, although even that might not save him from the vengeance of the Chief.

Canice stood up and straightened his shoulders like a man. He would take it on the chin, accept his medicine – no, more, he would ask for the medicine. He would kneel down before the Chief and beg to be punished. Treason, that was the name of his crime. He had betrayed Ireland, he had betrayed the Chief. And after after all the Chief had done for him, for all of them over the past five years. Quietly he began to weep again.

6

Like the polar bears at Dublin Zoo, Bill O'Reilly swam on his back, up and down, with monotonous regularity. Unlike the polar bears, however, this behaviour was not an outward sign of psychosis; Bill O'Reilly and his world were doing fine.

Known to his ministers and backbenchers as Chief, he had governed Ireland for five years, and during those five years he had brought about a transformation in the fortunes of the nation. Inflation was lower than in any other EC country, unemployment was at the same level as Germany and falling. Throughout the land cement mixers were busy erecting shopping malls and office blocks. The streets were choked with cars, the pubs were full of happy drinkers. Ireland for the first time since independence was prosperous and stable. Some commentators said it was all due to external forces, the strength of a now closely united Europe and the health and stability of the EMS. The Left, shrinking daily but still quarrelling among themselves, said the whole thing was a chimera. One day soon the bubble would burst.

Bill had no such fears, nor did he think that the miracle had been brought about by any phenomenon other than himself. Bill believed in his own greatness.

He had always had faith but had suffered many years of frustration during which nobody seemed to share his faith. He had watched as lesser men were brought into the sun, listening to himself described the while as overweeningly ambitious. He had persevered. He had concentrated on images from the past: Lenin arriving at Finland station; Hannibal crossing the Alps; Jesus Christ spat upon and mocked. He was reassured by an awareness of his own selflessness. He did not seek fame, nor power nor wealth. He sought only to make Ireland great.

How he loved this little country! He could weep and often did when he thought of all her past suffering. In his bath he would sing the old songs, moved, moved to pity and a sense of his own destiny. He was fond of a bit of nookie but he had never taken a wife. He had often been advised to, warned that he would never make it without the reassuring presence of the wife and kids. Despite this advice and partial though he was to a well-tanned haunch, he was wedded irrevocably to Kathleen Ni Houlihan.

For all his patriotism though, his respect for The Language, his desire for Unity, he was a pragmatist and he knew, moreover, what the Irish people wanted. They wanted money in their pockets and their children at home in jobs. When the economy was sorted out he would worry about the North and the revival of the Irish language – all in the fullness of time.

And they were nearly there. It had not been easy and he knew that even now he could not afford to relax; nevertheless he was moderately pleased with his achievements to date.

He was a changed man from the one who had tremblingly received his seal from the President five years ago. Then he had set about selecting his Cabinet, choosing colleagues for their expertise and intelligence. He had known that he would have a struggle on his hands and he had been ready to fight on all sides. Drawing his Cabinet round him he would see off an intractable and destructive Opposition, an entrenched Civil Service, all variety of power groups from the Church to the farmers to the trade unions, and a whining public that stood like Oliver Twist asking for more.

His first lesson in the shortcomings of democracy came when he realized that his real trouble would come from none of these groups but from his own Cabinet.

He would have men around him (Bill believed that the era of the Irish woman had not yet arrived) who were quick and keen, and now he found that these men were quite prepared to kick him in the balls. They didn't mean to, it was just that they were so eager, so full of ideas, taking their power and their portfolios a shade too seriously. With his unwavering vision Bill knew what he wanted, but every time he made a suggestion to one of his ministers he replied, 'Yes, Chief, but . . .' and proceeded to outline his own ideas, which formed no part of the master plan.

Time is of the essence, Bill said to his reflection every morning, and after a year of listening to himself and to his ministers snapping and snarling he decided that democracy had had its innings. So he gathered his colleagues round about him to explain to them the facts of political life and the nature of Cabinet responsibility. They could decide all manner of minor things, they would have discretion in the bringing of sweeteners to their constituencies, but all major policy decisions were to be made by Bill O'Reilly.

Some didn't like it and retired gracefully or sulkily to the backbenches; others, pondering the brevity of life and the comfort of their Mercedes, decided to give it a bash. Bill filled the vacancies which arose with men who were loyal and would be pliable. At the first meeting of his reformed Cabinet he addressed them thus: 'Now, lads, it's like this. I know you're all fine men, bursting with things to say and you *can* say them within this room. But it's like this – I have to get on with clearing up the mess left by the last crowd so I need your co-operation. Time is of the essence. I want each of you to make a personal sacrifice for Ireland – just do what I say. Trust me, lads. Go out there and read what's been written for you and read it with conviction.' (He was lucky in that most of them were already fluent readers.)

Any other man would have wilted at the amount of work Bill now found on his lap – he eyed it with gusto. He started the day at five a.m. with a swim in his pool. He was at his desk by seven and was usually still there working away at seven that night. He familiarized himself with every department and, as he had suspected, he found that it was comparatively easy to get things done when you didn't have to waste your time arguing to convince others. The Civil Service turned out to be a help rather than a hindrance, delighted to be answerable to only one man and a man moreover who knew his mind and didn't chop and change. No wonder Mussolini had got the trains running on time.

When he had subdued his party, he went on television to address the nation. He started by confirming the superiority of the Irish race, went on to apologize for the mistakes of past Taoiseachs and promised that from now on things would be different. He needed the help of the plain people of Ireland: if they would only give him their support, tighten their belts a few notches, then together they could get the show on the road and save this great little country from ruin.

He ended with a grand and irresistible flourish. 'And to start the ball rolling, we are doing away with the notion of ministerial cars. From now on my ministers will use a car pool – five to a Mercedes. The garda drivers released will be put back on the streets to fight crime. As for me, I'll be coming to work from now on on my motor bike.'

In that instant he won the national heart. What an image he presented, so twenty-first century, so American. That the image was never made flesh was irrelevant. It hung on the national retina so that ever afterwards when the Irish people thought of their Taoiseach they imagined him whizzing into the Dáil in his black leather jacket and crash helmet.

Wouldn't you do without your dinner for such a leader? And indeed, this is what it amounted to for some folk. Taxation went up, social services were not improved, but still the people cried, 'Bill will look after us – the good times are coming and the faraway hills are getting nearer every day.'

Bill had everything going for him. The World Bank loved him, the Brussels bureaucrats loved him, the people of Ireland loved him. The trade unions sent up piteous cries but nobody listened to them; the farmers swore that they were ruined but they had been swearing that for years. Bill, with fire in his belly and a light in his eyes, forged ahead, unstoppable.

Initially he did have a problem with his Cabinet's interaction with the outside world. He couldn't keep them locked up all the time, but he soon found that he couldn't let them loose on an unsuspecting public either, good and loyal boys though they were. In radio and television studios they would sit vacant eyed and open mouthed while some impertinent journalist made mincemeat of them. (Bill was finding the fourth estate less tractable than the rest of the nation.)

However, great leaders can read the times in which they live, and as Bill took time to study the problem he saw that the nature of reality had changed. Conditioned to looking at images and to listening to advertising jargon, appearance had become substance and was the new reality. People didn't expect to understand what they heard any more, much less to worry about its veracity. If the image on the screen was pleasing, if the voice on the radio carried conviction, that was enough.

So, firstly, Bill set about smartening up the lads. Teeth were crowned, the services of a smart tailor was suggested and they were all encouraged to take at least two holidays in the sun every year. This had the added advantage of making Bill, surrounded by all that tanned skin, look the only white man in the Cabinet.

When their appearances had been taken care of he sent them all off to media school, where they learnt to speak fluent nonsense, lengthily. So structured and complex was the nonsense that even the sharpest political journalist failed to unravel it. The nation, used as it was to advertising jargon and James Joyce, took it all on the chin. Besides, the lads looked so well, their flashing teeth and deeply tanned manly faces staring unflinchingly at camera, eyeballing the interviewer and speaking such mellifluous gobbledygook.

The contrast when Bill gave an interview was enormous. Knowing what he was talking about, there was no need for bamboozlement and it seemed a great compliment to the man in the street that he could understand every word his Taoiseach spoke. Interviewers, so unused to getting any kind of answers, never mind such straight ones as these, rolled on their backs in front of him and wagged their microphones.

He was perceived as that rarest of birds, a genius who could communicate with the man in the street.

The Opposition parties gnashed their teeth and turned up the collars of their coats. For them, it was going to be a long, cold wait.

It was because of the Chief's high regard for loyalty that Canice had ended up in his Cabinet. He had been an acolyte of Bill's long before Bill's ascent to greatness; in fact you could say that he alone in those early days had seen that greatness.

On his first day in the House, Bill, then a junior minister, had slapped him on the back and welcomed him. Later that week he had invited him for a drink and given him some hints on political survival. Canice, given to hero worship since his schooldays, had found a focus for his yearning. Ever afterwards, even when the fortunes of Bill O'Reilly were at their lowest, when he was dropped in a Cabinet reshuffle, Canice had stood by him, encouraging him, defending him, believing in him.

It was inevitable that the Chief should feel that he had to offer some reward. He also saw the man's potential, his smiling, diffident personality, his desire to be liked, his decency.

The problem was that Canice was thick, even by the standards of the present Cabinet. Even after a lengthy session in media school, he could not be trusted to open his mouth in public. How could you give such a man a budget? He would probably lose the bloody thing.

The Chief, ever a man of ingenuity, solved the problem by creating a new portfolio: he made him Minister for the Arts.

This was a brilliant stroke. While it made Bill appear a cultured and sensitive man, it cost him next to nothing. So small was Canice's budget that it didn't really matter how he blew it. In general the people of Ireland were not preoccupied by things cultural – apart from James Joyce they could take them or leave them. (For some obscure reason James Joyce had entered the realms of Irish iconography and was up there now securely ensconced with Saints Patrick, Bridget and Colmcille.) As for the artists themselves and the arts organizations, on the one hand they were flattered to have their very own minister, and on the other they were too busy with faction fighting to attack Canice or look askance at his budget.

Canice was ecstatic; he had never hankered after power, desiring only fame. Soon he was opening so many exhibitions and launching so many books that he became the most photographed man in Ireland. At first nights and the opening of new wings in museums and galleries, his was a smiling, diffident presence, oozing sincerity and commitment. Logic was not sought and ambiguity was expected in artistic pronouncements and Canice's speeches were little gems, remembered on many a dark night by the artists to whom they were addressed.

'It is my pleasure,' he would smilingly begin, 'to open this exhibition/launch this book,' an appropriate phrase for each occasion, 'and to assure you that this government is aware of the importance of the artist, the role he plays, *must* play in any healthy society.' Pause at this stage for applause which was always generous. 'It was with a genuine sense of humility that I approached this work of genius/work which contains the seeds of genius,' depending on the eminence of the artist in question, how long he had been buggering around, as P.J. McGuckian, his old school chum, would have put it. 'It shows . . .' and there would follow six or seven sentences of uniform opacity, which Canice would deliver with gusto and assurance.

At the end of his first year in office, his ministry was deemed a great success and the country was awash with genius. Initially, the professionals – critics, men of letters, serious journalists – were wary of him, but his obscurity saved him. Listening to his incomprehensible speeches they came to the conclusion that this was no lightweight; such fluency, such a grasp of difficult concepts – at least that's what they thought all those sub-clauses must denote – marked him as a man of real intelligence and insight.

Soon he had become a feather in the government's cap. His television appearances increased; he was touted around Europe as evidence of Ireland's commitment to the arts. The British, naturally, sneered, but the French, a more rigorously intellectual race, were more sympathetic and an in-depth profile of him appeared in *Le Monde*.

And now all this was to be taken from him. Canice, unable to contain his outrage and grief any longer, turned his face up to the ceiling and howled out loud.

'Minister, Minister,' Rosaleen came running in. 'Are you all right, Minister? Is it your sinuses again?'

Canice pulled himself together. The sight of Rosaleen, sophisticated, beautiful and his very own personal secretary, made him realize just how much was at stake.

'Rosaleen, get me P.J. McGuckian on the phone. Stop all other calls, clear the line. If the Chief rings, tell him I've gone round to the doctor, that my sinuses were killing me. Now, good girl, stick with it till you get him.'

Canice poured himself a glass of water and dropped a soluble aspirin in. All this talk about sinuses had reminded him of his condition and he could feel them filling up now, pressing on the nerve endings around his eyes and nose.

Never mind. P.J. was at hand. P.J. would come up with some solution, as he always did. Canice sat back, stretching his legs and switching on a transistor radio on his desk. Canice smiled. 'Encore' was on, filled as usual with highlights from the past week's Al Brown shows. Canice often listened to Brown and he found this listening preference morally reassuring. There was something so admirably humble, so sound, in the image of a government minister listening to the Al Brown show. It was the sort of thing that could only happen in Ireland.

No side, the Irish, no humbug, no pretence. Helping one

another as best they could, kindly, forgiving. See how far it got an Englishman when he tried to stab one of them in the back. The Famine wasn't that long ago and race memories die hard.

Canice gave his paunch a discreet pat and decided to knock off the chocolate profiteroles.

He folded his arms and sat back to wait for P.J.'s call.

'It's lovely,' Noreen said faintly as she peered up at the dripping trees and listened to the doleful cooing of the wood-pigeons. In front of her the waters of Lough Eannach were a uniform grey, except around the edges where they sported a dirty, whitish frill.

'And it's full of bream. How do you fancy a bream for breakfast?'

'I'm not very hungry.' Noreen's voice sounded even fainter. The journey last night had been a slow and bumpy one, for the campaign for national regeneration undertaken by Bill O'Reilly had not yet reached the roads of County Cavan. And they had not left Dublin until well after nine because P.J. had wanted to eat before they started out.

Of all the surprises P.J. had presented her with during their married life, this house was surely among the least welcome. As she turned in the bed she imagined she felt it tilt. She wasn't at all sure that it was safe, built as it was on stilts embedded in the boggy shore. Last night she hadn't been able to see anything but this morning she knew that she did not like the view. From the back window the woods loured at her, sticky green branches blocking out the sky. And in front of her was that expanse of dull, grey water.

She didn't want another house and she certainly didn't fancy spending her days in this depressing spot. P.J. of course would be out on the lake, enjoying himself, bringing home all manner of slimy fish, filling the house with smells. He could be so exasperating at times.

'What is it, sweetheart?' P.J. inquired as she turned her back on him. 'Are you going to have another snooze?'

'No I am not, P.J. McGuckian. I wish sometimes you'd just listen – '

'As if I had a choice.'

'I want a serious conversation.'

'Isn't it a bit early for that?' He began to smooth back her hair.

'P.J., just listen.'

'All right, pet, all right. I'm listening.'

'Well. You know the way I've tried so many things over the years – gardening and tennis and – '

'Yes and they didn't suit you and there's no point in wasting time on things that don't suit you. Life is too short for that carry on.'

'That's the whole point. I feel that I'm wasting my time.'

'A beautiful woman can't waste time. Did anyone accuse the Mona Lisa of wasting time?'

'P.J., will you listen? I'm fifty years of age, I've nothing to do all day long, I'm bored and useless. I've decided I'm going to do something about it.'

'So have I.'

She stared at him.

'You're not useless, pet, but I know that you feel fed up sometimes. You think I don't notice these things but I do. And I've come up with the perfect solution – tea dances.'

'P.J., what on earth are you talking about?'

For answer he leaped out of the bed, lifted her in his arms and began to dance with her round the room. 'Da da da-da-da-da da da.' He bent her backwards. 'Don't you remember, Noreen, before Aube was born? Every Saturday night in the Crystal, dancing every dance till our feet were blistered, hardly able to find our coats in the cloakroom when it was all over. Do you remember, Noreen, do you?'

In spite of herself, Noreen found that she was responding, catching the rhythm of his body, keeping step with him, her feet as light as they had been thirty years ago.

'We're going to start dancing again, I've discovered these tea dances and we're going to start going. Never mind the old biddies in the Horticultural Society and the superwomen in the tennis club, you and I are going to dance off into the sunset together.'

Noreen was laughing. 'That's not what I had in mind.'

'But isn't it great, all the same?' He stopped and turned her round so that the light from the window fell on her face. 'By God Noreen, you should see what this is doing for you already. You were looking peaky there in the bed. Now your cheeks are rosy and your eyes are shining. Come over here and I'll buy you a mineral.'

He led her back to the bed. 'Do you remember, Noreen? Wasn't

I a lucky man that I bought you a mineral the first dance I met you at? And that you agreed to drink the damn stuff. Pet, pet . . .'

That afternoon in the local village a group of lads gathered outside the garage to tell a tale. They were idle young layabouts who usually spent Saturday afternoons outside the garage, sniggering among themselves and guffawing at the country people who came in to do their weekly shopping. Today, however, they were purposeful and important for they had real news to impart.

That morning on their way to the lake to fish they had stopped as they drew abreast of the new wooden house. There was a car parked outside and, curious to know who the owners might be, they had halted under the trees. A movement in an upper window caught their eyes. Enthralled they had watched as hairy buttocks, naked as a plucked chicken and framed by the bare window, rose and fell, rose and fell. In passion or what? And they swore that it had gone on for a good five minutes.

Their elders and betters, aghast, cuffed them around their ears and told them to mind their manners – surely they knew who had built that house?

It would serve them right if the place had been put up by the Germans or the Dutch, then they'd see how near they'd get to it with all the Keep Out and No Trespassing signs. Just because P.J. McGuckian was a decent man was no reason to take advantage of him. Let them keep their mouths shut and their eyes averted and thank God that an Irishman could at last live as well as any foreigner.

'Of course I'll take the call. Jesus, woman, he's a government minister and I'm only a building contractor. Stop getting ideas above your station on my behalf.'

Thus P.J. McGuckian accepted a call from the Minister for the Arts and thus he illustrated the strength and weakness of his formidable personality.

He was a man without imagination and without guilt. His physical size was an outward manifestation of his inner self – he was big-hearted, sexually voracious and, yes, big-brained. Many, seeing his lack of finesse and lack of understanding of his fellow human being, took these limitations for lack of intelligence. They didn't realize that he was simply not interested in people; he loved them in general as he loved fresh air and green fields, but analysing them, trying to find out what made them tick, simply bored him. For this reason he could appear stupid, which was all the more galling for those who envied his millionaire status.

Success had come to him easily for he had never doubted himself; perhaps this was because his mother, a widow, never doubted her only son. When other mothers said, mind, don't, you can't, be careful, his had said, go on son, you can do anything. He could swim, ride a bike, fire a gun, drive a car, years before any of his peers.

When P.J. boasted about having no arse in his trousers, he had been less than truthful. In fact, among his contemporaries his was the only warm bottom, for his mother had been well off by the standards of rural Cavan.

He was born in Chicago, where his father had a job on the railways. When P.J. was one, his father had been killed in an industrial accident and his mother had decided to return with her infant son and handsome compensation to the family farmhouse, long abandoned by her brothers in favour of an easier life in Birmingham and Sheffield.

In such a modest setting those American dollars spelled real comfort and so P.J. started life not only financially secure, but with no dark oedipal stirrings to disturb his idyll.

It was ordained that he would succeed.

It was at boarding school that he had first met Canice. The school was a diocesan college, one of the many which had been established throughout Ireland by the Catholic church. Their purpose was to prepare, for a small fee, the sons of the emerging middle classes for seminaries, where they would eventually train to become priests. The education was Catholic, rigorous, narrow and classical, for those were the days when church services were conducted in Latin.

P.J. had never had any intention of becoming a priest and possibly his mother could have afforded a school of more lustre. However, she was a modest woman and she knew that though book learning was important, it would matter less to her son than to other boys.

Canice's parents had sent him to the same school, scraping together the money once their son had announced his intention of becoming a priest. 'I have a vocation,' he told his mother when he was thirteen, and she, having thanked God, went off to badger his father for the money to send him to the college.

When he arrived in school, he spent many spare moments in the chapel. His innocence and good nature picked him out as a potential victim and within months he had become a fresh source of sport for all the school thugs.

It was when the bullying became really bad that P.J. had stepped in.

The two boys shared a happy disposition; they smiled at the world, expecting it to smile back. P.J. however had all the cop-on and intelligence that Canice lacked, and in any case his height and strength made him immune to bullying.

The school was a bleak, harsh place but no more so than the homes from which most of the boys had come. Getting up at six o'clock for Mass was preferable to getting up at the same hour and going out to a cold byre to milk the cows. Bellies filled with dull, badly cooked food were preferable to empty bellies. Chilblains and cold they would have suffered anyway, and there was the ever-present knowledge that these five years were the gateway to glory – a career in the Civil Service or as a National School teacher if one didn't quite make it to the ranks of God's Holy Anointed.

P.J. and Canice enjoyed their years at school; as men they had grown apart, but when they did meet there was still an affection between them. Indeed in Canice's eyes, only the Chief took precedence over P.J.

'How're you, P.J.,' he now inquired, shaking his hand.

They were meeting in the Arts Club, which had become the Minister's favourite watering hole. In his early days in the County Council offices, it had been a place to which more raffish senior colleagues used to adjourn when the pubs closed, and because he had not been invited along it had acquired the glamour of forbidden fruit. On becoming Minister his first action had been to give the club a grant, which had been spent on redecorating the gloomy, cat-infested rooms, one of which was named after him. It was in this lounge that they were now drinking.

'I'm sorry I wasn't there on Friday, Canice. I took off early, down to Cavan. Did you know that I've built a place down there?'

'No.'

70

'I have, not far from your old home. It's great country round there, you forget – ' P.J. paused as he saw Canice's stricken face, noticed his hands folded tightly together as if in prayer. 'Sorry, Canice. You wanted to see me about something in particular. Fire away.'

Canice took a deep breath, threw P.J. a look of desperation and began . . .

'Jesus, you're a right fool,' was P.J.'s reaction to the story so pathetically unfolded to him. 'What sort of an eejit are you to tell a pup like that a story like that? Going to confession together – can't you see them laughing all along Fleet Street or Wapping or wherever the hell they are.'

'But it was the truth, P.J.'

'What's that got to do with it, for Christ's sake? Wise up, will you? And remember, it's not just your reputation that's at stake, it's Ireland's as well.' As one of the country's most respected millionaires, P.J. had, perforce, acquired a degree of gravitas.

Poor Canice tore at his fringe. 'Sure isn't that the worst of it. Isn't that what's driving me wild. What should I do, P.J., what *can* I do? Should I resign on the spot and take the boat to England? I could send for Nuala and the kids later.'

At the preposterousness of this idea P.J. choked on his pint. He was about to let fly, to walk away even, when Canice's earnest, blue-eyed gaze, so open and trusting, caused him to relent.

'Stop worrying, Canice. It's not the end of the world.'

'But – '

'It mightn't be at all as bad as we think. I mean, nobody reads the – *Champion*, is it? – in Ireland. I've never even seen a copy.'

'What about the other papers, though?'

'I don't think they'll be all that interested. Haven't they enough scandals over there to keep the presses rolling day and night? No, I think that this may well blow over if we just keep our heads.'

'But, P.J., have you thought about the Irish papers? Some journalist over here is bound to see the story and then, if it's reprinted over here, I'm finished.'

'Listen – there's still a sense of decency in this country. Irish papers don't go in for that sort of filth. No, the important thing now is to see Honey and make sure that she keeps her mouth shut.'

'The Chief – '

'Never mind the Chief. Quit worrying and leave things to me. Just keep your head down and your mouth closed and I'll buzz round and see Honey straight away.'

'But – are we not going to try and stop it, maybe ring Jack Buchanan – '

'Muzzle the press, even the English gutter press – '

'Oh no, P.J., it's a quality weekly. I would never have agreed to give an interview otherwise.'

'Canice – sometimes I despair of you. Look, like a good man, just do what you're told and leave the rest to me. Do you think you can do that?'

P.J. sat back to ponder and finish his drink as Canice scurried out the door. He was not displeased to be presented with the problem – he would enjoy the challenge of coming up with a solution. His building empire had begun to bore him of late and the trappings of wealth meant little to him. He had bought the big house for Noreen, and as for the Mercedes, he preferred his bike.

What he did like about being a millionaire was the power and freedom it gave him; that and the knowledge that he had done something for the country, put money in people's pockets, made a dint in the unemployment register. The cynics would jeer at this of course, but it was the truth.

At fifty-three, full of energy and still in love with life, he had begun to think recently that he would soon have to be moving on. In what direction though?

Now such questions could be shelved while he concentrated on Canice's little problem, which together with the dancing should keep his restlessness in check.

He wasn't as sanguine as he had pretended to Canice. Even if the English press didn't take up the story, he wasn't too sure that it would be ignored in Ireland. It had been twenty years ago but much had changed during those twenty years.

He remembered the sudden and dramatic collapse of Honey's career, how it had been the talk of the country, confirming the earlier rumours about her pregnancy. In every pub in Ireland Canice's name had been coupled with hers, although this was often disputed and the name of a counter-claimant put forward.

Not a word ever appeared in an Irish newspaper, however, all of whom printed without comment the anodyne press release which Honey's record company had issued to announce her retirement.

Everyone knew but not officially, it was the way things were done. And because its status was unofficial no consequences flowed from the affair. If you didn't believe the story (and many didn't) you could dismiss it as malicious gossip. If you did, it was good for a giggle, but with a measure of sympathy for the erring pair thrown in. And when the baby died it was generally accepted that the whole thing was best forgotten.

No questions were ever asked in the Dáil; if Honey had wanted to resume her career, her fans would have welcomed her back with delight.

Now a whole generation had grown up who had never heard of Honey Fitz. These people had no sexual morality, as far as P.J. could tell, and what was worse, they were brazen-faced about their behaviour. They gave interviews to newspapers boasting of illegitimate children and gay liaisons. (Gay – P.J. could see nothing gay about the po-faced men who bored him with their lectures on tolerance and minority rights.) And these were the very people, P.J. knew, who would demand Canice's head on a plate. They were priggish and prissy and while they rutted day and night, there was a code which they wanted to impose on everyone else. Their great cant word was Truth. 'We must have truth, honesty, openness,' they cried, 'particularly in public life.'

What then would they make of Canice and his tale of woe? Of his monthly jaunts to confession, accompanied by his ex-mistress? P.J. could imagine their high moral tone mixed with gleeful contempt.

Oh the times were changing in Ireland and not for the better as far as P.J. was concerned. These prigs didn't know they were born. How did they imagine Ireland had survived over the centuries, except through compromise, double-dealing, chicanery and deceit? It was bred in the bone – Canice and the political party of which he was a member knew that, acknowledged it every day of their political lives. And this didn't make them lesser men in P.J.'s eyes but greater, more visionary, more understanding of what it was that made us what we are.

The new breed, though, was growing apace.

P.J. finished his pint, deciding that there was nothing to be done until the story appeared. Retrieving his bike, he hopped on and began to cycle the mile and a half across city to Honey's house. He hadn't seen her for years, but even in the old days he never could stand her. Everything about her irritated him, from her beseeching eyes to her soft flabbiness, to her deep, deep sighs. For all her tarty dressing and peroxided hair she was just an up-to-date version of Mother Machree, long suffering and addicted to religion.

Until today he had not realized the extent of her collapse after the baby's death, but this knowledge did not soften his heart towards her. Everyone had problems, for Christ's sake. She could have made an international career for herself instead of living off that poor fool.

He tied his bike to her railings and engulfed the tiny brass knocker in his paw.

'P.J.! This *is* an honour.' The eyes grew even larger and the pink skin blushed a pretty, deeper pink. She grasped at the silky material around her neck, futilely endeavouring to pull it higher.

'How're you, Honey?'

'Come in, P.J. Mind your head.' There were few traces of Cavan left in the soft voice which sounded more American than Irish.

'I'm not stopping – there's just something I wanted to say to you.'

'You'll have time for a cup of tea?' The voice had begun to tremble.

'Oh – all right.'

He watched her teeter out, then began to look round the room. None of the chairs seemed solid enough to sit on but he chose the biggest, shoving two lace-trimmed cushions on to the floor. There were knick-knacks everywhere, china shepherdesses smirking up at him, fragile-looking vases, bowls filled with pot-pourri, which must be responsible for the cloying scent now irritating P.J.,'s nostrils. He stood up to open a window and banged his head on the sloping ceiling. Swearing, he sat down again. The walls were arrayed with photographs of Honey in her heyday – singing into microphones, smiling up at celebrities, wearing ten-gallon hats. P.J. was relieved to see that there was no likeness of Canice anywhere in evidence.

When Honey came back she was smiling. She loved to entertain, but nowadays knew so few people that she seldom had an opportunity to indulge herself. She had pulled out all the stops for P.J. and now placed before him a lace-covered tray set with her best china, her bone-handled pastry forks and her embroidered tea napkins. She had homemade jam, homemade cake and homemade biscuits. No wonder she had put on a few pounds, wanly eating the goodies baked optimistically for guests who failed to arrive.

'You'd make someone a good wife,' was on the tip of P.J.'s tongue. He could almost feel sorry for her if he hadn't been so irritated by her fussing. She kept thrusting things at him – plates and forks and sugar bowls with tongs. There hadn't been many of those in Cavan, he thought sourly.

'Just pour me a cup of tea, woman – I'll do the rest myself.'

She sat back, placing both hands under her little fat thighs as if to prevent them from moving.

'Now, listen. Something's come up, nothing for you to worry about just so long as you keep calm and do what I tell you.'

Honey listened, her face growing pinker as P.J. talked. By the time he had finished she was crying and black mascara had begun its inky descent down her plump cheeks. 'I knew it. I knew something like this would happen sooner or later. That man is just too good and the good always suffer in this world. He's a pure saint, that's what he is – a pure saint. Oh my God, P.J., what are we going to do at all?'

'Quit that blubbering for a start, that's not going to help him.'

'I know, I'm sorry.' She dabbed at her eyes with the cuff of her negligée, thus distributing the mascara over a wider area. 'If he had abandoned me like many another man, this would never have happened. He's just too good – '

'Don't start all that again. Look – it may come to nothing yet. All I want you to do is be prepared and – '

'I've got it!' She stood up, hands held aloft, eyes shining, looking for all the world like the Honey Fitz who had wowed them at the Grand Ole Opry twenty years before. 'We'll say it was you, P.J., that you were the man.' Seeing his stricken face she gave him a playful push. 'Don't worry, they'll believe me the way I tell it. And I mean, we all grew up together and you two are so famous it would have been easy enough to get the two of you mixed up. Mistaken identity,' she savoured the phrase. 'Isn't that what they call it?'

For once in his life P.J. was speechless.

'And think about it, P.J. You'll be doing this not only for Canice but you'll be doing it for Ireland as well. Isn't that grand now?'

Not a word which P.J. found appropriate. Looking at her

beaming face, all that he could think about that pair was that they deserved one another. The sheer stupidity of it.

'Honey,' he began to speak slowly. 'I don't think this is a good idea at all.'

'But for Ireland, P.J. – '

Carefully he started to explain to her the importance of his own good name in Ireland's image at home and abroad, noting the apparent success of Bill O'Reilly's slogan, 'A sacrifice for Ireland is a sacrifice you owe yourself.'

'So you see, Honey, even if it did work, it wouldn't really be a good idea. I know I'm not as important a man as Canice, that anybody could do what I'm doing. Unfortunately in the world we live in, money rates high. Dragging my name through the mud would be bringing Ireland's credibility into question. Think of the effect on the Punt and the stock markets. Think of all those poor people who have invested all their savings. It's not on, Honey, much as I would wish it could be.'

'I hadn't thought of that,' Honey stared across at him, her face crumpling inwards like an ageing capsicum. 'I suppose so, there's no hope. Poor Canice. Poor, poor Canice.'

P.J., fearing that the tears were about to start flowing once more, took her hand and patted it awkwardly. 'Don't worry, Honey, you weren't listening to me. I'm going to look after this and I've never let Canice down in my life. Now, all I want you to do, the reason I came here today, is to warn you not to say anything to anybody. No interviews, no matter what plausible line any of them come up with. Do you understand that?'

She nodded.

'Good girl. Now, leave the rest to me. And stop worrying – nothing's happened yet.'

P.J. pedalled away, conscious of the distance he was putting between Honey and himself, relieved to have that part of the business over. And he would deal with the rest when it came up. Maybe nothing would happen. Maybe the Irish papers would ignore it. Maybe he could have a word in a few ears. Money spoke, even to the holier-than-thous.

Skilfully avoiding a pothole, he breathed in deeply and began to whistle a favourite aria from *Don Giovanni*.

.7

In his brief life Aubrey McGuckian had considered himself in love on three different occasions. Each time the passion had been short-lived and he would realize with hindsight that there had been something puny about its very inception. He also realized, now that he had been infected by the genuine virus, that what he had suffered on those occasions bore little resemblance to true love. And one could hardly apply the term suffering this time round: he was in a fever, yes, but all his senses were inflamed by pleasure rather than pain. The affair, the first grand passion of his adult life, had begun a week ago and involved not a flesh and blood woman but a city. Aubrey was in love with the Big Apple. He had crossed the bridge into Manhattan and he had been instantly smitten.

It seemed very strange to him that he had been so negative about America up till now. It had never engaged his imagination as Europe and the Far East had; he had never wanted to come here, not even to New York, whose great architecture he was so familiar with. Perhaps America, as the birthplace of P.J., had been spoiled for him and so he had set his face against it. Even the prospect of this trip had not engendered excitement. He had come out of boredom with Dublin and disillusion with his profession. Looking around for somewhere to escape to, he had remembered a long-standing invitation from Joe Delaney. He hadn't thought about the man for years, although at one time they had been quite close friends. Joe and he had qualified together, and after three months hanging around Joe had set out to try his luck in New York. Which must have been considerable if the SoHo apartment and designer labels in his wardrobe were an indication.

As with so many love affairs, the initial attraction had been physical. Nobody had told Aubrey how breathtakingly beautiful the city was. He walked around it open-mouthed, eyes forever raised, in danger of falling flat on his face but indifferent to hurt or ridicule.

'Does it still excite you, living here?' he asked Joe now. They were having breakfast in a café in the East Village, seated at the window, looking out on the already hectic scene, although it was not much past eight.

'Love, love, love it,' replied Joe, licking honey from his fingers.

'Ever think of coming home?'

'God no. Maybe when I'm old and tired and need a rest but not yet awhile.'

'Things are looking up at home.'

'Yeah? Know what I love about New York? Its energy. It's go-go-go day and night. Nobody ever does anything in Dublin except bitch about things in general and drink too much. No – ' He held up a bronzed hand. 'I admit that the McGuckians are an exception to that rule. Your old man was different and you are too – that's why you are where you are today. But I couldn't bear to go back there, looking at fellas crying into their pints. This town is simply magic, intoxication, electrifying. You know.'

Oh didn't Aubrey know! He had neither sniffed, smoked nor drunk any hallucinatory substance since his arrival and yet every time he went outside he felt himself floating a good two inches above the Manhattan pavements, high on the high-octane air.

At six every morning he went for a swim with Joe in a roof-top pool, thirty-six storeys up where Joe's health club spread itself across the two top floors.

Afterwards they'd have breakfast together at a café such as this and then Joe would head off to work. Joe walked everywhere, stepping out briskly in his business suit and thick-soled trainers, swinging his arms in front of his body and looking decidedly odd, except that nothing looked odd in New York. Left to himself, Aubrey spent his days wandering happily. He sat in the sunshine in Central Park, watching the children at play and realizing with a shock that New Yorkers, too, reproduced themselves. He took in a concert at the Lincoln Center and visited the Frick Museum or the Museum of Modern Art. With a map and his pockets full of dollar tokens he rode the buses and the subway. And incessantly he snacked. He had succumbed totally to this delicious American obsession. He stopped off for a b.l.t. sandwich or a bowl of Manhattan clam chowder; he devoured bagels and pretzels; he licked ice-cream cones and lowered sodas, all the while wondering at the elderly eating habits he indulged in back home – three square meals a day, eaten, sedately, at table.

At night his feeling of intoxication became more pronounced. He felt then as he looked up at the thousands of lights high over his head as if the city itself were afloat. The twin towers of the World Trade Center held more magic for him than Orion ever had. He wanted to walk and walk, and so apparently did everybody else for the pavements were as crowded as at midday.

Of course he was no fool and he didn't stray too far uptown nor venture into the Lower East Side.

He had seen the people sleeping at the entrances to subway stations; he had been accosted by crazy people and beggars who had stood full square in front of him demanding money; he had glimpsed Harlem from the window of a moving train and been horrified by what he saw. It reminded him of photographs taken of German cities after the war – half-ruined buildings, fires in the streets.

He had, however, agreed with Joe Delaney's robust defence of his adopted city. 'What do you expect, for Christ's sake? Look at the size of this city and its ethnic mix. Then look at little monoracial Dublin – there are more beggars in Dublin than in New York and just as many heroin addicts, given the comparative size. The amazing thing is that *more* people aren't murdered each day in a city this size and with people coming in every day from every corner of the globe. New York is a bloody triumph of civilization, that's what it is.'

'What about the poverty though, what about – '

'You get drop-outs and beggars in every society. If you want to fall through, then no safety net is going to hold you.'

'But – '

'Look. I'm not saying New York hasn't got problems but I was mugged in Dublin and I've never been mugged in New York.'

'Yet.'

But Aubrey didn't feel threatened walking round the streets of the ciy, and having heard of the legendary rudeness of New Yorkers he was quite touched to find them friendly, to find that people smiled at him and held doors open for him. In cafés and museums he was occasionally asked where he came from and once he told them, he would become the centre of an admiring, congratulatory circle. Everyone had Irish blood, everyone loved Ireland, and they especially loved this Irishman who was so demonstrably in love with their town.

And as is the way with love affairs, Aubrey began to learn about himself; New York gave him new insights into past behaviour, explaining to him why he had done something, taken some course. His turning away from modernism and back towards Palladio had been instinctive, but he now had a rational back-up for that behaviour. Viewed from the distance of three thousand miles, across the raging Atlantic, Europe came clearly into focus – an old world, small and imperilled, fragile as any rain-forest, not to be taken for granted or mucked about with. Over thousands of years it had taken shape, cleared, cultivated and built by man, who had recognized his own mortality and who had never forgotten the gods at whose mercy he was. Over decades he had built the Parthenon, the Colosseum, the great mosque at Cordoba, the cathedrals at Cologne and Chartres. The secular buildings that followed, the merchants' houses of Amsterdam, the terraces and squares of London, were lovely in their modesty and lack of assumption; even the châteaux of the Loire, the country houses of the English nobility, did not presume too far. An ordered, hierarchical society with death at its centre had created a world of great delicacy and beauty.

And Europe was still dying and must look backwards, not forwards; the Prince of Wales recognized this although he might not put it in those exact words. Nostalgia was right for Europe, a gentle patina of melancholy settling over the continent, which recognized that its best times were past, that its duty now was to preserve itself as best it could.

What place did giant steel skeletons clad in concrete blocks have in such a world? None. They stood out, ugly and ridiculed, while people, Europeans, demanded somewhere small to live, burrows they could hide and work and shop in. No wonder Aubrey's gifts had not been fully appreciated, for Aubrey was an inventor, a forward-looking man of vision.

In the New World history didn't weigh you down, there was space to create and death had no pre-eminence, being an un-American activity. Gropius and Mies had known this when they had emigrated here; Aubrey now knew it as he looked at the skyscrapers around him and saw that their creators were often wrong in their assumption that such buildings were a mere expression of the possibilities of technology; they were more than that – they were a recognition of New Man, a hybrid grafted from the old European stock but now a distinct species. They were an expression of his psyche, looking forward, optimistic, unshadowed. When Aubrey saw the AT & T building on Madison Avenue he had laughed aloud, admiring the audacity of Philip Johnson, its architect, seeing the joke straight away, wondering what Dublin would have made of *that*. The two buildings which had moved him most deeply, however, were the Guggenheim Museum and the Seagram Building, both of them already old by New York standards.

His first sight of the Lloyd Wright building had filled Aubrey with joy. And what a nice conceit it presented! You stood at the top and looked down and quite soon saw that art was no match for architecture. The pictures viewed on a slant assumed a self-importance, burlesquing their seriousness. Then, dismissing the painting, you looked at mankind, crawling along the inside of the building, antlike and fevered in his descent. Man diminished? Ha – but not by some malevolent deity, not by some gloating presence up beyond the Gothic spires. If man was diminished here, it was by the genius of his fellow man. Frank Lloyd Wright had put man in the very centre.

The Seagram Building had a different flavour. There was nothing playful here: the unbroken fall of the curtain wall lent an air of severity, a touch of the sombre. The dark, amber-tinted glass, the brass mullions, gave it an impersonal, cool dignity that suggested the ecclesiastical.

And one walked away chastened, reminded of one's duty to America – to commerce, to production and expansion.

For it was a mistake to believe that the Americans were a frivolous people – they were serious, in their jogging as in their diet, in everything they did. And because they were serious they could believe in themselves, and because they could believe in themselves they could create, make something from nothing. Whereas the Europeans, with their self-conscious appraisals, their ambiguities, were more suited to be curators than creators. Aubrey scowled as he remembered how often he had failed to pick up nuances in conversations at home, finding himself arguing earnestly while those around him laughed at some hidden joke.

Here his utterances were taken at face value. Other people didn't talk in code, they said what they had to say, straight up. Aubrey knew where he was and he liked the feeling.

'We're invited to a party tonight,' Joe stood up, straightening his shoulders, ready to walk.

'Me too?'

'Sure. It's kind of in your honour. Statia Hennessey – rich, rich, rich. You've no idea. And she loves everything Irish. She met your old man last time he was in town and she's dying, darling, to meet you. Have you brought a tux?'

'Naturally.'

'Good man. That's what I like about you McGuckians – you've got style. Just like Statia. There aren't many black-tie dos in this town, but Statia has standards. See you about six.'

Statia Hennessey could have been any age between thirty-five and seventy. She was tall and spare with a restructured, smiling face, an even golden tan and blonde curls. Her nails were long and scarlet and the fluid material of her palazzo pants was the only thing about her that suggested the freedom of movement. Any natural tendency of the flesh to sag or bag had been overcome by the best efforts of art and science so that there was a certain rigidity about her person which was at first disconcerting. For all that, Aubrey found her magnificent, her sexy, throaty chuckle, her turquoise eyes that looked straight into his soul. Jesus! He felt the hair on his scalp rise – a phenomenon which began to spread to other areas and organs of his body.

She took his arm and led him towards a window which opened on to a balcony. 'It's quite a small apartment but I like it for the view.' Together they looked down on the woody expanses of Central Park. 'It's terrific having the Park on your doorstep. I go for a run there every morning before breakfast.'

'Is it safe?'

'What a darling question. It shows your concern, your human-ity, Aube. Look, stand back.' From the mysterious shadows between her breasts she withdrew a tiny, silver-topped bottle. Extending it at arm's length out over the balcony she depressed the silver top; there was a deafening screech and the smell of ammonia on the air.

'And that's only for demonstration purposes. Anyone tries messing with this lady is going to find himself deaf *and* blind.' She popped the little bottle back and took Aubrey's arm once more. 'Now, come and have a drink. I allow myself two glasses of champagne a day and *that's it*. But I know boys of your tender age get thirsty.' Removing her hand from his arm, she placed it experimentally on his spine where it began a slow, sensuous descent towards his buttocks.

He felt sweat on his forehead and ran a finger round the inside of his dress shirt, wishing it were not quite so tight.

'Want to remove that tie? Take off the tux, too, darling – we're informal here. Pleasure is the only principle.'

What a woman!

'Look.' She extended a shapely foot. 'I never wear shoes in the apartment, the tactile pleasure from marble is enormous. Why don't you do the same? I'll bet you have the darlingest toes.'

The apartment was furnished with minimalist elegance, the colour scheme black and pink. Aubrey liked it, its lack of fuss and feeling of space. The drawing room, or playpen, as Statia called it, was presided over by a life-size statue of the Buddha whose emerald eyes followed one smilingly round the room. It did not strike Aubrey as a decorative piece but rather as a shrine and he noticed that many of the guests made obeisances to it as they passed. Aubrey felt encouraged by the divine presence. He knew somehow that the Lord Buddha would be more relaxed and more permissive than the Lord Jesus in similar circumstances.

The guests were a sophisticated bunch, cosmopolitan in flavour. There was an Argentinian poet who talked to him about Yeats, there was an Indian prince who didn't talk at all and there were several assorted Europeans.

And then there were the New Yorkers, so easy, so relaxed. 'How you doing?' they asked him. 'You having a good time? Good. So'm I – having a hell of a good time.'

He thought that this must be the secret of their happiness, this mantra that they offered each other. 'You having a good time? Yeah. So am I.' If it were said often enough it became substantial, filling the air around them.

It was the sort of thing they made fun of back in Dublin. Well, it was better than eternally complaining about the weather as far as Aubrey was concerned.

He was surprised at how early the party ended. By eleven o'clock people had started to drift away, by twelve there was only a handful of guests remaining.

Statia was lying on a sofa with her feet up; Aubrey was sitting beside her, stroking her toes.

'Hey, Joe,' Statia called. 'You going home or you want a bed for the night?'

'Going home, Statia.'

'You don't expect this poor baby to head downtown at this hour?' She turned her head towards Aubrey, her eyes widening in concern.

'Of course not, Statia.'

'He's staying with me. I'm taking him running in the Park in the morning.'

'Good idea, Statia.'

'This poor boy can't be expected to schlep back to SoHo tonight, Statia's going to look after him.' Playfully she began to tickle his tummy with her toes, the red nails disappearing into the folds of his dress shirt.

'Then I guess I'll say good night.'

Don't leave me, Joe, wait for me, Aubrey's eyes appealed to the disappearing figure of his friend. The door closed behind him and Aubrey realized that he was alone with his hostess.

'I think you need a shower, Aube.' With a graceful yoga movement, Statia sat up. 'Or maybe a tub would be more relaxing. In fact I think that's one of my better ideas – we'll both take a tub.'

Like a lamb to the slaughter he followed her from the room and down a long, pink corridor. Ireland's honour was at stake and oh God, what a weight for his frail shoulders. He shouldn't have drunk so much champagne; he should have eaten that spinach at lunch; he hadn't had oysters for over a year.

Statia pushed in a door and pulled him in after her. She depressed a switch and there was an explosion of Statias all around, on the ceiling and on all the walls.

'I hate damn tiles,' she said, 'they're so clinical. Give me the humanity of mirrors anytime.'

In the middle of the floor was a sunken bath, the size of a small swimming pool.

Statia turned and began to undo his flies.

Oh God, Buddha, anyone – help!

When he awoke he couldn't understand why it was already bright for he felt as if he had only been asleep for minutes. He closed his eyes again and turned over, but even as he settled down he heard the door opening. He peered up to find Statia standing there, dressed in white shorts with a pink and white sweat band clamping down her pretty curls.

'Hi! Good morning, lover. How do you feel this morning?' She bent over to offer him a kiss. 'Go wash your teeth. Then join us for breakfast, there's a robe at the foot of the bed.'

Us? Was her husband out there?

He began to panic, getting caught up with pink silk sheets as he struggled out of bed. Then as memories of the previous night came back to him he thought, if there is a husband out there he should damn well offer me a service medal – he can only be grateful that I stood in for a night. Statia was a wonderful woman – his assessment of the previous night was merely reinforced by the light of the morning – but she did take some keeping up with. She had told him last night that she had been on oestrogen for the past ten years; after his experience Aubrey was tempted to go on it himself.

They were on the terrace drinking orange juice. 'Hi,' said the man in the baseball cap as he stood up to shake hands.

'Aube, I want you to meet Congressman Savino. Matt, this is my friend from Ireland that I was telling you about.' Statia patted the chair beside her and Aubrey sat down. 'He couldn't make the party last night, he didn't get in from Albany until after ten. But he couldn't miss meeting with you, so here you both are.'

'How do you do,' said Aubrey, stiff and European. He had noticed that he only began to offer his first 'Hi' half-way through the day.

Statia sipped her orange juice, looking from one to the other over the rim of her glass. 'I'll tell you what I'm going to do,' she said. 'I'm going to let you two boys get acquainted over breakfast. I'm off to the Park. No, lover,' she dropped a kiss on Aubrey's head, 'you're being let off this one for good behaviour.'

Matteo Savino had brown, buttery eyes and a double chin. The rest of him was trim, flat stomach, firm thighs inside the stretch material of his jogging suit.

'Everybody in New York seems to love exercising,' offered Aubrey, uncomfortable in his newly exposed lover status.

'Sure, stay fit. You enjoy life more that way and get to live longer.' Matt smiled benignly. 'It's great to be talking to someone from Ireland.'

'You know Ireland?'

'One of my favourite places.'

'Any Irish blood?'

'Nope. Italian. Both sides. And you know what I'm gonna tell you, Aube, you won't believe this but fifteen years ago I hardly knew where Ireland was. Can you believe that? I mean *I knew* – you can't live in New York and not know about the Irish. When I was in grade school I used to get beaten up regularly by Irish kids. And they were Catholic and we were Catholic but I didn't like them much. Can you believe that?'

'Indeed. I can. I know what sociological studies say about – '

'So the Irish were around and they fought and drank too much and made a nuisance of themselves on St Patrick's Day, but I never thought much about it and I never thought about Ireland – the place. Then – now listen to this, this is going to break you up, Aube – then one day, one night to be precise, I was looking at a late-night movie and it happened. I just flicked a switch and for the next two hours I got the best history lesson a guy could hope for. The funny thing is, I can't even remember the name of the movie now but it taught me more about Ireland than the *New York Times* ever did.'

Aubrey nodded, mystified as to what the movie could have been.

'Then I started to visit, to get to know the place properly.'

'Dublin?'

'Belfast.'

Oh – oh. Trouble. There was only one kind of American who visited Belfast. And – Aubrey stared more closely at the smiling face. Hadn't he seen that face somewhere before? In the pages of some newspaper? Savino –

'You know, I never thought much about those sort of things. I mean, I never liked the Brits, the way they talk as if they have a bad taste in their mouth. You see them guys sometimes around Washington and I can't stand them. But I never thought of them as oppressors. I mean – we saw them off a long

86

time ago, right? I mean, the United States of America has no problem with little old Britain. But when I saw that movie, the wool was pulled from my eyes and I began to read and think – you could say I was very uneducated beforehand. And that's how my interest in Ireland began. It all started with a movie.'

Aubrey stared at him in fascinated horror. Interest in Ireland: Aubrey would take a bet that Savino's interest did not lie in the direction of Waterford crystal and the lakes of Killarney; Congressman Savino's interest lay rather in the direction of the Troubles, of collecting dollars here in America to buy Semtex and rocket launchers and Uzi machine-guns.

And Statia must have known. What the hell did she think she was doing leaving him with this lunatic? Unless she was in on it too . . . then what about Joe Delaney?

'Hey, Aube – you want the john?'

In his agitation Aubrey had begun to wriggle away from Congressman Savino. 'No.' He gripped the arms of his chair. *Where* had he seen that face?

Matt Savino beamed at him, offering him more coffee. Could he get away from him, walk out, pretending he had an appointment somewhere?

But Statia – no. He would challenge him. This was America after all, the land of the candid, where people asked you your age, sexual proclivity and bank balance without batting an eyelid. He would follow their example.

'Congressman Savino, tell me – '

'Matt.'

'Matt. Are you a member of Noraid?'

Congressman Savino threw back his head, displaying a bull-like neck. 'Me? In Noraid? You gotta be kidding, Aube. They're nothing but a buncha schmucks. Now what could have given you that idea?'

Had he been wrong then? Had he misread the signals? Perhaps Matt was just another example of an American (and after all, he was an Italian American) suffering from emotional muddle when it came to the situation in Ireland.

'So, Aube, what you say we spend the day together? This is my town, I'd like to show it to you.'

'Oh I don't think so.' Aubrey didn't fancy a day spent in New

York talking about the Brits and Belfast with Congressman Savino.

'Come on, fella.'

'But Statia. She'll be expecting me here.'

'That's all taken care of. She's meeting us for lunch at Elaine's. I guess she's going to be busy till then, counting her money. So come on, Aube. Let me show you a really good time.'

8

It was the strangest day which Aubrey was to spend in New York. It started with a drive back to SoHo in Matt's car, which they picked up in a garage a block away from Statia's apartment. In Joe's apartment they both changed, Matt retrieving what appeared to be a complete wardrobe from the back of his car.

'Ready for a coffee?'

'Dying for one.'

'Right. From now on we'll walk or pick up a cab if your feet get tired. Now I'm going to introduce you to a place where I have lots of friends and you will too. We're going to Little Italy.'

They had *cappuccino* and some of the most delicious pastries that Aubrey had ever tasted in Ferrara's on Grand Street. Sitting looking out on the passing scene, Aubrey had difficulty believing that he was still in America, that he hadn't somehow been transported across the sea to Italy. The people who walked by moved with that co-ordinated grace that he had noticed on the streets of Rome. They spoke to one another in Italian, the men's cologne coming in through the open window had the same sharp tang that he remembered sniffing the first time he had stepped off a plane on to Italian soil. Small Italian flags hung from doors, bottles of Chianti and Italian salamis were displayed in windows.

When they finished their coffee they began to walk, continuing in a downtown direction. Matt seemed to know many of the traders and their progress was slow as he stopped to have a word here and there, sometimes in English, but more often in Italian.

'How's your Gaelic, Aube?' he asked casually.

'Not very good, I'm afraid.' Meaning – I couldn't put two sentences together.

'Ah never mind.'

But suddenly Aubrey did mind. For the first time in his life he was ashamed that he couldn't speak Irish.

On Mott Street they caught a cab for the short journey to South Street seaport. There they boarded a little white and red steamer for a trip in the bay. There was a breeze on the water and Aubrey sat back gratefully, letting it play on the back of his neck.

'The best view in town, Aube. Feast your eyes.'

The island of Manhattan, familiar from a thousand movies and yet unknown in its dazzle and variety, began to float past. Aubrey looked up at the giant forest of steel and glass, surprised by the aptness of the image which had come into his head. They *did* look rooted, those skyscrapers, and they looked inevitable, a part of nature, something that had grown not by the efforts of man but by some mysterious natural law. He thought of seedlings breaking through the forest floor and growing tall and tall, seeking the light. And these were so light, so at one with the element into which they bloomed.

As Aubrey gazed he was gradually overcome by a sense of disorientation. He began to wonder how he had ever arrived at this spot, travelling as he had from an impossibly remote island. He couldn't even begin to imagine what sort of grey July day it would be back in Dublin, not as he looked into this brazen sun whose beams ricocheted off the tall glass towers and then pierced right through his skull. He thought: Ireland has ceased to exist, it has been annihilated by the vigour of this young giant. He thought: I can never go back or I too shall cease to exist.

He was glad when Matt, poking him in the ribs, broke into his strange mood. 'Hey, Aube, turn your head and look – the Statue of Liberty. What do you think – isn't she great?'

Aubrey stared, overawed by the unexpected size of the statue.

'Can you imagine what all those poor people fleeing from persecution and famine, *famine*, Aube, must have felt when they got their first glimpse of her? Liberty, freedom, Aube. You can say what you like about this country but it was founded on the highest of ideals – and we Americans still believe in freedom.' He paused, his little brown eye turning slyly to peek at Aube. 'I guess that's why I found Belfast so hard to take.' He got up and began to stroll along the deck, leaving Aubrey more confused than ever. Dublin was distant enough – he couldn't even grasp at the fact of the existence of a town called Belfast.

As they disembarked Matt said, 'We're never going to make it to Elaine's for lunch, I'd better ring Statia and tell her to meet us down here somewhere.'

'But – if we can't make it uptown, how will she get down here?'

'Because Statia being Statia she'll come by helicopter. She has one or can get her hands on one – I don't know which. I'll go call her now.'

They waited for her in the sunshine on the pier. She arrived wearing a large straw hat, tied, like Little Bo Peep's, under the chin. She was carrying a large wickerwork picnic basket.

She kissed them both and sat down between them on the bench. 'This is the darlingest idea. I lo-ove picnics.' She began to withdraw the goodies: pastrami, prosciutto, rye bread, bagels, cheeses, individually packed salads and, of course, champagne. 'I thought we'd have coffee in one of those places along here when we finish – somewhere with a view.'

They ate in silence except for the expressions of delight and approval from the two Americans. Statia from time to time would pick out a particularly choice morsel and feed it to Aubrey, watching him carefully until he nodded his head in obvious pleasure. Then she would dab at his lips with a napkin saying, 'M'm . . . goo-ood . . . m'm . . .' in that throaty way of hers.

It was not the most relaxing meal that Aubrey had ever had but he thought he might grow used to it.

They spent the afternoon wandering back, stopping here and there, to eat something, to look at something. When they grew tired walking they took a cab. On West Broadway Aubrey felt unaccountably delighted by the sight of a shamrock-bedecked pub sign which read 'The Treaty Stone'. Everywhere they stopped and chatted to strangers in the manner of New Yorkers, the other two always introducing him as 'our friend from Ireland'. Back on Fifth Avenue Statia took his hand and said, 'Come and light a candle with me,' and led him into St Patrick's Cathedral.

Unselfconsciously he walked beside her, knelt beside her, and when he too offered a prayer it hardly seemed strange.

'Imagine,' whispered Statia, pointing towards the Gothic ceiling, 'imagine, it was the cents and dimes of the poor Irish servants that built this cathedral. Doesn't it make you proud, Aube?'

And that's what he was beginning to feel – proud. Proud to be Irish. Today he had undergone a sentimental education. From the moment that he had looked back on the Manhattan skyline, his passion for New York had begun to metamorphose. As he looked at the Statue of Liberty and Ellis Island and listened to Matt talk of the immigrants who had arrived to be humiliated and deloused and had stayed to claw their way up despite the best effort of the Yankees, as he watched people's genuine warmth towards him once they heard where he came from, as he knelt beside Statia in St Patrick's Cathedral, he began to realize that it was not a case of 'off with the old and on with the new' but that the old and new were inextricably entwined and that his new love had suddenly made him aware of his old one. Never before having questioned his nationality any more than he would question the colour of his eyes, he now saw that it couldn't be taken for granted, or shouldn't be, at any rate.

That tiny island, that rocky Atlantic outpost – what a mark it had made on the world!

They came out of the cathedral and began to stroll again, enjoying now the comparative cool.

'Statia,' Matt made an expansive gesture towards Fifth Avenue, 'would you live anywhere else?'

Statia sniffed with apparent delight the polluted air. 'I can't imagine it. Europe's great but I'm an American, and for an American there is only one possible place to live – Manhattan.'

'Just the way I feel, only on account of my mother I'd better extend that to Brooklyn. She still lives there, Aube, and she'd kill me if I didn't say that. You know something? I go anywhere in this town, at any hour of the day or night, and I've never been harmed.'

Aubrey looked at him sceptically. 'Would you go to the Bronx at twelve o'clock at night?'

'Well now – '

'There you are – I knew it.'

'No, it's true, Aube, this is not a dangerous city once you use your common sense. I've never been scared here, but I can tell you I was scared shitless in Belfast.'

Belfast – there it was again, but at Matt's second reference to the city Aubrey suddenly found his interest aroused. 'Have you often been to Belfast, Matt?' Aubrey himself had only been once when he had gone as a student to see an exhibition about industrical cities in the nineteenth century.

'Sure I've been, more than a dozen times. But I had this one really bad experience.'

He put an arm round each of them and when the traffic lights said Walk, he guided them across the street. 'I liked Belfast the minute I stepped into it. I liked the people and the pubs. After a few days I got used to the soldiers and the checkpoints and I sort of stopped noticing them. I didn't know anybody and I was just there as a private citizen – I mean, nobody knew who I was or anything. But I had a friend who wrote this family he knew in West Belfast and when I was there a few days one of the sons came to the hotel and asked me would I like a night out listening to some Irish music. He took me to a club.

'It was kinda strange at first. An awful deserted street like you see in war movies and this building with the windows all boarded up and a sort of cage in front of the door. But once you got inside the door – funsville. Singing, dancing, booze, great dames. I got talking to this young guy who was fairly stewed and who started telling me how he was in trouble with his wife. He looked too young to have a wife but that's what he told me. His son was being christened at the weekend he said, and that afternoon he'd taken a music centre to the hock shop so's they could all have a good time at the christening. It was his wife's music centre but she told him it was OK to take it. She wanted a fine party for their first-born too.

'Anyways, on the way home, with the money in his fist, he had fallen into bad company, a lotta bad company, and they had persuaded him to go drinking. When he realized what he had done, he had put ten pounds on a horse that was still running and here he was now, afraid to go home to his wife.

'I felt sorry for the kid and the mess he had gotten himself into. He kept on grabbing me and saying to me, "Listen, Yank, I really love that wee girl and wee Liam too. I really do love them – sure they're all I have in the world."

'I thought that maybe if we could sober him up, I could slip him a few dollars and we could go home and face the wee girl

93

together. I was about to suggest this when this young fellow, now *this* one really was a kid, came up to our table and said, "You're in right trouble, Charlie. Our Bernie's on her way here and she's flipping mad."

'Our Bernie and the wee girl turned out to be one and the same and my friend Charlie had no intention of hanging around for a reconciliation. "Give us a lift, Yank," he said, dragging me towards the door. "Give us a lift anywhere." I'd hired a car earlier that day, so Dennis – he was the guy who'd brought me there – suggested that we all go back to his mother's house and that Charlie could have some coffee there and try to sober up.

'We went outside and Dennis and I got into the front of the car. Charlie got into the back and lay down on the floor. I thought this was a bit extravagant myself, but Charlie explained that Bernie's brother drove a black taxi and she would come looking for him in that and if she saw him in this car she would give chase.

'Well, we were driving along for about five minutes when we came to a barrier and soldiers flagging us down. Dennis told me to stop and play it cool, not give them any lip. I stopped and was about to roll down my window when what did that stupid Charlie do – he jumped out of the back of the car and went tearing off down the road.

'The kid was drunk and stupid and scared. At first I didn't know what was happening. There was shouting and the clatter of army boots and flashing lights. Next there was a burst of fire and Charlie had fallen, just as he was about to round a corner. He was lying there on the sidewalk.

'I tell you the next hour was the very worst in my life.

'The soldiers made us get out of the car and backed us up against a wall with our hands up over our heads. If I tried to open my mouth they told me to shut it and I did – pretty damn quick. Those guys sure were trigger happy. Dennis knew this and he just stayed shtum right through, but that's hard for an American to do.

'They wouldn't let us go to poor Charlie, we had to just stand there as they took the car apart. Then this officer type came along and I tried offering him an explanation but he got real mad, just hearing my accent. Made some shitty remarks about Americans always causing trouble. But I didn't mind that – I didn't mind any of that. I was just thinking of poor young Charlie lying there

94

and of the wee girl and the baby and the christening party that would have to be abandoned.

'It turned out that the army had lost some men that night. A jeep had been blown up near where we were stopped and two soldiers had been killed. But, Jesus, is that any excuse?'

Matt stopped in the middle of the Manhattan pavement and addressed his query to the sky. 'You listen to me, Aube. You people in Dublin – and that includes the government – you don't have a clue. You've no idea what's been going on up there over the years. You just don't have a clue.'

Aubrey opened his mouth and then closed it again. Matt was right, he didn't have a clue, and what was worse, his ignorance was culpable.

'Cheer up.' Matt slapped him on the back. 'How about we all go back to my place and I cook you up some spaghetti the way momma taught me how?'

Statia shook her head. 'I'll take a raincheck, Matt. I'm flying to Houston in the morning and I've got an early start. But you take good care of this sweet guy – you hear? And as for you, lover,' she ran a hand along Aubrey's spine, 'I'll be seeing you soon.'

Aubrey found himself almost relieved that she was going. He was upset and confused and he wanted time to think things out and his thoughts tonight would not be focused on the carnal. He turned towards Matt, resentful of him and the mixture of sensations he had been responsible for arousing in a stomach already prone to over-acidity. 'I don't think I'll come either.'

'Sure you will. The night's young and I'll see you're home by ten thirty. How does that sound?'

For the next couple of hours Matt backed off, but after they had eaten the spaghetti and drunk a few glasses of wine, he started again. Anecdotes, statistics, examples of British barbarity.

'All right, all right,' Aubrey held up his hands. 'I accept that you know what you're talking about, that what you say is true, but – so what? What are we supposed to do? Join the Provos? Start planting bombs and murdering fathers in front of their children? Is that what you want? I thought you said you weren't a member of Noraid, well, you're sounding very like them.'

'Hey – Aube – calm down, fella. I don't want to bomb anybody and I'm not a member of Noraid. I don't believe in the bomb or the bullet, although I sure as hell don't think there's any difference in a bullet fired from a Brit rifle or fired by the IRA. But I'm a man of peace and I believe in the power of propaganda. The South is the bastard – if you'll pardon my French – we gotta get working on the ordinary Joe Soap who lives in Dublin or Galway or Mullingar. Once he realizes what's going on, once he isn't handed all this one-sided propaganda, he'll *demand* that the British get out of his country.'

You could say that Aubrey McGuckian was an apple ready to be plucked. Just a puff of wind and he was falling, down into the cupped and careful hands of Matteo Savino. He was still not convinced but he would be, soon. He would mull things over, toss them around and come back again to the perfidy of Southern behaviour in the person of his father, the Irish millionaire. He would be excited by the concept of a Cause, passionately moved by the plight of the unfree, delighting in the space to indulge in a little old-fashioned nationalism. He would come to see as pallid his former smart lifestyle and wonder how he had ever got excited at the prospect of restoring Georgian Dublin. And he would have Matteo Savino, his new hero, to thank for all that.

At the end of the evening Matt seemed well pleased as he handed Aubrey into a cab with as much care and courtesy as if he were a high-school date. 'I'll see you in Dublin, Aube. And I'd like to meet your father. He's just the sort of man we need to get to – opinion formers, the influential ones.'

Aubrey sat back in the cab, slapping his arms across his stomach to squash the worm of suspicion that had begun to wriggle somewhere inside his colon. Matt had picked out *him,* had chosen *him.* The fact that he was P.J.'s son was surely incidental. Matt's final comment had been casual; it was natural that he should want to get to know P.J. He didn't yet know how difficult it was to separate P.J. from even the smallest amount of his money. But he would find out.

9

When Annabel McGuckian opened her eyes she thought that she was still at school in her convent at Epsom. Then she saw her pink curtains with the black and white pierrots and she knew that she was home. She smiled at the pierrots' sad faces, then she stretched and yawned.

She intended to stay in bed for a month in order to recover from all those early mornings at school, if, that is, one ever recovered from such rigours. First of all, though, she must go to the loo.

On her return journey she stopped for a peek in the dressing-table mirror. Oh God – did she really look that hideous? Closing her eyes tightly she groped her way back to bed and collapsed.

She was, in fact, a pretty girl, a mixture of her father and mother, with P.J.'s black curls and dimpled chin and Noreen's blue eyes and fine, fair skin. At five foot seven she was two inches taller than her mother and she moved well and confidently, surveying the world with just a hint of arrogance in her blue eyes.

Sometimes this arrogance was real – when her skin behaved itself and she felt all the power of being eighteen years old; mostly it was a pose, protective covering to hide uncertainty and occasional unprovoked flashes of timidity.

She loved both her parents, accepting their adoration as her due, but she found it hard to forgive P.J. for having passed on his curls to her. She loathed her hair, she pined for sleek, straight tresses, cut off just above the chin. It was impossible to look sophisticated with a headful of curls; you couldn't flick them back, the silly things just grew there, defying gravity.

She had noted bitterly that all the really exotic curls around were the result of art, not nature. She would see a style she admired, approach the owner hopefully and inquire how such effects were achieved, only to be informed that this was 'not natural of course . . . a perm'.

The world, for Annabel, had no objective reality, did not exist except in relationship to herself. She was not a selfish young woman however, merely self-centred, and if you smiled at her she smiled back, if you praised her she was your friend for life. She did not like to be found fault with and the only rows she ever had with her mother were when Noreen wilfully refused to accept her view and evaluation of reality. With P.J. there was no such problem: all she had to do was smile at P.J., wrap her arms round his neck and kiss his rough cheek and he would capitulate to any excess, any foolishness.

The nuns had struggled with her mind but it had remaind largely virgin territory, as indeed was her body in its entirety – a fact of which she did not boast. Annabel intended to gather wisdom from life, not from books, and she intended to start this summer now that school was a thing of the past.

When June brought in her breakfast tray she was sitting up on plump pillows, practising idleness.

'Hi June.'

'Good morning, Miss Annabel.'

Annabel dropped her knees in amazement, causing some of the coffee to slop over on to the linen cloth.

'Will you mind what you're doing.'

'It's your fault. What's with this Miss Annabel?'

'I'm to call you that now that you've left school.'

'Who says so?'

'Ma.'

'She's daft.'

'I know. It runs in the family.'

For some time now, an uneasy alliance had grown up between those two, after years of warfare. They had known one another since they were eight years old, when Mrs Donovan had started working for the McGuckians, bringing June with her at weekends and school holidays. Soon the little girls were playing together and at first June had accepted Annabel's top-kid status, overawed as she was by her new friend's playroom, clothes, vocabulary and general air of authority. She grew fed up, however, when she saw that they never played her games and that Annabel was only nice to her as long as she did as she was told. Eventually she made a stand and refused both to accompany her mother or to wear Annabel's cast-off clothing. When she eventually returned as her mother's helper the ground had shifted. Now she had the street cred – the tight skirts, the make-up and the boyfriend. Annabel, though she would have died rather than admit it, was impressed.

Over the last year they had begun, warily, to accept one another, not exactly friends, more allies, launching similar attacks but on different battlefields.

Annabel patted the bed and June sat down.

'How's Jack?' Jack had been June's boyfriend when Annabel had been home at Easter.

'I got rid of him.'

'Oh?'

'Yeh. He was more trouble than he was bloody worth. And he drank too much. We never went anywhere except the pub and he was always telling me what to do and what to wear. Grow my hair long, show off my legs. He was a real pain.'

'But I thought he was dead sexy.'

'There's more to life than sex,' replied June with a wisdom beyond her years.

This was not a widely held belief in Annabel's school, where the very thought of a sexual encounter could cause pimples to erupt on chins and hair to grow limp overnight. Many of the girls had done it, or claimed to have. Those who hadn't, waited in anticipation for the great day. Annabel's attitude was more ambivalent. She too was dedicated to finding the love of her life but so far she had been unmoved by both her friends' pin-ups and by the real thing, specimens of whom used to foregather on the borders of hockey pitches and tennis courts to ogle. She thought she might prove hard to please – as well she might with P.J. McGuckian for a role model.

'Anyway, I think I prefer the older man. I fancy your Da no end.'

'Do you? What about Aube?'

'God, no. No offence, Annabel, but he's just not my type. Anyway, he's an architect and I don't like architects.'

'How can you not like someone just because they're an architect?'

'If you had to sleep in my house last night and been kept awake not only by your oul fella snoring but all the oul fellas in the row, you wouldn't ask me that. And when anybody goes to the jacks, you'd think the house was going to fall.'

Annabel smiled. 'I think, probably, Daddy built those houses. What do you say to that?'

'So what – I'm sure it was Aube that made the plans. Anyway, come on Annie, hurry up. I haven't time to stand nattering here all day.'

As June closed the door, Annabel turned on the radio, lay down and shut her eyes. She smiled as Al Brown's voice crackled at her. Other girls of her age might prefer music stations but coming home meant Al Brown and Annabel always listened to him on her first morning back. Breakfast in bed and Al Brown, it was a ritual.

'No, honestly,' a woman with a thick-vowelled accent interrupted him. 'I'm not talking morally, I'm not on about that at all. It's healthwise I'm talking about – things like that aren't good healthwise.'

'Come on now, missus, twenty years married and two children with two years in between – you must have been using something.'

'Nothing. I put my trust in God and said three Hail Marys before and after and they never failed me yet.'

'Yet. What age are you then?'

'Al – I'm serious. Three Hail Marys before and in thanksgiving afterwards and no trouble.'

'Was it that good?'

'What?'

'That you had to give thanks immediately afterwards?'

Annabel giggled. Nothing ever changed. That was the great thing about coming home. Nothing ever changed.

The mills of God grind slowly but they grind exceedingly small.

Canice O'Keeffe had never understood what those words meant but they seemed appropriate now, with their apocalyptic ring, for Canice knew that he was a ruined man.

Until Sunday, he thought he might have escaped. *The Champion* had come out on Thursday, devoting three pages to his story and using a most unflattering photograph which they had dug up God knows where, one that had made him look like a half-witted ferret.

On Friday morning and again on Saturday he had torn through a mountain of newsprint with trembling hands; by the time he had finished examining the Irish papers and the English tabloids on Sunday morning, he was beginning to breathe more easily, believing that P.J. had been right and that he had got away with it. He was washing his inky fingers when Nuala's voice had sounded his doom. 'Canice,' she had called up to him, 'you'd better come down here and have a look at this.'

Having found nothing in the tabloids he hadn't even bothered with the *Sunday Times* and he might well have overlooked this, a small item in a gossip column. The journalist had obviously read the article in *The Champion* and been amused by it. He was playful, even affectionate, but damning none the less. This would not be missed in Ireland; the *Sunday Times* brought out an Irish edition and was sold outside church gates throughout the country. This was the general exposure that Canice knew would bring ruin.

Now at ten o'clock on Monday morning his worst fears had been confirmed. Rosaleen had already had several telephone calls from the press, one from *The European*, the others, more ominously from Irish newspapers.

'Rosaleen,' bellowed Canice.

'Yes, Minister.' She came running.

'I'm going out. If anyone wants me say I'm out on business and you don't know when I'll be back. If it's the Chief tell him I've gone to the doctor about my sinuses, that I've been in agony all morning. And Rosaleen.'

'Yes, Minister?'

'Could I have your keys? I want to borrow your car.'

He felt more exposed than ever inside the tiny, fragile vehicle, but no one seemed to notice him as he left the car park and headed for P.J.'s offices.

P.J. saw him straight away, dismissing an architect who shrank away from Canice as they passed in the doorway – Canice had already begun to display certain signs which suggested incipient madness.

'Would you like a cup of coffee?' P.J. began to fold away some plans.

'No. God, no.' Canice in his agitation was dancing up and down. 'Did you see it, P.J., in yesterday's *Sunday Times*?'

'It was only a small reference, nobody is going to notice it.'

'Wrong. It's started already, the persecution has started already. I knew this would happen, I said so all along. P.J. – you've got to help me. You're my only chance.'

'Calm yourself man, for God's sake.' P.J. freed his cuff from Canice's grasp and pushed him into a chair. 'Try to get this thing into perspective, Canice. Didn't I tell you the tabloids wouldn't be bothered with you and wasn't I right?'

'But the Irish papers, P.J.'

'It's different in Ireland, Irish papers are decent. You're well known and well liked in this country. Nobody is going to do a hatchet job on you over here.'

Canice had a sudden vision of the Chief, chasing after him with a tomahawk.

'Now, how about that coffee?'

Canice followed him to a coffee machine. 'But you don't understand, P.J., they've started phoning Rosaleen this morning, looking for interviews with me. It's started already, I tell you.'

'Drink your coffee and calm down. I still maintain that nothing is going to happen. Maybe you should give an interview – well, maybe not. No comment unless you have to.'

'But what'll I do, P.J., if I meet one of them? What'll I say if they start asking me questions?'

'Remind them of their manners, remind them of who you are. Stand up to them like a man.'

'But if they – '

'Look – just quit worrying and calm down. I'm looking after you, I'm not going to desert you. As long as you keep your head everything is going to be all right.'

P.J. was correct in his assumption that the reticence of Irish newspapers on the sexual peccadilloes of public figures was governed by good manners. It was a long-standing code which was very seldom breached. Ireland was so small – an overgrown village inhabited by an extended family – that manners had to be observed. And although tinged with Jansenism the country was sufficiently Catholic to recognize the sinful, imperfect state of man and to acknowledge that kindness was more important than truth.

There was also the shyness in admitting to any sexual activity and this extended to writing about it. It was one thing to joke about it when you were half-jarred in the pub, quite another to coldly write it down and see it in print the following day. It was better in the long run to let those things be and politics was far more interesting than sex.

So P.J. had read the situation correctly, but unfortunately for Canice it did not apply to him. In his case the gaff had been blown by an English paper which was widely circulated in Ireland and Irish journalists were duty bound to respond.

The poor hoor was up the spout anyway, but more reputations than his were now at stake. It had to be made clear that decency and not incompetence had been responsible for the reticence of the Irish press.

They would do their duty without glee for, like themselves, they considered Canice a decent man.

A minority didn't and they would rejoice in his exposure. These were the moralists, the new breed whom P.J. had so contemptuously identified. As far as they were concerned, Canice had got his come-uppance and about time too. His sin, in their eyes, had nothing to do with sex, it was his hypocrisy which offended them. His was the party, after all, that had preached the necessity to protect Irish, Catholic values; that had fought against liberalizing the laws on contraception and divorce.

The moralists would bring them all down if they could; in the meantime, Canice would do very well as the sacrificial lamb.

And from behind her net curtains Honey peeped out at a representative of one of the moralists who had arrived early on her doorstep. She had been watching him for the last ten minutes as he rang the bell, raised the knocker and then stood back to survey the house. His enthusiasm showed no signs of flagging.

In the narrow hall the telephone was off the hook. The first call had come late last night, although where they had got her number she couldn't imagine. It hadn't been listed for years.

She peeped again. That boy – he looked young enough to be her son.

She fled to the bedroom and got back into bed, pulling the pink duvet up around her ears. She began to pray – that God would give her the strength to withstand this siege, that God would come to the aid of Canice, as He bloody well should, for when all was said and done, Canice was a pure saint.

It was now P.J.'s turn to feel persecuted. Since lunchtime, Honey had phoned him three times, Canice five.

'All right Canice, all right,' he shouted into the receiver, managing at last to silence the babble coming from the other end. 'Go and see Bill O'Reilly – you have to now anyway, once he's sent for you. Just tell him that you are handling it, that you have a master plan. Then come round here to me afterwards. And just don't talk to the bloody press.'

'But they're everywhere, P.J. Nuala says she's going to pour boiling water over them if they don't get out of the garden.'

'Call the Garda. Your garden is private property, they're all tresspassing.'

'They've no pity, P.J. We've had to send the children down to Nuala's cousin to get them away from all this. And Nuala's blaming me. I don't know if the Chief realizes how difficult it is for me.'

'I wouldn't take that tack with him, Canice. Just go in there and say you have it all in hand.'

'Will I ever be able to convince him, do you think?'

'By God, you'd better be.'

P.J. put the phone back, then lifted it again and placed it on the table. He needed to be free from interruptions to put the final gloss on his plan.

He was enjoying himself, sure now that if Canice's nerve held, they would have those self-righteous buggers.

P.J. was disgusted at the behaviour of the Irish press, whose members seemed to have learned many unsavoury tricks from their less salubrious colleagues across the water.

Canice was a fool but he was a harmless fool, as each one of them must know. He had been happily playing at being important, harming nobody and nothing – except perhaps Art, and Art as far as P.J. was concerned could look after itself.

The viciousness of the attack now launched against him had roused P.J., as the school bullying had done forty years before.

He had started off reluctant to become embroiled in Canice's problems but now, with his dander up, he would see those buggers shagged.

This was why he planned the party. Hoist them on their own typewriters; leave them with printers' ink all over their superior mugs. Set them up, let them think they were getting the muck, then pull the rug and let them fall right into it. Slime to slime – a fitting finale.

On the terrace Noreen was tidying brown bits off the clematis and Annabel lay stretched on a lounger, her face turned towards the last rays of the evening sun. Her cheeks were peach, a shade lighter than the towel which was wrapped around her head. She had coated her curls with a stiff, hot wax, offering to do P.J.'s too, assuring him that it was the best possible conditioning treatment for their contrary type of hair.

'Girls,' said P.J., smiling from one to the other, 'what do you say to a party?'

Annabel opened one eye, Noreen continued to snip tranquilly.

'Don't overwhelm me with your enthusiasm.'

'Do tell us Daddy – what's it all about?' Annabel kept her eyes closed.

'It's all arranged for next Saturday when Aube will be home. And it's your party Annie, to launch you.'

She sat up, laughing. 'I'm not a ship. Anyway, I thought I was launched.'

'This will make it official. You were at school for your birthday so this is like a delayed birthday party.'

'Ooh – I do believe I am coming out.'

'I do believe you don't deserve this party.'

'I do, I do. I'm utterly, utterly grateful.'

'Stop bickering you two.' Noreen sat down between them. 'You might have told us earlier, P.J.'

'I wasn't going to tell you at all, I was going to keep it as a surprise. Then I thought that wasn't such a good idea, that you'd need time to doll yourselves up.'

'What a divinely archaic man your husband is.'

'I just hope I've given you enough time. By the look of things I think you should start now.'

He escaped into the house before the missiles could find their mark.

And mother and daughter, foiled again, could only shake their heads over him.

In central Dublin the sky over Government Buildings had darkened and in nearby Merrion Square the little birds, sensing that something was amiss, had flown for cover and now peered out from the trees, chattering nervously.

In the Taoiseach's office, on his desk, *The Champion* was spread open, and the face of Canice O'Keeffe smiled innocently up.

The flesh-and-blood Canice was not smiling as he stood in the middle of the floor, wringing his hands, while his Cabinet colleagues formed a semi-circle round him and stared at him, some in sorrow, others in anger.

The Chief stood at one of the tall windows, scowling skywards and thus setting in train the aforementioned physical phenomena. In his hand there trailed a cutting from the *Sunday Times*.

He turned now and walked slowly back towards his desk, his scowl turning to a look of pain. As he sat down stiffly, his acolytes suddenly realized how much he had aged; this morning he looked every hour of his sixty-one years. Pain, pain and suffering exuded from the man. The acolytes growled and swayed threateningly in Canice's direction. Canice licked slyly at the sweat which was trickling down from his forehead; otherwise he remained immobile, his eyes bulging stoat-like as they besought his hero and Chief.

The Chief raised a hand and thick necks swivelled inside expensive shirts.

'Well, Canice?' It was almost a sigh.

'Chief.' The high-pitched squeak caused the Chief to wince and Canice cleared his throat and tried again. 'Please, Chief, as God is my judge, it will be all right. I have a plan, really I have.'

Chins dropped in incredulity at this effrontery, or was it sheer imbecility? With Canice one could never quite tell. The acolytes turned for guidance to their Chief and their faces grew stern as they noticed the red tide begin to stain his wan cheeks.

'Jesus Christ Almighty!' The Waterford crystal chandelier tinkled overhead. 'Have you gone stark, staring mad? What is this plan — to destroy me, is it?'

'No, Chief — '

'What have I done to you, Canice?' The voice was lowered to a growl. 'How have I offended you?'

'Chief, you've never offended me.'

'Ah but I must have. Why else would you seek to humiliate me, to make me a laughing stock before the world?'

'No, Chief, it's not – '

'Did I ever do you any harm, Canice? Was I not the first to welcome you to the House? Did I not offer you advice as a young man? Did I not take you into my Cabinet, creating a special portfolio for your particular talents? Did I not seek your advice and consult with you over the years? Jesus! Did I not offer you the hand of friendship?'

One or two Ministers were now openly in tears and Canice, unable to contain himself any longer, threw himself at his Chief's feet, sobbing and begging forgiveness.

The Chief rose and began a slow walk round the room. Some wondered if he was going to have a heart attack, others if he was going to murder Canice on the spot. None was prepared for the gesture when it came.

Turning on his heel, he slowly approached the kneeling Canice and, stopping beside him, stretched out a hand and touched his protégé's oily locks.

Te absolvo. Canice felt a balm of forgiveness spread like an anaesthetic along his spine.

The Chief withdrew his hand and smiled, and the sun came out again. A sigh went up around the room.

'Leave us, lads,' said the Chief.

The shuffling and coughing had well died away but still Canice knelt, his eyes fixed firmly on the carpet in front of him.

'Get up, you fool!'

The shove unbalanced him and he rose awkwardly, clawing at the leg of the desk. He looked across bashfully at his hero. 'It will be all right, Chief, really it will.'

The Chief let out a long fart and sniffed with pleasure. Since giving up smoking, farting was one of the few pleasures left to him. He grabbed Canice's lapels and glared into his eyes. 'Now. I'm a very busy man, although you mightn't think it. I've a country to run. The welfare of three and a half million people depends on me. I really have no time, Canice, to play silly buggers with you. I'm giving you twenty-four hours to come up with some solution

– not *you*, for God's sake. Go and talk to Andrew Boyle. Get this thing settled between you. Twenty-four hours, mind, not a second more. Now, get out of my sight.'

Outside the Taoiseach's office, Canice beamed at the wallpaper and broke into a trot. He had no intention of going anywhere near the Attorney-General, a man whose air of severity and reputed learning reduced him to a state of speechlessness, an unusual occurrence with Canice. He was going instead to P.J., who had promised to reveal his master plan today.

He summoned his Mercedes and sat into it with a sigh. The Chief knew and he was still alive.

As the car turned into the street, the waiting reporters lunged forward, then fell back in amazement at the sight of Canice smiling out at them, waving to them like royalty.

'Turn right now, go down by the canal.' He wanted time to savour the great, empty space in his innards that up till half an hour ago had been bursting with humoral emotions: guilt, fear, sorrow. Now the Chief had laid hands on him and all that was changed.

Tomorrow morning when he woke up, his Mercedes would still be there and Nuala would brush down his shoulders and send him off to Rosaleen, who would inquire about the state of his sinuses as she handed him a cup of coffee. The hideous nightmare that had been thrusting itself into his field of vision could now be stamped on. There would be no ignominious return to the County Council offices, no public ridicule nor private grief. *The Champion* had published its filth but how puny, how powerless it was when pitched against Bill O'Reilly. Canice had as yet no idea what plan P.J. would come up with, nor even if that plan would work. That no longer seemed to matter. Once he had the forgiveness of Bill O'Reilly everything else would follow. A man for our times, that was Bill O'Reilly – a moral and intellectual giant. Up till this moment even Canice had not divined his greatness. That he should have forgiven him! And even if that forgiveness was conditional, Canice was sure that everything now was going to work out fine.

Like the woman taken in adultery, he had been given a second chance.

10

A thousand lights had transformed Villierstown House so that its incandescence glowed into the dark world. Each window was ablaze and along the avenue the lime trees had been threaded with lights; at intervals on the gravel sweep a line of torches burned.

On the back lawn a marquee had been erected, with a resounding dance floor. Under the canvas a rock band, five young men with ponytails secured by green velvet ribbons, stretched and bent athletically, warming up for the gig. In the hall two sax players and a trombonist were already playing music from the 1930s and couples drifted across the black and white tiles, limp with pleasure.

It was a warm night, still and starry. The air was filled with the scents of honeysuckle and tobacco plant; music and laughter echoed under the canopy of giant trees. If nightingales had lived in Ireland, one would surely have sung tonight at P.J. McGuckian's bash.

There was a suggestion of the raffish about the gathering: ageing beauties with scarlet bleeding mouths; décolleté'd girls from P.J.'s office, excited and overtanned from the injudicious use of sunbeds; men in hired dinner jackets escorting ladies who, despite the warmth of the evening, clutched fur coats to their bosoms as they moved, delicate as hens, along the avenue.

There were also the sophisticates – young, successful professionals, polished from a stint in London or New York – a pop singer, the scion of a brewing empire and a fat prince from Schleswig-Holstein.

And then there was simple beauty.

You looked at Annabel and her convent friends – many of

whom had been flown over from England – and you saw the patina of wealth and privilege, you saw what could be made of mere human flesh. The gloss, the finish, the stance all proclaimed an inviolability a world away from mere assurance, for assurance was something which had to be acquired. Outside of the moral sphere, one did not attribute blame to these darlings nor chastise them for their shortcomings. As with any work of art, one simply admired.

Under the starry sky waiters circulated, seeing that glasses were kept frothing with champagne, or with whiskey in the case of the many of P.J.'s friends who looked on champagne as a sour version of lemonade.

For supper there was salmon, whole fish laid out on platters, their glazed eyes still showing shock – as well they might, for yesterday they had been swimming in the mild waters of the Atlantic.

The strawberries that followed were round and red and perfect and there were jugs of cream and ice-bowls of ice-cream. Decent food was what P.J. called it and Mrs Donovan approved. Tonight she was dressed in austere black, standing at the dining-room windows, keeping an eye on June but really too happy to worry about anything much. People came and went past her, carrying plates and glasses, going to find somewhere to sit down, *tête à tête* or in noisy groups. She herself had filled the boss's plate twice and she hoped that he would come back for more. It had been nice of him to invite June as a guest but not very wise. Flibbertygibbet that girl – Donovan through and through.

'God, you gave me such a fright.' She jumped as Aubrey, wearing a red cummerbund round his waist, came up behind her.

'Sorry Mrs D. We're going in to supper but I wanted to introduce you to someone. This is – '

Mrs Donovan didn't need to be told. She had been a fan twenty years ago and still kept the old records in a box under her bed. 'Honey Fitz! I never thought, I never really thought I'd see you in the flesh after all this time. And you know what it is – you haven't changed a bit.'

'Honey is going to sing for us – '

'She's not!'

'P.J. has persuaded her – isn't it a great honour? Do you think

110

you might get us some supper? I'm taking Honey into the morning room where she can be quiet.'

Honey tottered after Aubrey, precariously balanced on high, golden slippers. She was practically fainting from nerves. She had agreed to sing tonight because P.J. had said it would help Canice, but now that the moment had come, she didn't know if she could go through with it.

What would happen when she stood up in front of all those people? Would any sound come out when she opened her mouth? Would the old magic reassert itself? She rubbed her damp palms together and sat down on the sofa Aubrey pointed to. She eased the pink satin round her bosom and tried to remember if she had felt like this in the old days. 'I think I am going to be sick,' she said, looking away from the plate of food which Mrs Donovan was now holding out to her.

'You creature,' said Mrs Donovan, thrusting two plates at Aubrey. 'You come away down to my kitchen and I'll get you a nice cup of tea and I'll tell you about the last time I heard you singing – I think it was in the Ierne Ballroom. And I've never heard anyone sing like that since. It was pure magic.'

Canice O'Keeffe was also on the point of collapse. He hadn't wanted to come tonight but he had been bullied into it by Nuala.

'We're going and that's that. P.J. said it was important and we're going to do exactly as he says. Anyway, it'll make a nice change getting out of this gaol for a night. You might not have noticed it but all this hasn't been fun for me, either.'

'Oh Nuala, don't I know it. You've been a good wife to me and explanations are due – '

'They'll keep. I may well murder you myself when all this is over but you need have no worries till then. It's not only Country and Western singers who stand by their men.'

'God, Nuala.'

'Enough. Go and get your dinner jacket so's I can see if it needs to be pressed.'

So against his better judgment he had come and his judgment had been proved right. The first person he had clapped eyes on as he was handing his silk scarf to a waiter was Honey Fitz. Sweat broke out on his forehead; he stumbled and might have fallen if it were not for Nuala's iron hand in the small of his back. Jesus – where was P.J.? He'd be dug out of him.

'Calm down, will you.' P.J. handed him a glass of whiskey. 'Everything's under control.'

'What are you trying to do, P.J.? Are you trying to ruin me entirely?' Canice whimpered, tugging at his fringe.

'Knock that back, and for Christ's sake pull yourself together. Just do what I tell you and never mind whatever happens. This is all part of the plan.'

He steered Canice into a corner. 'Lance the boil, Canice, let all the pus out. Then you'll be left with a nice, clean wound which will heal in no time.'

Although a lover of poetry and difficult prose, Canice had no idea what P.J. was talking about. He swallowed some whiskey. 'I saw a photographer, P.J.'

'There are one or two around. Nothing for you to worry about – they like to cover this sort of do for the social columns.'

'Oh God no, P.J.'

'What?'

'I'm going home. The Chief wouldn't like it at all if myself and – ah – should be snapped by one of those fellows. I'll have to go.'

'Jesus! Are you a man or a mouse?'

'P.J. – I'm a politician.'

P.J. acknowledged that therefore Canice fell into neither category. He put an arm round his shoulder. 'Look – you'll have to trust me, Canice. Have I ever let you down before?'

'No, P.J.'

'There you are then. Trust me, I know what I'm doing.'

'Oh God, P.J.'

'And go easy on the whiskey. I want you to have a clear head. Now go on back to Nuala, like a good man.'

As twelve o'clock approached, the guests began to squeeze into the marquee. The young men, swishing their ponytails, stepped down, except for the one at the keyboard who came forward to help Honey Fitz.

A murmur went up from the crowd as the large, pink figure made its way uncertainly across the platform. Older people started to nudge one another. Was it really . . . ? Could she still . . . ?

Honey stood, trembling, her little plump hands tearing at a scrap of pink lace. The young man at the keyboard gave her a chord, began to play a tentative introduction. Honey raised her chin and took a deep breath.

The voice was the same – pure, untrained, with that quality of innocence that had caught at the heart twenty years ago. Her eyes swept the room as sound poured from her throat and suddenly she had ceased to be a middle-aged, overdressed figure of fun. The upturned faces now caught the hurt from those eyes, the pain in that voice, and each person in the marquee thought how brave it was to expose this hurt, to share it with a crowd of strangers.

Everybody except Canice, that is, who had his eyes firmly closed and, hedging his bets, was praying fervently to the Blessed Virgin. If P.J. didn't come up with the goods maybe God's holy mother would come to his assistance.

> My lover's gone and left me but he'll be back some day,
> And when he does return I'll know he's here to stay.
> He's just gone on vacation, a short break away,
> A walk on the wild side of life –

Honey sang. Women sighed and remembered, men nodded and sipped their drinks. Canice opened a surreptitious eye, anxiously wondering if anybody would consider late-night sittings in Dáil Eireann as life on the wild side.

Holding a microphone aloft, Honey came forward to the front of the platform. She opened her arms in a gesture to the crowd. 'I want all of you to join me now.'

The guests sang Happy Birthday and Mrs Donovan wheeled in a huge cake, blazing like a liner afloat on a night sea. P.J. held back his daughter's black curls as she leaned forward to blow out the candles.

And Honey threw herself forward into the arms of Canice O'Keeffe.

What could he have done? Let her fall on her face? As he steadied himself, offering her a decent, friendly, gentlemanly squeeze, a flash-bulb exploded inches from him. Canice shied, as from a machine-gun, then in a gesture of gallant desperation planted a kiss on Honey's flushed cheek. 'That was wonderful, Honey. The voice is as good as ever.'

More flashes went off as P.J. came to his two old friends, an arm round his daughter. 'Honey, I don't think you've met Annabel.'

Annabel thanked her prettily.

'And say hello to the Minister, Annie.'

Canice winced; the phrase sounded like a death knell in his ear.

'Isn't it a great night? Everything's going fine. Here, Honey, here's Aubrey to ask you to dance. But remember – I want one before the night is out.' His eyes were still on Honey as he felt a pull on his jacket. 'A fine woman, don't you agree, Canice?'

'I don't know what's happening but I need another drink.'

'Right you are and you can relax now – I've sent those photographers off. You've done a grand job tonight, Canice, yourself and Nuala. Everything's going according to plan and I'll be in touch tomorrow. Now, off you go and enjoy yourself.'

Canice trotted off, having to accept the mysteries of P.J. McGuckian. Was it any wonder that P.J. sometimes felt like God?

He swept his daughter into his arms and then captured Noreen. As the three of them danced together laughing, he thought – I don't give a shite about anything or anybody else, just what I am holding in my arms. I am a happy man.

At around two o'clock the party seemed to get a second wind. Slack jaws had more make-up slapped on to them, jackets were discarded; a breeze had arisen outside, lifting the sated trees. Some of the younger guests began to roam in search of food, the trio launched into a Jellyroll Morton number and the house began to heave once more.

P.J. caught Honey as she was making her way out, wrapped up in glitter like a Christmas present.

'Sneaking away, were you, without giving me that dance?'

'Oh P.J. – I didn't think you were serious. I was just going to look for Noreen to thank her for such a lovely evening.'

'And it's not over yet. Come on.' He unhooked her cloak and swung her on to the floor. 'You were great,' he said, dancing her away from the music, to a quieter part of the room.

'It was great for me too, P.J. I haven't felt like this for years. I didn't know if I could sing any more and now – well, it was just terrific being up there again.'

'I'm going to tell you something now, Honey, and I hope you won't be offended. I was never much of a fan of yours and I

114

wondered at the time how Canice could have been such a fool. But, by God, I've changed my mind tonight. You've got guts, Honey, and you can sing bloody well too.'

'Thank you, P.J.'

'And you'll do it again – sing, I mean?'

'I don't know. But I had a most strange sensation up there. It was as if I'd never been away. And the way you feel when you're up there in front of an audience – I'd forgotten that too.'

'This is a whole new beginning for you, girl. You can't lock yourself away after this. You're going to go out there and give it to them. Amn't I right?'

Guests began to leave with the dawn and when P.J. closed his bedroom door, the birds were taking an encore on their morning chorus. In the grey, uncertain light of the bedroom P.J. looked down at his wife, lying across the bed, still in her dance dress.

'Come on,' he said, 'I'll give you a shower.'

'But P.J. – '

'Come on, pet.'

When half an hour later she lay warm and deliciously sleepy, she opened an eye to find P.J. getting dressed again. 'What are you doing?'

'I'm going for a cycle.'

'But – aren't you whacked?'

'I can't miss this opportunity. It's years since I've been out at this time – the hour of creation, Noreen. It's going to make me feel like a boy again, being out there at this hour.'

She listened to her husband's departing clatter, smiling as she recalled the tenderness with which he had soaped her back. Such intimacies still embarrassed and delighted her. What right did she have to so much happiness, thirty years of life with P.J. McGuckian?

And tonight had been so perfect, even Aubrey had seemed to be enjoying himself. Perhaps his trip to America had helped to relax him.

'Please God,' she prayed as she always did before she fell asleep, 'look after them for me. And look after me so that I can continue to look after them.'

Before P.J.'s bicycle wheels scratched across the gravel she was asleep.

At his bedside Canice O'Keefe was also praying, though in a less intimate fashion. He had failed to escape earlier for the second whiskey he had taken had gone straight to his head – anxiety he supposed – and Nuala had kept him in a corner, pouring cups of coffee down his gullet, reminding him that he had caused enough commotion for one night.

'Spare me, O Lord,' he now besought. 'Spare me so that I can continue to do Thy work, so that I may feed the hungry, clothe the naked and visit the sick.'

That he did none of those things bothered him not at all. He prayed as he spoke, metaphorically. And, as a Minister in the Chief's government, wasn't he indeed doing God's work?

Canice, like his Chief, believed that a people had to be led, pointed in the right direction. And who but the Chief and his Cabinet could protect the country in these perilous times, preserving the old, Christian verities, saving the beloved land from messers, communists, anarchists and loose livers?

'Will you get into bed, Canice,' said Nuala, losing patience, unable to get to sleep with the continuous snuffling and shifting at her side. 'It'll soon be time to get up.'

'I will, Mammy, I will,' replied Canice, hopping into bed with some agility and planting a chaste kiss on his wife's forehead before settling down with his hands joined on his chest, as he had been taught to do years ago by his sainted mother, in case he should die in his sleep.

He sighed a sigh of pure pleasure, thanking God as he did so that all carnality with its myriad snares and ramifications was entirely a thing of the past as far as he was concerned.

In Dun Laoire the sun was coming up over the sea and Aubrey McGuckian, gazing at it, seemed, like his father, to have few thoughts of bed. He peered out, past the Kish lighthouse, past some small craft at anchor, wondering whimsically if in the sharp morning light he might get a glimpse of the coast of Wales.

It was a scene familiar to him since childhood, but this morning he was seeing it as for the first time through eyes from which the scales of frivolity had fallen. From the moment he had stepped off the plane, restraining within himself a strong desire to bend, like the Pope, and kiss the soil, from that moment he

116

had known himself to be a man with a mission – a born-again Republican.

He had been reading a most interesting and learned book before setting out for his sister's party, and now as he began a gentle walk along the pier, his thoughts returned to it.

The book had dealt with the Indo-European origins of Irish society and the continuing strong Vedic influences on early Gaelic life.

Happily copulating gods and goddesses had not been confined to the Indian subcontinent apparently but had cavorted the length and breadth of the Four Green Fields until the malevolent twin arrival of the Brits and Christianity. Or maybe it was Christianity and the Brits.

Aubrey had taken against Christianity and specifically against Catholicism. There had always been an alliance of interests between the Catholic Church and imperialist Britain, ever since Pope Adrian IV had sent Henry II over to Ireland to bring the native bishops to heel. Throughout the centuries the Church had sided with the oppressors – look at their attitude to the Fenians, their breaking of Parnell, the ambivalence of the bishops towards the men of 1916. And today it was the same: with the exception of one or two principled clerics, the Catholic Church ignored or condemned the armed struggle in the six counties. Its priests ranted from their pulpits about IRA violence but seldom bothered to mention the atrocities committed by the forces of the British crown.

Aube glared down at the blameless water and then, raising his head, emitted a huh of contempt as he remembered the carry-on last night. What a pathetic spectacle the birthday party had proved, with the hosts and their guests outdoing one another in an effort to display their colonial mentality. Aube had heard that phrase on the radio yesterday morning and it had caught his fancy. Some woman, a *Bean Ui Dhalaigh*, had rung up Al Brown to complain about the colonial mentality which she found so prevalent in her native city. Well, if she had been in Villierstown last night she would have come into contact with it in epidemic form. What a disgusting display of materialism she would have witnessed – men and women in ridiculous get-ups, stuffing themselves with champagne and salmon and dancing to foreign music. Where were the ideals of nationhood gone? Why must the Irishman forever ape the foreigner? Why couldn't he dress –

But here Aube's imagination revolted at a vision of P.J. McGuckian in saffron kilt.

Well – it *had* been pathetic. And his own sister talking as if she had been reared in the Home Counties. The only authentic person there last night, the only one in touch with herself, was Honey Fitz. Aubrey had been charmed by Honey, by the manner in which she had clung to him, confided in him, asked his advice. He was willing to overlook her musical impurity which, anyway, was less offensive than all that jazz and rock.

Aube was glad that Matt Savino had been spared last night's craven display. Matt would be arriving in Dublin in ten days' time, coming specifically to be introduced to P.J.

He had written to tell Aube about the inauguration of the Manhattan Pikemen, a society of peace and justice which he had founded but which was proving hellishly difficult to get off the ground. Money was needed and money would be sought from P.J. Pike was an acronym standing for Promote Irish Knowledge Everywhere and Matt felt that it was neat, with its historical and military overtones. Matt promised Aube that he would be running things in Dublin, playing a pivotal role in the whole organization.

Looking into the morning sun, Aube felt that the force of their enthusiasm and the justice of their cause must make P.J. part with some of his dosh. And then, '*Tiocfaidh ár lá,*' said Aubrey McGuckian, shaking his fist at the Irish sea. 'Our day will come.'

He was thinking as much of his own dilemma, it must be said, as of his country's, and he used the Provos' slogan for although, like Matt, he was a man of peace, he shared the ideals of the combatants.

A herring gull, taking fright at the angry cry, swooped off towards enemy territory, for birds, like people, are notoriously fickle and this one now chose to ignore the generosity of Aube, who had been feeding it scraps of salmon for the past five minutes.

Aubrey did not notice its desertion. He had turned his back on the sea and begun to walk with new resolution towards his Lamborghini, trim and shining in the morning sun.

'*Tiocfaidh ár lá,*' he incanted again, smiling now, reassured by the warmth and generosity of the Gaelic vowels. A mean language, English, even in the mouths of Irishmen; fit for conquest, yes, but not for pleasure.

Annabel was not asleep either. She was sitting up in bed eating chocolate biscuits and chatting to her two friends who were sharing her bedroom, despite the fact that seven bedrooms lay empty around them. This was more fun though, one sleeping on a chaise-longue and the other tucked in at the bottom of Annabel's bed.

'I do think he's dishy,' said Teresa, licking each finger carefully.

'Who?'

'I told you – your Pa. He's *so* hairy. I've never seen a man with such hair. They say it's a sign of virility, hairiness. Athough,' she widened her eyes at her friends, 'I don't know if I should be talking like this to two virgins. It's different for those of us who've done it.'

'Stop boasting.' Alice threw a cushion at her and Annabel kicked her as viciously as her small foot would allow.

'But seriously,' continued Teresa, unperturbed, 'do you think I stand a chance, Annie? Does he fancy them young?'

'Well I certainly don't fancy you as a stepmama, so lay off.' Annabel pouted, pretending displeasure.

'You're a bit shop-soiled by now, anyway,' Alice winked over Teresa's head. 'I think he might prefer someone fresh like me – what do you think, Annie?'

Annabel lay back giggling and closed her eyes. She was delighted by Teresa's remarks. No one else had a father such as she – handsome, fun and a terrific dancer. And not a bit stuffy like other people's fathers. All her English friends had remarked on his lack of stuffiness – even the nuns were not indifferent to P.J.'s charms. She had seen Mother Bernadine blush as Daddy had bent over her hand and they were forever popping into the guests' sitting room when P.J was visiting.

She allowed a pleasant wash of nostalgia to sweep over her at the realization that her schooldays were over; but it was no match for the wave of excitement which pushed it aside at the thought of what the future would bring. Freedom, adventure, love and sex and . . .

Teresa swept the biscuit from her suddenly limp fingers and popped it into her own mouth. Then she too closed her eyes.

And the three young women slipped effortlessly into sleep, untroubled by sticky fingers and chocolate-coated teeth.

Questions had been asked in the Dáil, not of the limp, rhetorical variety but probing and accurate. The Opposition, smelling blood, sat straining on the benches, waiting to be summoned in for the kill.

'But where *is* the Minister?' asked the Leader of the Opposition. 'That's what I want to know. That's what the people of Ireland want to know. Has the Government, perhaps, lost him? Has he emigrated to more exotic climes – Nashville, Tennessee, perhaps?'

Growls from the Government benches, cheers from the Opposition.

'Would it not be in his own interests to show up in this House, to answer these – stories – which we have all been reading about with such deep distress? We, on this side of the House, worry about his good name, we are jealous of the reputation of all our colleagues in Dáil Eireann. It is, Taoiseach, a question of honour.'

Bill O'Reilly stood up. His pale blue eyes grew paler still as the corneas began to ice over; his voice too held shards of frost. 'I have come here today to discuss the Book of Estimates. We have been elected by the people of Ireland to govern the country of Ireland and we would not be thanked by the people of Ireland if we wasted our time on idle gossip. I can understand why the Leader of the Opposition wishes to waste time on trivia but I'm afraid I cannot indulge him.'

'I demand – '

Bill O'Reilly sat down. Let him rant. Eventually he would tire himself out and Bill would get to his feet again and resume his reasoned debate.

He closed his eyes and marvelled at his own resilience. It was a wonder that he could talk coherently, that he wasn't foaming at the mouth, three days after O'Keeffe's disappearance, four days after those photographs had appeared, photographs in which were juxtaposed Canice's well-shaped nose and Honey Fitz's generous bosom.

Bill had seen an early edition of the papers but by then O'Keeffe had gone to ground. When Bill had sent his driver round to haul him back by the ear, the O'Keeffe house had been deserted. The only contact anyone had had with the fool since was a note left on Bill's desk. 'Don't worry, Chief, all will be revealed. Have patience for my sake and for Ireland's.'

Perhaps he was dead. Bill began to feel more cheerful. Perhaps he had drowned himself, thrown himself into some bog hole in his native Cavan. For the moment all Bill could do was wait – by moving too soon he might wreak even more destruction. He must withstand the pressure and wait, until Canice O'Keeffe came to his senses, or, an altogether more satisfactory scenario, until his body floated to the surface of some dark pool.

At that very moment Canice's body was indeed floating, not in a bog hole but before a full-length mirror in the bedroom of a house on a suburban housing estate.

He had been whisked there at dead of night by P.J.'s secretary with Nuala driving behind, watching his back.

It was a nice little house, warm and cosy, and Canice had begun to feel quite at home. The kitchen was well stocked with goodies, the lounge with videos and magazines. These were to keep Nuala happy – Canice had no time for such frivolities. He was busy up here, concentrating on restoring, indeed enhancing the prestige of his country.

He took another turn in front of the mirror, raising his arms in a graceful arabesque. He offered one profile, then the other. He raised his chin, lifted an eyebrow. He tried on various expressions – sadness, amusement, righteous indignation. Then he cleared his throat and began to practise his speech.

In the lounge Nuala turned up the volume on the television set and stared unseeingly at the screen. She sat, as she always did, neatly, hands folded, feet together; only her mouth moved as she pleated her lips inwards, taking little agitated bites.

She pined for her own house, longed to be busy tending it and her garden, her pride and joy. Here there was nothing to do except defrost the TV dinners and worry about Canice. She worried about the children too, although they were at this moment probably sitting on a beach somewhere in Portugal with her sister. But would all this have blown over by the time they returned?

She hated to be beholden to people, particularly to that creature.

121

P.J. had said, 'Oh we can depend on Honey, Honey won't let us down, she'll be discretion itself.' What the man didn't seem to realize was the fact that Honey wouldn't even know she was being indiscreet, however good her intentions were. She was so thick she would blab away, not knowing the damage she was doing. And half of what she said would be imagined – those sort of people lived in a fantasy world. God knows what harm she could do, what wild stories she would invent once she got going.

Honey had been sticking tenaciously to the historical truth, in fact. Since that night when she had been reborn, when she had found her voice again and felt Canice's lips on her cheek, she had wanted to tell her story. She had been pursuing cameramen and reporters; when they called at her house she had invited them in and showered photographs, records and souvenirs on to their laps. She had offered to sing for them, begged them to wait so that she could get into her costume, the one that had been presented to her by the mayor of Ithaca, Alabama. She told them of being on the Grand Ole Opry and asked them had they any contacts in the music world – she was sort of out of touch herself.

When they asked her questions about Canice, she didn't even hear them as she clutched at their sleeves, trying to persuade them of how good she had been and would be again, now that she had found her voice. She wondered if they knew the finer points of Country music and offered to explain them. Her cheeks grew pinker, her eyes shone a little crazily, it seemed as if she couldn't stop talking.

Finally the journalists admitted defeat – they had met their match. Honey, deserted, tweaked nervously at the net curtains, peering out, wondering what had happened. She didn't worry any more about Canice for she had done her bit and P.J. would do the rest. Soon she had ceased to say her nightly rosary for him and had begun to offer it up instead that God might help to relaunch her in the world of Country music.

The Taoiseach stared in disbelief at his press secretary. 'He did what?'

'He's issued a statement saying that he's appearing on "Brown Sunday" to address the country on a question of grave, national importance.'

'Jesus – what in God's name is he up to?'

Maybe he was staging a *coup d'état*. Maybe the thought of losing the Mercedes had finally pushed him over the edge. The Taoiseach's head was suddenly filled with a vision of Canice O'Keeffe, a bandeau round his forehead and a machine-gun belt round his waist, signalling on a group of wild Cavan men.

Warily he opened his eyelids as if fearful that he might be confronted by the reality of his imaginings.

'Well, what do you want me to do, Taoiseach, what statement will we put out? Did he clear it with you first? Or do you want the whole thing quashed?'

'Do we know where he is?'

'No.'

'Well we can hardly kidnap him on the way to the bloody studio. We have no option – do we? Yes, Minister O'Keeffe naturally discussed everything with me, he would do on a question of grave national importance. Go on, Tom,' he waved a hand. 'You know what to say. Blah, blah. Just make it sound good.'

As the door closed, Bill put his head down on his desk. It might be the last statement he would release as Taoiseach, depending on the capers of O'Keeffe. God alone knew what he intended once he got behind the cameras. Maybe a tango with Honey Fitz, a red rose clasped between his expensive white teeth.

And to think that he had introduced him to his own dentist. He should have left him with his yellow, Cavan fangs. He should have left him in Cavan, but then he had assumed the man to be merely stupid, not stark, staring mad. Imagine – a government minister having himself photographed with a half-naked, superannuated floozy.

Bill O'Reilly shuddered and reached into a drawer to bring out a bottle of Paddy. He gulped from the bottle, twice, then put away the bottle once more.

The whiskey calmed him and he closed his eyes the better to grapple with the mind of Canice O'Keeffe. Unknowable, impenetrable as the Gobi desert. And the most dangerous aspect of the whole affair was his perceived closeness to his Chief. He was seen as his man, his protégé.

Bill O'Reilly got down on his knees and began to pray. He admitted his own unworthiness, his lowly status as a sinner, but he then reminded God and His holy mother that it was on Ireland's behalf that he was asking for help, a country which, whatever its faults, had always been faithful to the One, True, Church.

A playful God sent a skitter of unseasonal hailstones against the Taoiseach's long window, making the poor man jump.

Getting to his feet he pulled down his waistcoat, straightened his back and smoothed down his thinning hair. There was still a country to be governed and he would not be found wanting. He took a breath, in through his nose, deep into his stomach and expelled it through his mouth. Then he picked up his phone.

11

It was raining, soft, summer rain. The low sky merged with the lake water and from the house the world outside seemed blurred. The overhead trees, swollen with water, bent threateningly towards the roof. Although it was only three o'clock in the afternoon, twilight had already descended.

In the kitchen, with the light on, Noreen was viciously slapping bread dough on to the table. She lifted it and banged it down, wishing it was P.J. she was slapping as she listened to his irritatingly cheerful whistle from the living room. He had been congratulating himself on the weather since getting up this morning, smiling into the greyness, ignoring her sighs. It was perfect fishing weather.

He came into the kitchen. 'Where's Annabel?'

'She's gone for a walk.'

'In this weather?'

'You know she loves the rain.'

'But she'll catch cold – '

'She won't, stop fussing. She's young, let her enjoy herself. Come back here, P.J. – I want to talk to you.'

'I thought we'd go into the town, have a few jars in Maguire's, take a stroll along the boulevard. Then I'll have done my duty and I might be allowed a little fishing.'

'Did anyone ever tell you how maddening you are? You can go fishing once we've had our chat. And I don't want to go into the town or to Maguire's. This is a serious chat.'

'So? Maguire's would make anyone serious. Go on Noreen, go and get into your glad rags. You don't seem to understand that we have to display ourselves down here. We're not going to hide ourselves away like bloody foreigners. We're going to tog ourselves out and put ourselves on display so's the locals can take us to bits and criticize our taste and our ostentation. It's the least we can do. Now, go and see if you can find a Christian Dior raincoat.'

'What about Annabel?'

'We'll leave the door open. That's what I keep telling you, pet, relax, you're not in Dublin now. Nobody is going to rob us or mug us around here. We're home.'

In the woods Annabel was trying to climb a beech tree. Impeded by her yellow raincoat, she took it off and bundled it into a cleft low down on the trunk. Now she found it easy to climb, her legs unrestricted in their jeans, the soles of her trainers successfully gripping at the bark. Six feet from the ground she found a sturdy branch which, with her back against the trunk, provided a steady perch. She would be quite dry under the interlaced umbrella of leaves.

She peered around her, into the empty echoing woods and the still lake beyond. She was conscious of the ancientness of this world, the springy woodland floor that had been building up for hundreds of years, the deep, mysterious lake, deserted and sunless, even on the brightest day. She loved it here, supplying her own sunshine which dispersed any gloom so that she laughed at shadows and mocked the sorrowful pigeons that cooed above her head. Surely this was the very place for a great adventure?

She plucked at a leaf and began to chew it, savouring its cool juice. The lake water would be colder, icy. She imagined plunging in. Her parents had forbidden her to swim in it, the fussy old darlings. 'It's dangerous, there are currents,' Noreen had warned her daughter. 'You think you're in your depth and you stand up and suddenly there's no bottom. People have disappeared in lakes in Ireland, their bodies never found.'

How exciting. Perhaps they had been transported to another world, an underwater world of submerged cities and –

Annabel sat up and blinked as a movement out on the lake caught her eye. She manoeuvred herself forward. There it was again – something black and sleek breaking the surface of the water. A seal? No. She shook her head in disbelief – it was a man. A boy. As she watched he turned on his back and began a vigorous backstroke towards the shore. Annabel's eyes followed the arc of his arms, the diamonds of water that fell from them. He was a powerful, graceful swimmer, moving rhythmically, pushing the water away from him, transforming it as he mixed its greyness with light. An alchemist.

He turned again, dived, resurfaced and began a gentle breast-stroke which brought him to the rocks. Like a pole-vaulter he hoisted himself up, stood for a moment, a narrow flash of white, and then disappeared among the trees.

She could feel her loss as she watched the green downy blanket re-establish itself. 'Wait,' she called from her perch. 'Come back here.'

Nothing. She shook her head as if to clear her vision. The trees, the lake were still. Had she really seen him? He had appeared from nowhere out there in the middle of the lake and disappeared with equal completeness. Where had he come from? Locals didn't use the lake once they knew the McGuckians were down, respecting their privacy. Perhaps she had imagined him or he was a ghost. No. No ghost could swim like that. She had to see him again – maybe tomorrow.

At Mass next morning she searched for him among the wor-shippers, craning her neck this way and that until Noreen dug her in the ribs and whispered to her to behave.

'I'm going for a last walk,' she said after lunch.

'Make it a short one,' P.J. advised. 'I want to be home in good time for "Brown Sunday". Remember, tonight's the night.'

She took the opposite path today, walking with care, careful for him as she would be for a rabbit or a hare. Behind the white rocks where he had stood yesterday she found a tree and started to climb, taking her raincoat with her this time, seeking total concealment.

She folded her arms and closed her eyes and began to wait, concentrating all her energies on listening.

She didn't know how long she had waited, she thought she might even have dozed for a few seconds, when she heard the sounds: twigs snapping, a rustling and then a low whistling as the other sounds ceased. It came from just below her. She held her breath and screwed her eyes tighter. More rustling, then an explosion of sound, deafening in the forest silence. She opened her eyes as his body smacked on to the water.

His head broke the surface, he shook it and shouted, a sound joyous and shocked. She could feel his shock, imagining how his body felt as it came into contact with the water. He disappeared then reappeared, threshing then settling to calmer movements. From her perch she could see his face, his black shining hair, his teeth as he drew back his lips in shock or pleasure. He dived underwater so that for a second she saw the soles of his feet. When he reappeared he was nearer to her, turned on his back. She saw him stretch into a float, arching his neck, staring up at the sky. Now that he was nearer, he seemed more than ever a creature of this lake, these woods. She could imagine how clothes would diminish him; she believed that like a swan he must lose some of his grace when he quitted his watery domain.

He had begun to swim again with gentle strokes that hardly disturbed the glassy water. She caught snatches of a song that he was singing in a voice surprisingly high for a man. As he raised his head she saw his neck stretch, white. She felt a sudden shiver of fear as she imagined the power of his wings, how they could injure her if she angered or frightened him. It was a surprise to see, as he heaved himself out of the water, his legs appear, followed by his feet, unwebbed. She giggled. A boy.

He shook himself and stretched towards the sky. As he walked towards her she began to study him with interest. She had only seen pictures of naked men before and her initial reaction was – how lovely. His skin was white, a thick, creamy white, and his whole body suggested solidity and yet lightness. Out of the water his grace had not diminished but he moved with stealth, placing his feet with sureness, hardly making a sound. His arms were shortish, she thought, his legs long and slim, and his sex – she looked away quickly, giggling, scandalized.

He reminded her now not of a swan but of a cat, soft and dangerous. Why did she keep on getting this charge of danger from him?

Perhaps it was the intense focus of her attention that caused him to look up, for now with a sudden jerk he raised his chin and blue gaze met blue. She smiled and he smiled back until, remembering his nakedness, he put his hands in front of him and dropped his head.

'I'm sorry,' said Annabel, looking down on the wet, black head, 'I didn't know anyone swam in this lake.'

'My clothes are just over there.'

'Look – I'll keep my eyes tight shut, I'll bury my face in my hands and you can get dressed. I really didn't mean to embarrass you.'

On top of the world and on top of the situation, that's me, Annabel told herself as she listened and tried to analyse the small sounds coming up to her. She felt deliciously grown up and at ease. She would have to put him at his ease when they faced one another. Maybe she should invite him up to the house for a cup of tea? Or –

Why had all the sounds suddenly stopped? Had he fled? Had she frightened him away? She opened her eyes and craned forward.

'Isn't it a good job I was here to catch you?' he said, stepping forward as she jumped down from the tree and stumbled on landing. But he didn't try to hold on to her, just set her gently back on her feet.

They smiled at one another for the second time.

'I'm Annabel McGuckian.' She put out her hand with formal good manners. 'We have a house up there.'

'I know.'

'You do?'

'Naturally. P.J. McGuckian is fairly famous around these parts.'

'Oh.' Was he mocking her?

'It's a small place, everybody minding everybody else's business. And with your father coming from around here – it's only natural.'

'Are you from here?'

'From the town. Seán Flanagan. And I shouldn't have been swimming in your lake, I'm sorry.'

She knew very few boys; when she met them it was usually in packs, often drunk, always aggressive. Now all she could do was marvel at this handsome creature who smiled at her so easily.

'Do you want to come for a walk? I'll get cold if I hang around – that water is always freezing.'

He led her the long way round, making a circle of the lake. He didn't say much but he didn't need to, for there was an instant ease between them. It seemed as if they had known one another for years, for ever. She knew what he was going to say before he spoke; she anticipated his jokes. She wondered how a stranger could share so many of her feelings.

'I'll leave you now, so.'

'What do you mean?'

He smiled at her panic. 'I only mean you're home – look. There's your house.'

'Won't you come in?'

'No.'

'But – '

'I'll see you when you're down next time.'

'Where?'

'The lake. I'll bring togs.' He smiled again.

'Do you promise?'

'To wear togs?'

She blushed. 'You know what I mean.'

'I promise if you promise something.'

'What?' Anything.

'To come in for a dip with me.'

'Of course.' She would defy more than a mother for him.

'That's a promise then.' And he was gone.

This is ridiculous, Annabel told herself as she slipped into her bedroom to pack. He's only a boy. But how lucky that he *was* a boy, flesh and blood, not some woodland sprite that she might never meet again.

Just a boy – be cool.

When would they be coming down again? Could she persuade them to come down next weekend? Perhaps she should have made a definite arrangement – how would he know when she was down? But, just a boy, lots of them about.

She would tell no one about him; she would keep his existence secret. She must buy a new swimsuit – she certainly wouldn't appear in that old school thing. And no cap – she was bad enough without a cap.

On for goodness sake – just a boy.

'I met a boy today.' It came out before she could stop it, because she had been thinking about him, she supposed.

'What?' The Mercedes swerved dangerously across the pock-marked road. 'Where?'

'In the woods. He was swimming in *your* lake, Daddy. In the nude.'

'Jesus Christ!' The car shuddered and slewed to a halt.

Noreen reached back and shook her daughter. 'That was really bold, Annabel. We could have crashed.'

'I'm sorry.' She didn't sound it.

P.J. jerked on the handbrake and turned to examine his daughter. 'What exactly are you telling me, that you were accosted by some naked youth?'

'For goodness sake. Of course I wasn't accosted.'

'Was he naked?'

'Yes, but – '

'Right, Miss. Then we're turning back and you're coming with me to tell the Garda all about it.'

'Daddy!'

P.J. thumped the steering wheel. 'Straight back.'

'Daddy. Mummy – tell him what a scum idea that is. Tell him I won't – '

'P.J., calm down, your blood pressure.'

'Jesus.' He turned his wrath on Noreen. 'Will you stop talking about my blood pressure. Are you two trying to kill me? First of all my wife tells me that she's not satisfied with the life I've given her, that she wants to go and get herself a job. *My* wife. Then my daughter informs me that she's been swimming with a sex maniac.'

'Daddy.'

'P.J.'

It was not easy to calm P.J. down. The more he thought about what he had been told the more outraged he became. He got out of the car, as much to get away from those two exasperating women as to find something to kick. He sent a stone clattering down the road, finding some relief in imagining it to be a soft, nude bum. Wait till he got his hands on that fellow, he'd soon settle his hash.

'Daddy.' Annabel took his hand, looping her fingers through his. 'It wasn't a bit what you imagine – he's a very nice boy.'

'Nice boys don't swim naked.'

'But he didn't know anyone was there.'

'It's my bloody lake. I'll have to put a sign up saying that it is not a nudist colony.'

'And he nearly died of embarrassment when I appeared.'

'So he should.'

'Anyway, I won't see him again if you don't want me to. You'll always be my best fella – you know that?'

P.J. coughed – embarrassed, vanquished. 'Come on, get into the car or we'll never get home.'

Noreen turned her head towards the window, smiling. If P.J.'s enemies could only see him now, putty in the hands of this eighteen-year-old girl. Where was his devastating ruthlessness, his low cunning? It was easy to misjudge P.J., as indeed she had herself. Only yesterday morning she had been worrying about telling him of her plans and when she had eventually blurted them out, her fear had made her appear aggressive. P.J. had merely raised an eyebrow and enquired, 'So, when can I take you off the payroll? Does this mean I can retire earlier?'

He hadn't liked what he had heard and there would be plenty of grumbling along the way, but she believed now that he wouldn't oppose her.

She turned back towards him, still smiling. He was nothing but an old pussy-cat.

P.J., who saw himself more as a tiger, would not have been pleased with his wife's metaphor, but warmed by her smiles and by his daughter's kisses he could feel his pulse begin to slow down. 'I'd want to know all about him, mind. I'd want to meet him before you have anything more to do with him. Has he asked to see you again?'

'No, Daddy.'

'At least he has some decency. Flanagan you said – it's Flanagans that own the hardware shop in the town – great notions that crowd had when I was growing up, thought themselves the local gentry. Now, Annabel,' he shook a stubby finger at her, 'I am quite serious. You will have nothing more to do with him until your mother and I have seen him. Remember, I know what it's like to be a young buck, I was there and it's dangerous country. And they can be a bit crude round here, not what you're used to. So, no more meetings until I've had a talk with him.'

'I'll remember, Daddy.' Annabel assumed an air of meekness.

P.J. put the car back on the road, grateful to know that she would be safe in Villierstown for the next week at least.

It was a *coup*, it was a dazzling success, it was an occasion which made broadcasting history. It was compared by some to the abdication speech of Edward VIII, by others to Padraig Pearse's oration at the grave of O'Donovan Rossa. It was perfection.

132

Instead of sending an underling, Al Brown came out to meet him and stood peering through the glass doors of the television centre, waiting for the ministerial car to appear.

Al was aware what a *coup* too for 'Brown Sunday' was Canice's decision to appear on it. He could have gone anywhere else, he could have held a news conference, but his instinct had led him here. Al believed that he was to be congratulated on that instinct for Al knew that, despite an undercurrent of murmurs to the contrary, 'Brown Sunday' was still the most important forum for the Irish people.

Although he preferred the warm, dark intimacy of radio, Al was proud of 'Brown Sunday'. And every time the whingeing critics reached a crescendo, Al turned around and pulled out a plum, like tonight's . . . but never as juicy before.

Al, who always felt better, healthier, more *real* in the presence of microphones, leapt forward now to open the car door for Canice. Walking respectfully behind him, he ushered him along dingy corridors to a room lined with mirrors where his make-up was to be applied.

Canice was seated and bibbed. 'Where's Louise?' he asked. 'Louise knows this old mug – she'll do a job on it.'

Al Brown returned with coffee in a proper cup. 'Now Minister, I'll just run through the format with you, if I may. We're not in the usual studio because of not having an audience tonight – all right? I'm going to do a brief intro and then it's over to you. No interruption, no commercial breaks.'

Canice nodded, not listening. He was calm but exalted. His face had acquired a look of tortured nobility like that of a Christian martyr in an El Greco painting. His eyes held the sheen of ecstasy.

He floated behind Al Brown down another corridor and sat where he was told to, beside a table with a glass and water carafe. In front of him and to his right, Al Brown stood, microphone in hand. He waited for his cue then smiled into the camera, a smile which managed to convey both welcome and weight.

'Tonight is not our usual "Brown Sunday". Tonight is a very special occasion, one which, I am sure, you will talk about in years to come. Tonight a well-loved man has come before you to tell his story. On your behalf I would like to welcome – Minister Canice O'Keeffe.'

133

Canice O'Keeffe raised a noble chin and stared out at the nation with a mixture of resolution, sadness and quiet pride. Widening his eyes, he smiled, a trifle hesitantly and then, in clear, unhurried tones he began to confess all.

He told of his childhood in Cavan, of his happy marriage and then when madness struck, of his illicit passion for Honey Fitz. He spoke of her beauty and his weakness, of their mutual fight and failure to be good. He touched on the magic of their affair and went on to reveal the birth and tragic death of their love child.

He broke down then, weeping – the nation wept with him. In pubs throughout the land hard cases stopped with their pint glasses half-way to their lips; in love nests adulterous daddies surreptitiously fingered their miraculous medallions and promised, promised.

Canice, shaking tears from his eyes, told of their new resolution, of their going jointly to confession, of their years of restitution and their continuing, chaste friendship. He said that they had been marked by the experience, though Honey more profoundly than he, motherhood being a more profoundly moving experience.

He paused and took a sip of water and the nation held its breath. Then he raised his chin again and told the Irish people of his overwhelming love for his country and of his gratitude to his Taoiseach who had allowed him to put his puny talents to its service. He spoke of his years of hard work and of his sense of privilege in being allowed to pursue this work.

Another pause followed by what seemed like a thunder clap bursting in the studio; it was, however, Canice O'Keefee's stentorian indignation rising as he approached his dénouement.

'I have always, as long as I can remember, believed the best of people I meet. I like to extend the hand of friendship – that is my way. And I did just this to a well-known English gentleman, the proprietor and editor of an English weekly called *The Champion*.

'I met him in Trieste and there I offered him Irish hospitality. Under the roof of the – ', he paused reverently, 'James Joyce House, we broke bread together. I poured his wine; we discussed literature. At the end of the evening we said good night and I thought no more about it.

'When a reporter from *The Champion* came to interview me, I innocently imagined that he was interested in my work for the arts. Imagine my profound shock when I was presented with such

134

a scurrilous article a week later. It was unbelievable. I had been betrayed and to this day I do not know why.

'So I do not at all blame the men and women of the Irish press for misinterpreting this photograph.'

Canice's face was replaced on screen by the blown-up photograph of Honey and himself at P.J.'s party.

'Having read that dreadful article, you were not to know that what you see here is me congratulating a tragic and beautiful woman who, after years as a virtual recluse, has found the courage to start all over again. P.J. McGuckian gave her this chance, P.J., who was at school with both of us. And do you notice that smiling lady by my side? That is my wife Nuala, out of focus but there for anyone with a sharp eye to see. Nuala was just waiting to add her congratulations.'

Nuala, who had been barely visible in the original, was identifiable on the television screen.

'As I said, I do not blame the Irish press – I know with what reluctance it was forced into this whole, sorry mess. I know it is not the way of Irish journalists to persecute a fellow countryman, to try to destroy someone with lies and half truths and filthy innuendoes. You have never sunk to the level of some of your colleagues across the water, you have been a credit to your profession, every one of you, fearlessly seeking truth but avoiding muck-raking in the process.

'On many an occasion I have been grilled by you, have felt the sharp tip of your pens – and quite right too. But I know that you would never have sought to discredit me in such a fashion if you had not been led astray by the disgraceful antics of a foreign so-called newspaper. I realize that and I do not want you to blame yourselves for any misinterpretation of facts that you may have printed. We are all, in the final analysis, only human. Some of us have suffered more than others. Some of us may never fully recover', Honey's face was momentarily flashed on the screen, 'from the cruel hand dealt out to us by fate. But we must always remember that we are Irish and Irish people have always helped one another throughout the long, dark years of suffering . . .'

He broke off, wiped a tear from his cheek and blew his nose.

'I thank God for all His goodness, I thank my Taoiseach, Bill O'Reilly, I thank my dear wife, Nuala, but most of all I thank you, the people of Ireland, for allowing me to serve you and for listening to me tonight. *Slán agus beannacht Dé orainn go léir.*'

The country went wild, there was ecstasy throughout the land. If Canice O'Keeffe had but said the word, the British Embassy would have been burned down all over again.

It was a great moment to be Irish, for this man had given them everything: he had made them proud of their country, kicked England in the balls, proved that the wages of sin was death, demonstrated that demi-gods had feet of clay and that they could weep real tears. Most of all, he had given them a shove towards the twenty-first century.

Throughout the last twenty years, in various progressive western countries, heads of state and government ministers had been caught in varying degrees of *flagrante delicto*. Their public-spirited newspapers had, naturally, reported their carryings on and each sinner had taken it on the chin, confessing on television, weeping in some cases and always begging for forgiveness.

The reaction to these public confessions in Ireland had been complex. Lying chastely on the edge of Europe, protected by its watery *cordon sanitaire*, the collective soul of the nation was filled with a mixture of smugness and wistfulness. Yes, we were the only truly Christian country left in the entire western world; yes, this was something to be justly proud of . . . but . . . but . . .

Wouldn't a *soupçon* of public sin liven things up without doing any damage to the national fabric? Wouldn't it give us the sheen of sophistication which would add the final touch to our status as nation state and full, equal EC partner?

And now, tonight, Canice O'Keeffe had solved the problem. We had our own confessed adulterer, but better, more noble than the foreign variety and sanctified by tragedy and the sacraments of the Church.

Perfection. Nothing hick about this little country now. The island of saints and scholars had come of age.

The people were delighted, the press, most of them, were relieved. It wasn't their style, this snuffling around amongst Canice's fleshly sins, they had always felt uneasy about it and were glad to be off the hook.

Among the minority of journalists who had seen the Canice affair as a crusade against hypocrisy, confusion reigned. How had he done it? They were sure this time that they had him nailed. And he had emerged, if anything, more sanctified and sanctimonious than before. The bastard had got away with it. They thought that they had read the situation correctly, had correctly interpreted the public mind, but apparently Irish morality continued to shift, like the sands of the desert.

They would try again, they would retrench; for the moment though, they admitted defeat.

From his half-tester bed, the Taoiseach flicked off his remote control and stared across the expanse of his bedroom to a portrait of himself on the opposite wall. However, instead of his own handsome features he saw, momentarily imposed on the workmanlike oil, the simpering, silly face of Canice O'Keeffe.

The man was a total enigma. He had always thought of him as plain thick and until three days ago had no reason to change his mind. By this morning he had begun to grapple with the probability that he had appointed a madman to his Cabinet, had even begun to toy with the idea of seeing if he could have him locked away.

And now this – this, most chillingly, was not the performance of either a madman or a fool.

He began to think back over the career of Canice O'Keeffe, remembering the fulsome praise he had received over the years from various journalists.

Bill O'Reilly had always had a satisfactory relationship with the press. On a philosophic basis, like Pilate, he doubted the existence of truth so he was seldom upset by what he read in his newspapers. He had never liked journalists, however, believing them to be underworked, overpaid and self-important, and it had been a source of satisfaction to him over the years to realize how successfully he had sold them a pup in the person of Canice O'Keeffe. Every eulogy on Canice, every picture of him staring like a sick calf at some lump of granite or twisted iron bar, would have him laughing bitterly, remarking, 'Far from art the lot of yiz were reared.'

His sense of omnipotence would be reinforced on such occasions, his belief in his own right to rule.

Now he was not so sure. Self-doubt began to well up through his gut. He burped and propped himself against the pillows. Maybe the fellow *was* a genius. How else could his performance tonight be explained? Surely only a genius could produce such a delicately balanced mixture of bathos and patriotism, just the thing to appeal to the Irish nation? And it had been delivered with so much sincerity and resonance.

Bill O'Reilly reached for an antacid pill, then paused, his hand half-way to his bedside table. Hang on though: Canice was an accomplished actor who had always been able to say his lines with conviction but whose lines had he been reading tonight from the teleprompter?

Not his own, surely – the style was wrong, lacking the man's usual lofty abstruseness. Perhaps that style was reserved for matters artistic? Even so, he still could not believe that O'Keeffe was capable of producing any sort of coherent prose. He was incapable of coherent thought. Bill had yet to hear him string three intelligent sentences together.

Then who? Who had the necessary judgment and subtlety? Not that many people who could – of course. His side-kick, McGuckian.

Now there was a man of genius. A self-made millionaire, an acknowledged crook, one who had destroyed his capital city and emerged a national hero. Bill could see it now – the whole thing: the bringing together of the two, the photograph, the speech tonight, all obviously part of the one plan. What a man!

He had often been grateful in the past that McGuckian's role in politics had extended no further than contributions to the national collection; grateful not only because it had helped the party through many a lean year but because Bill knew that there was simply no room for any more genius round the Cabinet table. A great bloody race, the Celts. Full of genius.

Bill smiled and felt his stomach settle. He had been misjudging Canice there for a while and he should have known better. Above all else, Canice was loyal. And he had done very well tonight. On impulse Bill picked up his phone. He would get in with his congratulations straight away. It was no more than the decent fellow deserved.

'I'm sorry, Taoiseach, no, but I imagine he should be home any minute now. Will I get him to ring you back?

'That's very kind of you, Taoiseach, and I will of course. Thank you, thanks very much.'

Nuala O'Keeffe smiled as she patted the phone back into place then returned to her task of scalding the teapot. She was looking forward to her cup of tea, for listening to Canice always gave her a fierce thirst.

Not that she could complain about his performance tonight and Bill was clearly delighted with him.

She popped the cosy on to the pot, placed everything on a tray and carried it into a large room which with much tuition Canice was at last learning to call the lounge. Government Ministers, even if they were born in Cavan, did not have front rooms.

Nuala sipped her tea and sighed with pleasure. Of course she had always known that it would blow over, but it had been sticky enough while it lasted and as far as she was concerned Canice was still not out of the woods. Men were such fools and Canice more so than most; she wondered where he would be today if she had not taken pity on him all those years ago and agreed to marry him.

Such a lot of nonsense had gone on. If she had wanted to she could have put those reporters straight, for well she knew that Canice had retired in the sex department years ago. Like many a decent Irishman before him, he had taken to religion. That and art. And Nuala had come to the conclusion that art was an even more efficacious passion killer than religion.

Canice and she had never actually discussed the affair – there had been no time with so much else happening. Listening to him tonight though, getting the full story for the first time, Nuala wasn't buying it. She didn't believe a word of his rigmarole to the nation. He was a good liar, she had always known that, and he was an old softie who felt sorry for Honey, had done for years.

But she knew her husband and all this talk of a carnal relationship and love children rang false. Canice was far more comfortable on his knees than astride a woman. Even in his heyday he had never been energetic, pleading sinusitis on those very nights when she knew she was in her fertile period. It had taken her five years to conceive Cliodna.

They were notoriously clannish, Cavan people. She wouldn't be a bit surprised if the whole thing had been a plot, cooked up between P.J. and himself in order to ignite Honey's moribund career.

Cavan people all three. And even in her twenties she was fat and Canice had never fancied fat girls. Sloppy and sluttish, it wasn't difficult to believe that Honey had had a love child . . . neatness he admired, small waists, slim hips, modest bosoms.

But he had made her suffer over the last few weeks, herself and the children. She had kept going through fear, knowing that if she collapsed worse would ensue. So she had outfaced the reporters, withstood the siege, shipped off the children to her sister and helped Canice to go to ground.

He might think it was all over now, he could simper at the nation but he still had her to deal with. Nuala, who was as tough as the Kerry crags amidst which she had been reared, had a strong sense of justice, especially where her children were concerned. Canice's job was secure, his Mercedes would remain in the garage; his debt to his family had yet to be paid.

Finishing her tea Nuala stood up and moved to survey her figure in the glass doors of the drinks cabinet. She had not put on one ounce since their wedding day, in fact, if anything, she had lost weight.

She sat down again, raising her feet on to an embroidered foot stool. Her eyes began to move around the room, lingering with pleasure on matching details, toning effects.

No reason to let Cavan people get you down.

12

P.J. was in a grump before he ever set eyes on Matt Savino. 'Why does he want to bring him here?' he had complained to Noreen. 'I didn't build this house to entertain Aube's friends – nor Annabel's boyfriends either.'

'I want you to be nice to both of them.'

'A bloody circus, that's what we'll have here tonight.'

'You said you wanted to inspect young Flanagan and you should be glad Aube wants us to meet his friends.'

'Yanks.'

'Just behave, P.J.'

Aubrey introduced Matt as if he were producing a rabbit from a hat. 'Mother, P.J., I want you to meet Congressman Matt Savino.'

'Hi! Call me Matt.' Matt waved a hand – large, genial, expansive, American.

P.J. stared at him sourly. Jesus. Tweeds and a cap – who did he think he was? Victor McLaglen in *The Quiet Man*? And sporting a miniature tricolour in his buttonhole, for Christ's sake.

'Here, sit here, Matt,' Aubrey pointed towards a chair. 'Can I get you a drink?'

He was dismayed by his parents' reactions. His father's rude stare was not unexpected, but why on earth had Noreen made a dash from the room without even a word of greeting to her guest? He examined Matt. Nothing wrong, fly buttons not undone. What the hell was going on?

As Matt and Aube had walked into the living room an unpleasant odour had wafted in with them and assaulted Noreen's nostrils. The pike – she had forgotten all about the pike. She sniffed. Ugh!

Horrible. Why on earth had she listened to P.J.? She looked wildly around her, then made a run towards the kitchen.

Earlier in the day she had said to P.J., 'I think I'll give them lamb tonight.'

'By God you won't.'

'What do you mean?' P.J. never interfered with her menus.

'Pike, that's what we'll have, that fine fellow I caught last night.'

'But I've never cooked pike, P.J., and you said we'd bring it back to Dublin with us.'

'Ha – but that was before I was aware of the arrival of our honoured guests. That'll soon sort out the men from the boys.'

Noreen had not at all liked the look of the long-snouted brute. Where she had been brought up there had been a prejudice against pike, accompanied by tales of rats found whole in their bellies when they were split open.

'I've no recipe for pike, P.J.'

'But I have, my love – the most famous recipe for pike in the world – Izaak Walton's.'

He had cleaned and scaled the fish and then presented it to her, together with his copy of *The Compleat Angler*.

'Look what he says, Noreen – "too good a dish for any but anglers, or very honest men". We'll soon see if our Yank friend is an honest man because I'm damned sure he's not an angler.'

'He might be.'

'A friend of Aube's? Come on now, girl, listen to this.'

As he read out the list of ingredients, Noreen listened incredulously. The fish was to be stuffed with herbs, spices, oysters, anchovies, a pound of butter, then larded with strips of bacon and roasted on a spit.

'We haven't got a spit and you're not going to get oysters anywhere in Cavan. Anyway, it's August.'

'No problem, my love. There's three tins of oysters in that press and we can cook him on a barbecue.'

As it turned out the pike had to be manoeuvred into the oven, for by four o'clock the rain had settled in and no barbecueing was going to be done for the rest of the evening. P.J. shoved in its tail, shut the oven door and declared that everything would be grand; Noreen was not so sure.

Now, as she stood in the middle of the kitchen, having left the

142

living room so precipitously, she sniffed the air, trying to identify smells. But the amalgam was so overpowering that she could not identify any of its ingredients nor could she tell whether it was pleasant or otherwise. And something, the spices perhaps, was stinging her eyes, causing them to water.

She was struggling with oven gloves and weeping copiously when the guests began to cram into the kitchen, herded forward by P.J.

'You're going to be crowded here, it was never intended for guests,' he told them rudely. 'I built this house for the family, not for entertaining strangers.'

Matt, however, was oblivious of any rudeness. His face had assumed a beatific expression as he turned his nose in the air like a pointer. 'Is it – pike?' he asked tremulously.

'Yes.'

'Oh my gosh, Mrs McGuckian, Noreen, this is a real treat.'

Noreen, Seán and Annabel ate hardly anything; Seán shared Noreen's prejudice and Annabel was fully occupied admiring Seán. The other three, however, made up for their abstemiousness. Aubrey chewed his way through a second helping, anger fuelling his appetite; P.J. ate through spite, his appetite and his digestion ruined by the sight of this Yank enjoying his food; and Matt ate through sheer delight, pausing every now and again to roll his eyes heavenwards and exclaim '*M'm*-m'm.'

'Do you fish?' P.J. asked Matt as Annabel and Seán began to clear the table, irritated beyond endurance by the expression of satisfaction on the American's face.

''Fraid not,' Matt belched gently. 'I've never had the time.'

'Oh, I see, yes. A busy man.' He looked towards Aubrey. 'I hope your friend won't be bored here then, Aube. Nothing much to do around here except fish . . . but then, we're not very busy around here anyway. Not being as important as the Yanks, we've nothing much to do except throw out a line.'

'I told you, P.J.' As usual when he was distressed, Aubrey's voice had risen to a squeal. 'Matt's going to Belfast in the morning.'

'Do you know Belfast well, Matt?' Noreen offered her best social smile, noting with alarm that storm clouds were darkening the grey of P.J.'s eyes.

Aubrey threw down his napkin in disgust. Was she doing

this deliberately? 'Mother – have you forgotten who Matt is? Congressman Savino – you know? You remember? For God's sake, he's been fighting Ireland's cause in the United States Congress for years.'

'Oh, of course.' Noreen laughed and tried to looked intelligent. '*That* Savino. And we're delighted that you could stay with us, even if it's only overnight.'

P.J. was having none of it. 'And what cause would that be now, Congressman Savino?'

Matt was all charm. He smiled deprecatingly and turned his full brown gaze on P.J. 'Aube here is exaggerating. I'm just kinda interested in what goes on up in the north of Ireland. I help where I can, raising people's consciousness, making Northern Ireland a political issue.'

'I see.' P.J. wiped his mouth with the back of his hand, deliberately, it seemed to Noreen, ignoring the napkin on his knee. 'Well, I suppose that must be a great comfort to all those people up in Northern Ireland to know that you're taking such an interest in their affairs.'

'I just think that this is such a beautiful country and such a beautiful people that it hurts me to see what is going on up there. It really hurts me.'

P.J. stared at him in disbelief, then, still looking at him, changed his expression to one of concern. 'Well, we can't have that now, we can't have you going round hurting.' He stretched across the table and tapped him gently on the forearm. 'My advice to you is this, Matt: when things get too much for you, don't brood over them – go fishing. If you took up fishing I can guarantee that you'd feel a lot better about that sort of thing – you'd find you wouldn't be in nearly so much pain.'

They didn't stay for coffee. Aubrey said that he wanted Matt to sample the pint in Maguire's bar. Nobody pressed them to stay.

As the kitchen door closed, Noreen glared at her husband. 'That was disgraceful, P.J. No – I mean it. You were downright rude to that poor man.'

'Arra, I wasn't.'

'Yes, you were – I was ashamed of you.'

'Well, I'm sorry. I suppose I just lost my temper – but, do you blame me, Noreen? These bloody Yanks coming over here, telling

144

us how to solve our problems. Then they hare off back to the States and leave us to clear up the mess.'

'He's Aube's friend.'

'Right, I'll apologize the next time I see him. Now, how about a cup of tea?' He beckoned Annabel over to him and planted a smacking kiss on her mouth.

'What's that in aid of?'

'For being such a good daughter. Now, off you go and help your mother, I'm taking this lad for a walk.'

Although distracted, P.J. had been observing Seán throughout the evening and he was pleased with what he saw. The boy was quiet, not pushy, but able to speak up for himself when addressed. There had been something about him which had been puzzling P.J., something familiar, and only seconds ago as he caught his profile at the window had he realized what it was. He reminded him of himself at that age, same physique, same black hair, same accent even. Not as handsome of course. Bugger the Yank, this was more important.

'Come on, lad, we'll leave the women to get on with it.'

They walked along the lake, taking the same path Annabel had chosen the day that she had met Seán.

'So,' P.J. turned to look at the boy, 'you're a Flanagan of Flanagan's Hardware?'

'Yes.'

'I knew your father. Decent people.' P.J. smiled. 'So you and Annabel have become friends?'

'Yes.'

'I'm glad. She knows no one around here – I'm glad she's found a friend. What do you do – Seán?'

'I'll be repeating my Leaving Certificate starting in September.'

'You failed this year then?'

'No – I just didn't get enough points to go to college.'

'And you want to go to college?'

'*I* don't. My parents want me to.'

'And you?'

'I'm a poet. I'd quite like to do an Arts degree but they want me to do medicine. A doctor in the family still counts for something in rural Ireland, Mr McGuckian.'

P.J. looked at him, half admiringly. 'Begod. A poet. I suppose you'll be looking for a rich wife so.'

145

Seán's laugh was natural, amused. 'To tell you the truth, Mr McGuckian, I'm not thinking about marriage just yet – I'm only eighteen after all. Anyway, when the time comes I won't be looking for a rich wife. I'll marry for love, Mr McGuckian – isn't that what you'd expect a poet to do?'

P.J. stopped and clapped him on the shoulders. 'You know what it is, son, I like you. You've got spunk and I like that. But regarding Annabel – she's only out of the convent. She's young for her age and I want you to remember that. Enjoy yourselves over the summer, but if you harm her in any way, if you make her unhappy as only young pups can, then I'm warning you I will seek you out and personally break every bone in your body. Is that understood?' He paused for breath, then added, 'Not that I think you're a young pup.'

Seán nodded, hiding his amusement, far surer of his love for Annabel than of her father's ability to break his bones.

'So enjoy yourself this summer and you're welcome up at the house any time, lad.'

Aubrey was wondering how he would word his apology to Matt. They were sitting in the Maguire Roadhouse in the Lassoo Lounge. They had chosen this in preference to the Rodeo Bar or the Six-shooter Lounge, each area distinct and divided by louvred swing doors that stopped a foot from the ground. The threat of 'Live Music Tonite' had not materialized; the artists' van had broken down and they were at this very minute stranded on a lonely Sligo road.

The only other revellers in the Lassoo Lounge were a young couple with their three children, plump subdued mites who sat steadily eating crisps and drinking Coca-Cola, staring with well-behaved vacuity at a blank television screen.

'I want to explain something to you, Matt,' Aubrey began. 'About P.J. – he wasn't getting at you – '

'Forget it.'

'No, really, Matt.'

'I said forget it. I'm a big boy, Aube, I can look after myself.'

'I brought you there, I subjected you to his rudeness.'

'Look – fella, I told you.' Matt's voice was sharp with irritation. 'Just let me look after myself. I mean – it was kind of embarrassing back there the way you were going on. As if I couldn't speak for myself. P.J. didn't bother me. If you'd left us alone, we'd have gotten on fine.'

Aubrey excused himself and headed for the Gents. It was the most authentically Wild West corner of the roadhouse but Aubrey was unconscious of its shortcomings as he stared at his reflection in the damp-spotted mirror.

Life was so unfair. Matt was displeased with him now and P.J. as usual had come out a winner. Rude, bad-tempered, shallow, selfish – how could Matt say he was all right?

Of course, Matt didn't know him, didn't realize the depths of his perfidy. If he was hoping to get money out of P.J. he would be waiting a thousand years. P.J. would not part with a penny, especially not for the Cause; his colonial mentality would only allow him to spend money on vulgar birthday parties, aping a time and a people that had already sunk into oblivion.

A colonial mentality. Aubrey had by this time made the phrase his own and found that repeating it at fraught moments brought him solace. And it fitted the old man so perfectly.

Aubrey straightened his back, beginning to feel a little better. He turned on the single tap on the hand basin, but hesitated as he saw the thin stream of brackish water which had begun to flow.

'Are you OK?' Matt manoeuvred himself into the small room. 'Jesus.' He looked round him. 'You'll catch typhoid if you stay in here any longer. Come on. Let's get back to the house – I aim for an early start in the morning.'

P.J. had been dozing. The rough closing of the front door woke him and his listened to the footsteps ascending the stairs. They weren't coming in then. A pity. Chastened by Noreen's remarks he had been waiting for them to come in so that he could make amends. He had been prepared even to share his brandy with Matt and listen to his silly blather.

Aubrey was probably offended. The boy was like a bloody Reverend Mother – if you looked crooked at him he took offence.

Not that even Aubrey could annoy him this evening. It was a perfect evening: the brandy was good, his daughter was safely tucked up in bed and two hours ago he had made love to his wife and enjoyed it. There was something particularly satisfying about making love to a wife of thirty years and enjoying it.

And tomorrow was going to be another perfect day, perfect, that is, for fishing. Clouds would gather and the rain would fall and the little buggers would begin to bit. He mightn't go back to Dublin till Tuesday. Annabel would like another day here, now that she had found her Seán. And Seán? He was fine for the time being; when the time came to dispatch him, P.J. didn't think that he would have any trouble.

A pity Aubrey had never taken up fishing, it might have calmed him down. But he didn't have the patience, he was forever running around chasing his tail. Whereas Annabel – Annabel had the gift of stillness. She could sit in a room without blinking an eyelid for hours on end. She could teach her brother a thing or two, except that poor Aubrey was incapable of learning.

P.J. stretched and heaved himself from his chair. Noreen would be asleep now and he would slip in beside her and snuggle up to her as he had done for thirty years. As a man of principle, a moral being, P.J. McGuckian had never slept with another woman. He had shagged them, caressed them, licked double cream off their nipples, but he had never laid down and slept beside them when it was all over. His snores were reserved for his wife and he felt proud now of his record. In every meaningful way he considered that he had been faithful to Noreen all his married life.

It was fitting that he should sleep so soundly.

Annabel closed her eyes and marvelled again that passion could be such a cool thing: incandescent and star-like, its fine, sharp slivers had pierced her body, shocking it into life.

She stared at her reflection in wonder, at her lips and her tongue and the rounded, pink tips of her fingers. Where had they learned their secrets? How had they acquired such skill?

'I'm a poet,' he had told her, drinking the drops that fell from her wet curls. 'That's why I'm repeating my Leaving. It'll give ma a year off before they throw me out and tell me to go and get a job.'

He swam between her legs and she was fearful again of webbed feet bruising her; then he popped up beside her, smiling, and kissed the tip of her nose.

He sat beside her on the rock, letting his feet float in the water, beside hers.

'You're my water nymph. Let's be buried in this lake.'

'I don't want to die.'

'You'll have to die some day.'

She showered him with lake droplets. 'I shall live for ever.'

They found a spot where the sun had broken through the trees.

'I cannot offer you immortality, but how about nine hundred years – like the Children of Lir? You remember the story, Annie? Three hundred years on this lake and then we can fly off to Lake Derravaragh – '

'No, no,' she shivered. 'I've always hated that story. It's cruel, they were so lonely, poor things.'

He began to rub her with a towel, between kisses. 'You've been too long at your English boarding school. I shall have to restore you to your element, little water nymph.'

This time the water seemed warmer. She dived and saw his legs, long and greeny-hued and boneless. She swam under him and reached out to touch. Warm, not fish-like, blood-carrying, despite the greeny hue.

He slipped away from her and she swam upwards after him. They turned together and lay back to look at the sky, a limitless and vacuous blue.

'The woods are friendlier,' he said, and taking her hand began to kick towards the shore.

He made a mossy bed for her and drew her down. 'We should run away. I hate family complications.'

'I couldn't.'

'You *wouldn't*.'

'I might.'

'You're a tease. Is that what the nuns taught you?'

Annabel had discovered that she was adept at games that had never been on the school curriculum. And such delicious games – demanding more skill than tennis, they were more fun than hockey, more subtle than chess. Annabel, who had never been bored in her life, wondered how she had passed the time before she had met Seán. How she enjoyed looking at him, running her hand down his thick, white skin, feeling the ting of his teeth against hers, watching his eyes change and darken as they looked down at her.

'You are not trifling with me, Annie?'

She laughed and shook her head. 'What a funny expression. Of course I'm not.'

'If you were, if you were merely passing the time, rich-girl fashion, then I should kill you.' His hands circled her neck.

She shuddered delightedly.

Annabel had never felt real fear but sometimes as a child she had willed herself on black nights to summon up witches. Then as she had stared out at the empty garden she had been excited by a fear that wasn't really a fear, more a new experience in pleasure, for she knew that Daddy would let no witch near his little girl.

Now as she lay perfectly still within Seán's encircling hands, she experienced the same thrill of mock danger.

'If you kill me, I shall come back and haunt you.'

'All poets are haunted.'

'And all poets are lazy as hell.' She slipped from his arms and ran once more to the lake.

'I love you, Annabel.' He was embarrassed by the involuntary admission, then disappointed when he realized that she would not have heard it. He looked towards the lake but there was no sign of her anywhere, no ripple on the still surface.

'Annabel,' he shouted, panicking. 'Annabel, where are you?'

As she popped up for air several yards from the shore, he shook his fist at her and started to run. 'I'll show you. Just wait till I get you.'

'As if you could.'

Their shouts were absorbed by the trees so that Noreen, sitting with her back to the lake in her suspended sitting room, heard nothing but the restless pigeons and P.J.'s gentle grunts as he tied a fly to his line.

Unexpectedly, and to P.J.'s annoyance, the sun had come out today.

'Come on, Mummy,' Annabel had pleaded, 'come on and I'll teach you to swim.'

'I'm not going near that lake and neither should you.'

'But look,' taking her hand she had dragged her mother to the window. 'It looks almost blue today. I'd hold on to you – you'd be safe with me.'

But Noreen had folded her arms and watched her lovely daughter dance down the steps, laughing at her mother, laughing at a sunny world, a world created specially for her.

Was she in love?

Seán certainly was. He heard nothing that was said to him, saw nothing around him when he was in Annabel's presence. You could almost feel the current of his passion when he entered a room.

No, Noreen decided, at the moment Annabel was not in such a state. At the moment she was playing at being in love with Seán but the person she was really in love with was herself. She was discovering herself, delighting in what she found, aware suddenly of her power, exulting in it one moment and doubting it the next. It was not a bad basis to start from but it would mean a bumpy ride for Seán. Annabel had a way of getting what she wanted – of smiling and beguiling and wheedling until in the end you just gave in. Noreen had a feeling that Seán would be no more successful at withstanding her blandishments than was P.J.

She smiled, then frowned as she remembered her other child. Sometimes she wished, meanly, that there were only the three of them, that Aubrey would take himself off somewhere, cut himself off, so that she no longer had to feel responsible for him. He was so unlovable – brusque, seeking out insults, ready to feel offended at every turn.

Was it her fault? Had she been too absorbed in P.J. so that the left-over love which trickled down to Aubrey had deformed and stunted rather than nurtured? She wished she could remember if she had neglected him, but when she thought back to his babyhood all she could remember was the surge of pleasure she used to feel after the night feeds when P.J. would be there waiting for her, keeping the bed warm, staying awake, banishing her tiredness as his hand crept up under her nightie.

Poor Aube – no man, least of all a son, could compete with P.J. McGuckian.

13

Aubrey gingerly uncrossed a knee, fearful of drawing attention to himself or of upsetting Matt, who had suffered enough upset at the hands of the McGuckians last night. He had pretended indifference but he had not fooled Aube and this morning his driving was even more erratic than usual. Were they still going to Belfast? At this stage Aubrey couldn't tell. When they hit the main road Matt might decide to head back to Dublin.

'Ah shit,' said Matt and turned on the car radio. He hummed along for a while then took his hand off the steering wheel and punched Aubrey playfully on the shoulder. 'Do you realize, fella, how lucky you are? Do you realize what a privilege it is to be born in such a country at such an epoch?'

'But I do – of course I do.'

'Most men, Aube, lead quiet lives of desperation. That's not my own, that's a quote but can't you see how right it is? Nothing meaningful ever happens to most people. They get born, get married, look at television some and die. It's not their fault, it's just the hand they're dealt. Born in a dull country and at a dull time. You, Aube, on the other hand, can play a role in history. Do you still want to come to Belfast with me?'

Did he want immortality?

It turned out to be a voyage of discovery. Matt, his good humour restored, began a lecture on Irish history and Aubrey, listening, aware of his own ignorance, could feel a cathartic surge of shame washing through his pores. He knew that he would emerge from this experience a changed man.

When they came to the border checkpoint he found it hard

to control his indignation as foreign adolescents with theatrically blackened faces asked for identification and the purpose of the visit.

'Cool,' Matt breathed in his ear as he handed over his papers. 'Stay cool, Aube.'

The soldier, a youth with a blond crewcut, seemed irritated by Matt's status and the questioning became more intense, each sentence ending with mock respect in 'Congressman, Sir.'

Matt smiled up at him, lazily. 'No need for all that sirring. Where I come from we don't go in much for handles – no lords or earls. Know what I mean? Log cabin to White House, that's the great tradition in my country so you can forget about the sirs.'

The soldier waved them through and when Aubrey looked back he saw that he was staring after the car. 'Good for you, Matt – cheeky young beggar.'

Suddenly they were on the motorway, then off it and right into Belfast. Aubrey stared at the passing streets, disappointed by their ordinariness. Grey and shabby, yes, but not like a war zone. Even the soldiers looked more like props than occupying forces.

'Hang on, fella,' Matt reassured him. 'I am going to introduce you to the face of the Oppressed.'

They drove to a housing estate, similar to many built by his father but unfamiliar to Aubrey, who had only joined P.J.'s firm when it had moved out of housing and into grander things. Matt turned into a cul-de-sac and stopped the car half-way along it, parking carefully in the short distance between two sets of double gates. Most of the houses had portions of their low walls replaced by these gates, to allow for off-street parking as far as Aubrey could make out.

Matt honked the horn. Immediately, as if by prearranged signal, doors began to open and people came streaming towards them, waving and calling Matt's name.

Matt got out. 'Watch this, Aube,' he leant through the car window. 'These are your oppressed and separated brethren.'

Aubrey blinked. Were they?

The people coming towards the car bore no resemblance to the faces of his imaginings but instead bore an unnerving similarity to the inhabitants of certain areas of inner Dublin, areas where you parked your car at your peril and where women didn't walk for fear of having their handbags snatched.

They were the sort of people Aubrey would avoid at home –
undersized, denim-clad, dyed blonde hair predominating. They
puffed on cigarettes and stared at him, hostile. Not looking at
all oppressed, looking as if they might any minute eat him
without salt.

Rows of women surrounded the car, the men lolled in the
background. Some of the younger women nudged one another
and sniggered; one pushed a cigarette at him through the open
window. He cowered from them, from their pale, aggressive faces,
their strutting stance, their high-pitched, squawking voices.

Matt yanked the door open. 'Come on, let me introduce
you. This here is Aube McGuckian, a friend come down from
Dublin.'

Aubrey stumbled out and stood naked before them. 'How do
you do – hello . . .'

There were some hoots of derision but most of them stared
at him indifferently and then returned their attention to Matt.
Everybody seemed to be talking at once, clamouring for notice.
Aubrey could understand little of what they were saying though
Matt seemed to have no difficulty.

They were invited into one of the little houses and given tea.
Their hostess, who kept on digging Aubrey in the ribs, exclaiming
'Isn't that right,' seemed to be complaining about having had her
windows broken. Matt made soothing noises and Aubrey drank
his tea.

Half-way through his third cup, which he had been too timid to
refuse, Aubrey began to relax. These people meant him no harm,
indeed they were welcoming, most of them. Early impressions
faded and he could soon tell that they were quite different from
the thugs and layabouts of the north Dublin neighbourhoods. He
looked into their faces and saw their individuality; he looked into
their eyes and saw their suffering.

The oppressed.

Ireland unfree shall never be at peace.

He felt his soul stir.

Later, having a drink in the Europa, Matt said to him, 'Well,
Aube, now do you see what I mean?'

Aubrey nodded.

'But did you know any of this back in Dublin? Does anyone in
Dublin know what's going on up here? No, because you won't

get off your – pardon my French – fucking backsides and come up and see.'

Aubrey felt he had been made whole. He was overcome as if by a religious zeal. He wanted to stand up there in the bar of the Europa and, raising his hands, give thanks that his eyes had at last been opened. Praise Matt, praise the Lord.

'You've got this thing about nationalism down in the South,' Matt continued. 'All you college types that should be leading the revolution, you think nationalism is gone out of fashion. You're so busy being good little Englishmen, good Europeans, that you can't see what's happening under your noses.'

Aubrey took a swig of his whiskey, waiting to have his eyes opened further.

'It's all that conditioning. You think there's something shameful about feeling nationalistic. Tell that to the Germans, or try calling the Falklands the Malvinas and see what response you get from a Brit.'

Brits. Aubrey stared wildly around to see if there were any of the hated species near enough to spit on.

'So what's wrong with Irish nationalism, what's different about that? All you rich guys, all you college types, you all need to be deprogrammed, so that you can see this war up here for what it is and stop all that shit about terrorism. A word, for Christ's sake. One word and you're all running for cover.'

How chastening were *those* words to Aubrey McGuckian's ears. He thought what a bitter lesson he had learned: to find his soul he had had to journey three thousand miles. He smiled with gratitude at Matt and ordered two more whiskies. He had been so moved in that little house, sitting in the parlour, fingering the touching ornaments made with such loving care by young men who would spend the best years of their lives behind bars. He was a man of peace but, by God, there were limits.

'What will I do, Matt?' He swept the whiskey off the counter and downed it with one swallow. 'Tell me what I must do.'

'Stick with me, fella. I've got plans.'

It was a different man who returned across the border twenty-four hours later, a man changed by experience, touched by the hand of fate. He knew himself to be different, now, sitting in his father's dining room, watching without anger the pitiful charade

155

of ascendency manners unfolding in front of him . . . linen napkins, polished rosewood, silver. He did not know precisely how he wished them to break bread – although fleetingly a collage of *scian*, stone floors and flagons of mead formed in his mind – he just knew that all this was false, false.

He marvelled at the complexity of his emotional response, contempt tempered by pity for that poor man, his father. Poor in spite of his millions, his life empty and meaningless.

P.J., enjoying a particularly tender leg of lamb stuffed with a mixture of apricots, rice and rosemary by Mrs Donovan, was irritated by the presence of his son. He had arrived unannounced, invited himself to dinner and had sat for the last twenty minutes with a pained and pious expression on his face. Any time a comment was made by someone he simpered and flapped his eyelashes like a lovesick girl. If P.J. were the type to worry, he would worry about this strange behaviour; as it was, he just wished that Aubrey would take himself off and quick.

Noreen was doing her best with him, asking him questions, making inquiries about the Yank – in fact all the chatter was beginning to get on P.J.'s nerves. He liked to eat in peace, believing that silence was an aid to digestion. He finished his meat and pushed his plate away. Good grub but he had probably overdone it.

'A pot of tea now and I'll be a happy man,' he said, loosening the waistband of his trousers.

Aubrey sniffed. 'I'm surprised it's not coffee.'

P.J. felt the hot flush of blood to his face. Jesus. How could he have fathered such a total imbecile? What did he *mean* by remarks like that?

Noreen, noticing the flush, touched his hand. 'Tea coming up.'

P.J. smiled and looked across at his other child. Consolation there, more than consolation. His lovely girl, sitting as the nuns had taught her, straight backed, hands on lap. He could feel himself relax as he looked at her with pleasure.

'Well, Annie,' he began, unaware in his absorption with Annabel that he was cutting across Aubrey, who had launched into an account of his visit to Belfast. 'Tell us now, how is that boyfriend of yours? When are you seeing him again?'

Annabel giggled.

'He's not a bad lad, I've decided.'

'What do you mean he's not a bad lad? He's wonderful. Almost as wonderful as you, Daddy.'

Annabel stood up and walked around the table to plant a kiss on her father's head; then, to even things up, she stretched over and kissed Noreen's cheek. She smiled kindly at Aubrey.

Annabel was in love, and the world which had always been a pleasant place had become a sparkling, shining orb. She had discovered that being in love with Seán caused her to fall in love with humanity and with all sorts of inanimate matter – with trees and sand; with the immaterial too, light and wind and the warmth of sunshine. She did not miss the beloved, so overwhelmed was she by her own good fortune, and in any case she phoned him twice a day.

'You're a chancer, Annie.'

'I am, Daddy.'

Noreen had been listening to the exchange between father and daughter while at the same time casting an anxious eye at her son. He was sulking now, cheeks bunched like a little boy. He had been in such good form when he arrived, as if he was actually pleased to see them all. She hadn't expected him to stay to dinner and had been delighted when he had suggested it, but now his mood had changed, suddenly and without warning.

"What do you think of Matt's suggestion, P.J.?" she decided it was time to intervene.

P.J. looked startled. 'What suggestion?'

'You know – what Aube was just saying, about all of us getting involved and – '

'Forget it, Mother,' Aubrey interrupted, pushing back his chair. 'Obviously he didn't think much of it, he didn't even bother to listen to it.'

As he disappeared through the door, his entire back view, his hunched shoulders, lengthened spine and tightened buttocks managed to convey an air of offended dignity.

P.J. shook his head in genuine bewilderment. 'What did I do now? That fellow is as touchy as a pregnant Girl Guide.'

Aubrey, hurrying to his Lamborghini, had to remind himself that it was his father, P.J. McGuckian, who was in need of pity. He was the betrayed, not the betrayer, and his son must remember that. A dupe after all, eventually an object of ridicule.

He would not be written about by historians; his name would not be remembered when his hideous buildings were pulled down to be replaced by something more inspired. Amassing a fortune would not confer immortality on him and he would be forgotten before that money was spent.

Quiet lives of desperation. He liked that phrase, and although he didn't think it applied to his father's life, it bloody well should. He must be made to realize just how banal his existence was.

Nipping out on to the main road he glared at a woman in a Ford Fiesta who had blown her horn at him. He took a bend too fast, then skilfully settled the car and increased speed as he approached a straight stretch of road. By the time he had arrived in Stephen's Green and found a parking space straight away, his good humour had been quite restored.

'Then I said to myself, "No Matt, you won't chicken out. It's your duty to stay and do something." That's when I got the idea.'

Matt Savino was pacing up and down his hotel bedroom, shirt sleeves rolled up, hair tousled from constantly running his fingers through it, a sign to those who knew him that he had been indulging in serious intellectual stimulation. The recycled, faintly perfumed air of the room had given Aubrey a headache, but Matt seemed impervious to its toxicity. His bulk and determination overwhelmed the room, his gestures sending ashtrays and table lamps flying. He turned now and lifted Aubrey from the bed, shaking him gently by the shoulders. 'Wake up, Aube. Listen to what I'm saying. This is going to be big. This is going to be meaningful. A symbolic gathering right on the border. Can't you picture it? A joining of hands, a coming together. I can get this networked back home – it'll be on every TV channel from New York to LA. Can't you just picture it, Aube?'

Aubrey thought he could, though the focus was not too clear. 'It sounds wonderful. What – ah – exactly do you have in mind?'

'Look – this whole thing started, the germ of this idea, when we were pub hunting up in Cavan. You remember? You wanted me to see this real nice old pub and we went that back road and crossed the border and back again and I never would have realized it if you hadn't said. Remember, Aube?'

'I remember.'

'I thought then – Jeez – this can't be for real. This is one little

158

country, one intact island. How dare the Brits plonk a border down just anywhere? It kinda brought the whole thing home to me and it made me real indignant. That's how I got my idea. Something, isn't it? They'll march from the North and they'll march from the South. They'll meet on a lonely country road which will also be the line that divides their little country and they will shake hands across that invisible line.'

As he talked, Aubrey began to catch his enthusiasm. A symbolic coming together of a divided people; a platform straddling the border; music; orations, declarations and the world television cameras there to record the proceedings for posterity.

'I haven't worked out the finer points,' Matt continued. 'It's all going to take some time. I was thinking of something to highlight the symbolism, some kinda mascot. Like an Irish wolfhound standing across the border. Anyway, I want to do this thing right – no hitches. It's gotta impress people, then we'll wake them up down here and we'll see the dollars begin to flow from back home.'

Aubrey had a most unusual gift – almost indeed an extra sense. At certain crucial periods during his life, when he stood at a crossroads, when vital decisions had to be made, he would go to bed and in the course of the night he would dream, a dream of such inspirational force that when he awoke in the morning he knew that he had found the answer. This had happened to him most notably on the night that he had been visited by Palladio. And now, again, his gift did not forsake him.

He left Matt at about ten that night and was in bed by twelve. Sometime before dawn he awoke. He sat up in bed, throbbing with excitement, the vividness of the dream still possessing him. The Táin Bó Cuailgne – the epic tale of the brown bull of Cuailgne. There was Matt's perfect mascot. No, more than a mascot, the perfect embodiment of the symbolism inherent in the pageant.

He leaped out of bed and over to a bookcase under the window. Yes, there it was, a book on Irish myths and legends. Impatiently he turned to the index, leafing his way to Táin, to try to find out more about this early epic tale.

It wasn't all that helpful. Scholarly and discreet, it talked of varying versions, badly damaged eighth-century manuscripts, contradictions, excisions and additions over the centuries. There was enough there though for Aubrey to know that his hazy childhood memory had been right.

It seemed, reading between the scholarly, cautious lines, that Queen Maeve and King Ailill of Connacht had invaded Ulster. With their armies they had gone on a giant cattle raid to try and steal the great brown bull of Cuailgne. Much bloodshed had ensued, with many heroes killed on both sides in pitched battles and single combat. The bull had eventually been taken from the men of Ulster, but Maeve had not brought him back to Connacht for he had been killed in combat with another bull.

What a marvellous story. What a marvellous opportunity to make restitution to the people of Ulster. The Bó Cuailgne would be returned over the border.

The symbolism, with its echoes down through the centuries, was perfect. Aubrey pictured the noble animal, a tricolour round its horn, a Union Jack hanging from its tail, being handed back to the warriors of Ulster.

Even hardened Unionist hearts must be touched, must recognize the generosity and good will of the gesture. And if they weren't, that was all right too, just proving what the nationalists said all along, that they were a crowd of bastards. But they would be given a chance.

Matt shared his vision 'This is simply the best idea. Tell me about that old bull, Aube.'

Aubrey obliged.

'This is going to slay them. And it is going to show what serious pacifists we are. I mean, are we touting machine-guns? Not while we've got the goddam bull.'

Aubrey's inspiration had a therapeutic effect on his psyche, cleansing his innards, getting rid of all the bile which he churned out daily, a symptom of the malaise of being his father's son. Now he felt soothed and sweet as he had immediately after his dream of Palladio, although he knew that he would never return to the business of designing houses. It didn't seem important any more what Dublin looked like, whether it was defaced by his father's ghastly egg cartons or rose again a gracious classical town.

A preoccupation with appearances seemed wickedly frivolous when the spirit and heart of the nation was on the point of death.

160

Brick, cement, granite, sandstone – what did they signify in the march of a nation, in the search of an ancient people for its identity?

In fact, as far as Aubrey knew, the ancient Celts had not been builders; they pitched camp when the need arose and then they moved on. They had left no cities behind them, nor ancient cathedrals. These were the legacy of the invaders: the Normans, the English and the fiendish Roman Church.

The Catholic Church had achieved pride of place in Aubrey's demonology, although up till three months ago his attitude towards it had been one of benign indifference. Growing up in an era when it no longer hectored and bullied, he had not thought much about it since he had stopped going to Mass. And this had happened more through laziness than through any conscious decision.

Since his awakening, however, urged on by Matt, he had sought an explanation for the apathy which surrounded him, which indeed had been his own state until he had met Matt. He had come to the conclusion that the Catholic Church must take much of the blame. He began to listen to the moral pronouncements of bishops and priests and he found, running through much of what they said, a simplistic condemnation of the IRA.

What really cheesed him off though was their concern for the poor, suffering people of the Third World. Priests marched against American imperialism in Nicaragua, they collected money for the starving in Ethiopia. What about the poor, suffering people of west Belfast, their own people? What about them?

No wonder P.J., who constantly flouted God's law, still maintained a respectful attitude towards His holy anointed.

Holy anointed? Tools of the establishment: birds of a feather, P.J. McGuckian and the Catholic clergy. You scratch my back and I'll scratch yours and who cares if God is ignored and the country's going down the spout? Let's all shout for freedom for Nicaragua and maintain the *status quo*.

Aubrey was, in fact, being unfair to his father, who had only a hazy idea as to where Nicaragua was and who never listened to clerical pronouncements of any kind.

He lay in bed now, although it was ten o'clock. Wakening with a headache, he had been persuaded by Noreen to take a lie in and he had agreed, for the sky was grey. Good for fishing, but he was stuck in Dublin.

Covertly he watched June's behind as she bent down to retrieve a pillow.

She had come on, had Mrs Donovan's little girl. Lovely, blooming skin and what a backside!

No! He sat up in bed and reached for his breakfast tray. That would be fouling his own nest and P.J. had strict ideas about such behaviour.

Fouling one's own nest, it was an expression his mother had been fond of.

'Never foul your own nest, P.J.,' she would say when he was threatening to leave this country and clear out to England.

'Never foul your own nest,' she would reiterate as he slicked Brylcreem on to his curls, staring into the kitchen mirror in preparation for the Sunday night dance.

He had always assured her that he never would, while wondering what the hell she meant. Now he clearly saw that a quick fuck with young June would certainly be encompassed by the phrase.

'Tell Mrs McGuckian that I'm not sick and that there was no need for breakfast in bed – though I'm going to enjoy it. Now, off you go, there's a good girl.'

He whacked her behind and she shimmied out of the room, well pleased with how her campaign to seduce her employer was progressing. June had recently discovered romantic fiction and with it a new dimension to her relationship with P.J. Wronged virgin as heroine: she fancied herself in that role and she didn't see why a small technical detail like a broken hymen should stand between her and it.

P.J. poured himself a cup of tea. He had been thinking of his mother increasingly this summer, since building the house in Cavan in fact. She had been an exasperating woman, but wise. Never foul your own nest. Look now how that phrase had given up its meaning after more than thirty years.

Wise. What then would she make of her only grandson? Would she have advised P.J. to have him put away somewhere, in some home for harmless poor fools? Would she have had some saying, some ancient wisdom which could have explained the weakness in his head, his slackening hold on reality?

He had taken now to raving about bulls and borders and Queen

Maeve of Connacht and for some reason was pursuing P.J. with this rubbish, popping up at unexpected hours, the Yank by his shoulder, grinning and nodding. Since Noreen had put her foot down P.J. had had to be polite to the Yank and, to be fair, he knew he couldn't blame him entirely for his son's imbecility, but his presence, his unrelenting cheerfulness somehow got P.J. down.

He wondered if Aubrey had stopped working, he certainly didn't spend much time in the office these days. And he had begun to look strange, his cheeks permanently flushed, his eyes bright and crazy. He reminded P.J. of a picture he had seen somewhere of St Sebastian, with arrows sticking out of his body.

Martyrdom – that was it. The lad fancied himself as a martyr. Not for aesthetics though, that day was past. For old Ireland? He shuddered at the possibilities of this scenario.

Kicking back the covers, he hopped out of bed. He would not go into work today, he needed some distraction, something to take the taste of his son and heir out of his mouth.

He'd take his girls somewhere – for a spin and a picnic. The sky was now quite blue. The sea, perhaps. He loved to swim but hated the stink of chlorinated pools. He'd take his chance any day in the Irish Sea, even if it was, as they said, the most radioactive stretch of water in the world.

P.J. McGuckian didn't worry about such things, believing that the superbly engineered human body could take anything that was thrown at it. He had grown weary of the messages of doom with which he was daily assaulted. He was surrounded apparently by dangers: tobacco, alcohol, vegetables sprayed with chemicals, dead animals who had ingested hormones and antibiotics in their brief lives. The air was poisoned, the sea was poisoned, the planet was doomed, he was constantly being told.

And bollocks replied P.J. McGuckian. Have some faith in the Man above and look at the beauty which surrounds you.

A sound digestion and belief in the deity was P.J.'s prescription for a happy life. And not too much delving into the whys and wherefores.

P.J. stepped out of the shower and began rigorously to towel his back. This caused the black hairs to fluff out and thus increased his likeness to a fine, mountain ram. He slapped his belly and began with some reluctance to fight his way into a blue silk shirt. Getting dressed was always a battle, as if his body resented being covered, no matter how fine the feathers. Maybe he and Noreen should retire to some South Sea island where the sun was hot and the natives none too partial to clothes. There they could live in bliss, just the two of them. P.J. did not imagine them growing old but rather becoming more and more invigorated with the sunshine and a diet of coconuts and passion fruit and –

'Come up here, woman,' bellowed P.J., striding out to stand at the top of the stairs.

Noreen, emerging from the morning room, looked up and her alarm turned to scandal as she saw her husband, clad only in his shirt, his member sticking out through the fine oak banisters.

'P.J., for heaven's sake go back into your room. What if Mrs Donovan or worse still, young June, came out and saw you? Thank God Annabel is gone into town.'

She ran up the stairs towards him and he smacked a kiss on her mouth.

'And what would they see only a grand useful tool, well maintained and ready for action?' He smiled as he watched her cheeks grow pink. He could still make her blush like a schoolgirl. No wonder he was as mad about her as ever.

14

Matt Savino was homesick. His butter-brown eyes looked down forlornly at the prim flower-beds in front of Aube's apartment building. He wished he was back home, sipping a *cappuccino* in Ferrara's or eating a bagel in Ratner's Dairy Restaurant. He longed for the familiarity of the Manhattan streets, the warmth and movement and life. The longer he stayed in this sodden land the more alien he felt.

Matt looked around him nervously as if his unvoiced treason might somehow have been divined.

He had never felt like this before; on other trips he had been hot and zealous, committed to the cause and energized by it. This time he had lingered too long. The awful Irish lethargy had got to him, zapping him, turning him into one of themselves.

And what upset him most was his ambivalence towards the Irish – that really made him feel bad. He still loved and revered the Irish nation, ancient and wronged. It was just that he didn't like the goddamn Irish.

They drank too much, they whined incessantly and they were slippery as eels. You couldn't pin them down. At night he would be drawn into dark corners in smoky pubs, and words, promises, plans would be whispered into his ear. Offers of help and money; ideas and commitment. The next morning it was as if he had dreamt it all. Nobody had said anything; at the ends of telephone lines people were out or unknown. In the light of day men who the night before had been preaching sedition, urging him to a sampling of semtex as if to a Tupperware party, now smiled at him pityingly when he approached them, implying that *he* was the lunatic.

And it wasn't as if he were seeking out bullets and bombs; all he wanted was a field that straddled the border, a bull and some music. It didn't seem a lot to Matt and yet, after three weeks of negotiations, no concrete offer was on the table. Fields seemed to shift position, bulls became cows, so that what was offered last night was withdrawn next morning.

A new thought struck Matt as he turned away from the rain which had begun to fall, as it always did at some point during the day. What if his experiences this time were due, not to the length of his visit, but to the fact that it was taking place in the South? Geography, not time span, was the key.

On every other visit he had flown to Belfast or scooted straight up in a hired car. And in Belfast he had never found anything but straight talking. You knew where you were in Belfast – you mightn't get as many compliments thrown at you but you knew where you were. Southern climes. Goddamn it, hadn't his Momma, who was born in Lucca, always warned him against southern Italians, clinching her argument by pointing out that the ancestral home of the Savinos was on a rocky hillside in Calabria?

The force of her argument came back to him now. And who in their right minds would choose to settle down in Kentucky or Alabama, for example?

It seemed to be a law of nature: the moral degenerates had a way of sliding down to the southern portion of any given country.

Matt shook his head – Jeez, this was weird. He was beginning to sound like one of those Unionists.

He walked back to look out the window, seeking something that he might find lovable. Grass, green, almost fluorescent. It figured, with all that rain. People, scurrying and scowling past, hurrying back to their holes like so many bad-tempered, dyspeptic mice. And overhead the sky hung like a dirty raincoat.

He would be off, he couldn't bear another gloomy, grey minute. Except that he couldn't run out on Aube. He owed it to that kid, a good, committed guy, he owed it to him to stick around. Look how he had insisted on offering him hospitality, moving out of his own bedroom to give it to Matt. And that tough-guy father that he just couldn't handle. He would have to stay on. Aube needed him.

Cheered by a new sense of purpose, Matt headed for the kitchen to fix himself a snack. Aube seemed to have no interest in food and when Matt had moved in he had had to spend the first three days shopping in supermarkets and specialist food shops. Now the cupboards and worktops had plumped out nicely, filled with jars of gherkins and olives, mustards and mayonnaise, cans of frankfurters, sauerkraut, rounds of salami sausage, bottles of ketchup, toothpicks and paper napkins and low alcohol beers.

Matt was an inspired and dainty snacker. He took it as a challenge, approaching it seriously, turning it into an art form. In Ireland, if you refused an offer of booze the only alternative seemed to be tea and some indescribably awful confection, limp and undercooked, that they called biscuits. Matt saw that he could change all that; even if he failed to bring about the reunification of the country he could introduce it to the delights of inventive snacking.

Looking into Aubrey's tiny freezer he rejected the ice-cream, although he had found a good homemade brand whose chocolate chip he was particularly partial to. Now he felt like something savoury. He cut some brown soda bread, spread the slices with cream cheese and covered this in turn with smoked salmon. This was his own adaptation of the New York favourite, bagels with lox and cream cheese, having sampled Dublin's bagels and found them wanting.

He had just settled at the table when Aube put his head round the kitchen door.

'Want something to eat?' Matt dabbed daintily at his chin, noting that this boy brought out a sort of maternal streak in him which delighted Matt, who knew that the male and the female were present in all rounded human persons.

'Problem solved.' Aube threw his jacket over a chair and loosened his tie. He looked at Matt with a mixture of triumph and expectation. 'What we should have realized all along is that money speaks. God – how could I fail to make the connection with my father in front of me as a living example?'

'Did Hugh Sherwin agree then?'

Hugh Sherwin was the owner of the most suitable field, well drained, level and straddling the border.

'Like a shot, once I mentioned the green stuff. Hugh Sherwin and P.J. McGuckian, two of a kind, Cavan backwoodsmen who will do anything to claw their way out.'

'How much?'

'Never mind, Matt. You've spent enough already. And to think all along that we were naïve enough to believe that they would be insulted by offers of money, that they would want to become involved out of a sense of patriotism.' He laughed humourlessly and waved away a sandwich which Matt was offering.

'Then all we need is the bull.'

'Matt, I could set myself up as an Andalucian bull farmer with all the offers I've had since word got out that I'm offering money. What a disgusting shower they all are.'

Matt shook his head wisely. 'Eight hundred years, Aube, it's a long time. A hell of a lot of conditioning went on in that time, it can't be undone in a day.'

He was not upset, there was nothing wrong in his book with a little private enterprise. And besides, they could now get the show on the road, which was the important thing.

He swept the food aside and got out a notebook and ballpoint pen. 'Let's get down to business, we gotta start planning right away, Aube. Hey,' he stabbed the pen in the air. 'I've had an idea. How about involving your sister? She's such a looker, Aube, can't you just see her up on a platform?'

'The old man would never allow it. You don't know how fussy he is where she's concerned and he's not going to approve of any of this in any case.'

'He don't have to allow it – she's eighteen, isn't she?'

The idea appealed to Aubrey. He had never thought very much about Annabel; being so much younger than he, he had always dismissed her as just a kid. He knew of course that she was P.J.'s favourite, Noreen's too if he came to think about it, and up till this summer he had been ready to dismiss her as a spoilt brat. But he liked the spunky way she had stood up to the old man, choosing a boyfriend from among the people, not some little socialite P.J. would have preferred. She had led a useless parasitic existence till now but she could hardly be blamed for that.

Perhaps she could be moulded, perhaps her eyes could be opened, as his had been. She could be made to realize that there was more to life than swimming and tennis and partying. And what a slap in the teeth that would be for the old man. Two children with a sense of values; two children who rejected materialism and the vain and empty lifestyle of their parents.

'Do you know what I think – she'd make a wonderful Queen

168

Maeve. What do you say, Matt? We could have her actually handing back the bull – a grand gesture of reparation.'

'You've got it, fella. And she looks like a queen, the way she walks just slays me. And she won't have to say anything – no offence, Aube, but we couldn't have her talking in that poncy English voice.'

'You'll have to go.'

'Me, Chief? God, that's a great honour.'

Bill O'Reilly stared at his Minister, seeking for any suggestion of irony. He could find none. The small green eyes expressed dog-like devotion, the capped teeth twinkled innocently.

'Well, we want to keep it in the realm of the cultural, do you understand, Canice?' A vain question but one which he asked as a matter of form.

'Oh yes, certainly, Chief.'

'We don't want these Americans stirring things up, but he's a Congressman and we have to be nice to him. He's organized this pageant thing and he's invited churchmen and MP's from the North and God knows who else. Now what I want you to do is go up there as my Minister, emphasizing the historical and cultural nature of the event and making fraternal noises.'

'The what, Chief, exactly?'

'Being nice to the bloody Unionists.'

'Just so.'

'I do not want this to become an incident, do you understand, Canice? Play it down, pour plenty of oil, take charge, man. Feed the American plenty of bull. Bull – that's a good one. Talk, Canice, and plenty of long words.'

If anyone in the Cabinet could outbore the American it was surely Canice. Bill O'Reilly, on the eve of flying to Brussels on important business of state (he was looking for more money while at the same time reaffirming Ireland's firm and principled stand on neutrality), was reasonably sure that Canice would spread enough mystification to damp down any trouble that might arise in Cavan.

Canice stood up. 'I'll go so and just start preparing my speech.' He walked towards the door, then turned to look back, sheepishly. 'It's a God-sent opportunity for me. It's the first time I've been back in Cavan since – well, you remember, Chief.'

As if he could forget. Life had not been easy for Bill since the night of the famous broadcast. Although Canice's tale had won most hearts, there was still enough malice around, inside and outside the Dáil, to want to keep the issue alive and Canice had to be convinced that his position was still vulnerable. Bill had endured much acid indigestion before Canice had agreed that for the foreseeable future he must avoid kissing babies and confine his enthusiasm to works of art and that the best way of dealing with the jibes of the Opposition was to ignore them. He had also to be convinced of the dangers of giving interviews, no matter on what topic or however apparently innocuous.

Things had quietened down now and Bill hoped that they would remain so. He had always believed that there was sufficient decency and good manners left in the country to see that the affair would be dropped, provided it hadn't continued to be reported in the English press. And thank God it hadn't. The tabloids had never had any interest in it and *The Champion* had found a new crusade.

Bill had become a subscriber to *The Champion*. Buchanan seemed to have lost interest in all things Irish but what, Bill wondered, had Canice done originally to bring down such wrath upon him? What had he said that night in Trieste to cause Buchanan to send a reporter over here to dig for dirt? The liberties he took with the English language were hardly sufficient cause.

Whatever the reason, *The Champion* had now turned its interest towards American English, a phrase Buchanan described as the equivalent of Australian champagne. Each week now he published a photograph of some notable American with a bubble of nonsense coming from his or her mouth. Underneath he printed a prose translation of the nonsense.

Canice O'Keeffe was apparently of no further interest to him.

'How is – ah – Honey?' Bill now thought it only mannerly to inquire. 'Is she keeping well these days?'

'She's gone, Chief.'

'Gone?'

'To America, to a place called Tupelo. Did you ever hear tell of it, Chief?'

Bill shook his head.

'I didn't either but it's the town where Elvis Presley was born. So you can understand.'

Bill didn't think that he could.

'After that night she was a changed woman. She knew she could sing again and she wanted to and the offers started to roll in. But the publicity wouldn't die down and she kept on getting asked about – you know. Everywhere she went she couldn't seem to get away from it. Then she got this offer of a six-month engagement in the Green Lizard Lounge in Tupelo – I think she might have worked there once, years ago. Anyway, she jumped at it and she's out there now and as Nuala said to me, isn't God good, all the same?'

'Indeed.' Bill made a mental note not to take any leisure breaks in Tupelo during the next six months.

'So you can see how grateful I am, Chief, for this opportunity to make an official appearance in my own county.'

'Just remember, Canice – caution. Even in your own county you'd be surprised at the amount of begrudgers there are around.'

'Ah, you don't know Cavan, Chief. But I'll be careful all the same, you need have no worries whatsoever.'

'Good man.'

'Thank you, Chief.'

And Canice O'Keeffe trotted happily off to his office thinking how lucky he was to have such a boss; how blessed Ireland was to have such a leader.

'No,' roared P.J. McGuckian and stamped a giant foot down on to Noreen's antique kilim.

Annabel put her tongue out at him, then running over to him began to kiss his scowling face. 'Please, Daddy.' She put her arms around his neck. 'Please, please, please. It will be such fun and it won't do any harm.'

Noreen smiled at the two of them, knowing that at any second now P.J. would capitulate. One more troubled blue look and he would have collapsed.

'Go on, P.J., let her.' She intervened to make it easier for him, to protect him from his son's smirk of satisfaction when he had changed his mind.

P.J. and Aubrey, what was she to do with them? Since the arrival of Matt Savino the smouldering animosity had been ignited into open war: P.J. growled and roared at his son and Aubrey snapped back, reminding Noreen of a Jack Russell terrier she had once had. She had loved him dearly but eventually had to have him put down when he reached the stage of being unable to resist an ankle.

171

Where had she gone wrong with Aubrey? She looked at her daughter, smiling and rosy-cheeked, and thought how unfair nature was. She smiled at Aubrey and he glared back at her. He made life so difficult for himself. He eschewed all pleasantness, charm, good manners as if they would contaminate him and he had about him an aura of righteousness which was off-putting, even to a mother.

He began to lecture them. 'This will not be fun, Annabel.'

The child nodded, then shook her head, ready to agree, to hide all signs of pleasure if that was what he wanted.

'I want Annabel to take part because I want to give her an opportunity. This could affect the course of Irish history.'

'All right, all right.' P.J. held up both hands. He turned to his daughter. 'So you fancy yourself as Queen Maeve?'

She giggled. 'I do – it will be such fun.' Then looking over at Aubrey she added, 'I mean it is a great opportrnity for me to learn about Irish history.'

P.J. slapped her gently on the cheek. 'Annie, you're a chancer, just like me.'

'But will you let me, Daddy? Will you?'

'Go on then, off you go, the pair of you. Just make sure that the bull is well tied up, Aube, and don't let your sister anywhere near him.'

Noreen looked after her children and sighed as the door closed behind them. 'Poor Aubrey.'

'What's poor about him?'

'P.J. – could you make more of an effort? Could you try to be more patient with him?'

'For Jesus' sake, woman! I think I've been remarkably patient that I haven't murdered him already. The boy's a fool.'

'He's a talented architect.'

'And does he go into work any more? As far as I can see he's too busy chasing after bulls.'

Noreen sought to lay the blame elsewhere. 'Things will be different when Matt goes back – '

'And that's another thing. How is it that when Aube goes to a city the size of New York, he ends up befriending someone like Matt Savino? Isn't it a remarkable thing how they sought one another out? A knave and a fool, perfectly matched.'

'Matt's not really – '

'He is. He'll come over here and wreak havoc for his own political ends. Then he'll hare off back to New York and leave some fool like Aubrey to pick up the pieces. I'm sorry now I let Annabel have any part in it.'

'She'll be fine, P.J. And it's nice to see her and Aube doing things together. Come on, sit down over here with me.'

She led him to a sofa and began to rub his shoulders. 'Do you remember how I used to do this in the old days when you'd come home, tired out from work?'

'And don't try to *plamás* me, woman.' He shook off her hands. 'Sure soon you won't need to use any of those wiles, soon you'll have your own money and you can do what you like. How's the typing going?'

'You know perfectly well it's not just typing – I'm learning how to use a computer. Computer literate is what they call it.'

'And you'll need it. Listen to me, Noreen.' He turned her chin round and held it in his hand. 'I'm going to make you an offer you can't refuse. I'm going to retire.'

'P.J.!'

'I am. I've been in the shagging business too long. How would you like to take over? You've a good head on you, I'd trust you. You can walk into my shoes in the morning. I'm going to get in more fishing and Mrs Donovan is going to teach me how to cook. What do you say to that, then?'

'You're not serious?'

'I am. Come on now, give us an oul' rub. I need to be soothed.'

He closed his eyes and Noreen began to massage his neck muscles again. He could well be serious – it was the sort of thing he'd do. 'Do you know something, P.J.?' she said. 'You can be exasperating but you are never boring – I'll give you that.'

15

They had been swimming in the lake and clung now to the struts of P.J.'s boathouse, their legs floating behind them, disembodied in the green water. Seán had been telling her about the inaccuracies in the forthcoming pageant and Annabel had been sizing him up, not listening, playing a different game.

'I think you're pompous,' she said. 'And do you know how doubly silly pomposity sounds when spoken in a Cavan accent?' She kicked insolently and Seán lunged, catching her mid-back and dragging her downwards. 'I'll murder you.'

When they surfaced again they were spluttering, then kissing, then breaking apart and diving in different directions.

They were like young seals, sleek and playful, their eyes bright as they blinked water from their lashes.

Turning on their backs, they joined hands and lay there floating, looking up at the sky.

'You mock me.' Seán raised his chin.

'I do.'

'You don't love me.'

'I do.'

'You're an impossible woman.'

'I'll sink if I keep on opening my mouth.'

It had begun to rain, fat drops that bounced off the surface of the lake.

In P.J.'s boathouse she put her arms around him, wrapping him in her soft towelling robe. 'Don't you know I am going to be Queen Maeve? Don't you think I will make a wonderful Queen Maeve?'

'You are Queen Annabel, queen of this watery domain.' He

picked her up, walked with her to the edge and held her out, suspended over the lake. 'What are you doing out of your element? Shall I drop you back in?'

'Idiot. Let me down, I'm freezing.'

'*Do* you love me?' Serious now, straight black brows drawn together in a scowl.

'I don't know.' Annabel had discovered the delights of playing with cruelty, of edging forward then drawing back. It was dangerous if she went too far – male passion, she was discovering, was exciting, but frightening too.

'You are a cruel, heartless woman.'

'But think of it, Seán,' she kissed one cheek and then the other. 'Unrequited love is so much more useful to you. Think of Yeats. You could write poems about me and to me for the rest of your life. I'd be the source of your inspiration, even when I am old and grey and full of tears.'

'Ha! So they taught you something at that fancy English boarding school – you didn't emerge completely ignorant.'

'I did. I just like Yeats. I've always liked poetry. And poets. That's why I'm interested in you – for your mind, not for your body.'

'What's wrong with my body?' He struck a pose, throwing off his towel, thrusting forward a thigh and raising his profile.

Annabel stared across at him, at the white skin, perfect line, the slight swelling inside the swimming trunks, and felt her joyous mood desert her, to be replaced by a feeling of desolation.

It can't last then, she told herself, it was all an illusion. We are two separate creatures, after all, and one day we will be dead and then our love –

'I do love you, I do,' she declared, reaching up to kiss him.

In this moment she had passed from girlhood to womanhood, and as she clung now to Seán and felt the confident support of his arms she experienced lonesomeness for the first time in her young life.

'Let's go back,' she said soberly.

And hand in hand they climbed the steps to P.J.'s house on stilts. They found him in the living room, legs stretched out in front of him, staring at his son with a mixture of incredulity and amusement.

Aubrey loomed, defiant and charged.

'Come over here you two,' P.J. gestured, 'and tell me that my ears are not deceiving me. Aube here and his friend Congressman Savino cannot decide whether to use a black bull painted brown or a genuine brown bullock for the great occasion. Of course the brown bullock would only be genuine as regards his colour.'

'Stop being horrid, Daddy,' Annabel said, but she was smiling.

'Wait, that's not the best of it. Whatever they decide, the beast is going to be decked out in ribbons, a tricoloured green, white and orange from his horns and a blue and red one from his tail. Now, Aube, I think you should reconsider that one as a symbol of unity, it might be misinterpreted by some sections of the northern community. Would you not consider reversing the order of the ribbons?'

P.J. wiped tears from his cheeks and Aubrey kicked viciously at the leg of a table, looking, from the expression on his face, as if he wished it were P.J. he was kicking.

Getting his voice under control, he spoke coldly. 'We are simply having some difficulty getting a brown bull but it's a minor detail, nothing to get so excited about.'

'Oh *I'm* not getting excited and will you stop breaking up the furniture, although honest to God, I'd forgive you anything at this moment, Aube, you've given me such a good laugh.'

Annabel went to stand beside her brother. 'It's going to be a big success, just you wait and see. And have you forgotten that I'm Queen Maeve?'

'As long as you can tell a bull from a cow.'

Aubrey glared round him, including the innocent Annabel in his displeasure. 'It is going to be an event of considerable importance, sorry to disappoint you, P.J. It's going to be networked on American TV and all sorts of dignitaries have already said they're coming. The government is sending Canice O'Keeffe.'

'O'Keeffe? Bejasus! That's a real coup.' P.J. started to laugh again. 'Once you've got O'Keeffe, Aube, you can be sure things will go with a swing.'

Aubrey stood up. 'I'm really too busy to stay here nattering with you, P.J., I must be off. Believe it or not, some of us think about other things besides making money. Some of us believe that you have to give something to society, not just take with both hands. It might be good for you if you thought of somebody else, just for a change.'

But P.J. was not at all put out. He was still laughing when his son banged the front door behind him. A vision of Canice O'Keeffe sharing a platform with a black bull painted a shiny brown and sprouting ribbons was a vision strong enough to withstand the irritation usually caused by his son's foolishness.

'You two, go and change out of those wet things. Go on – we don't want you catching cold at such a crucial time, poor old Aube is having enough problems with the bulls. Do you know what it is, I haven't laughed this much in years.'

'Yeah. Sure. Gotcha.' Matt put down the phone. Things were going nicely.

That telephone call had confirmed that the pageant would be carried on American television; RTE had already confirmed and that would probably mean that British television would pick it up too.

The American Ambassador had declined his invitation but then, learning that the Irish government was sending its Minister for the Arts, he had decided to throw in a third secretary. The local Catholic bishop was leading a pilgrimage to Lourdes but the parish priest was coming, and Matt's biggest triumph had been the reply from the Protestant archbishop, who lived in the North but whose diocese lay on both sides of the border. His Grace would be delighted to attend.

Matt had been advised that the pageant must take place on Saturday.

'If you hold it on Sunday,' Aube had told him, 'it's going to offend a lot of Protestants. Keep holy the Sabbath day – they take that very seriously.'

'That's all very well,' Matt had argued, 'but what about the Jews? They won't even ride in a cab on the Sabbath, the religious ones I mean, and I guess they'd be the religious kind around here.'

'There aren't any Jews around here.'

'Oh. Right.'

Matt's biggest problem had been in finding a recipient for the bull. In theory it had seemed simple enough. You just got someone, anyone from North of the border, to stand on the platform and receive the bull. Matt thought that it would heighten the symbolism if the person chosen lived just across the border, and with this in mind he and Aubrey had gone knocking on doors.

He had been astounded by the response. Rich and poor, Catholic and Protestant, he was met by the same half-embarrassed, half-hostile negative response.

'Jeez,' he had said to Aube after the twentieth door had been closed in their faces, 'what's with these people? I'm beginning to feel like a Jehovah's Witness. I can see that maybe the Prods wouldn't be too keen but what's with the goddamn Catholics?'

Tight mouthed and tight arsed. Matt wondered for the hundredth time if these people were worth fighting for. Let them kill one another, the world would be a better place without their meanness of spirit.

Then he had a brainwave: he would bus in a contingent from West Belfast. He knew where he was with them, he knew they would be delighted to accept the bull. Open minded and generous, he reminded himself that *these* were the people he was fighting for, the Oppressed of West Belfast.

But – Matt sensed that the symbolism was becoming muddied: the South was offering to return the brown bull of Cuailgne to the North as a gesture of reconciliation, an extension of the hand of friendship – shouldn't the recipient then be of the Unionist persuasion?

For a while Matt worried about this; he even considered going up to Belfast and asking one of the Unionist politicans to accept the role. He knew however that his popularity was not high in that quarter and he decided to settle for what he had – a minor technical inconsistency perhaps, but with the best and most sincere of intentions and a genuine Protestant archbishop. Not bad.

'Aube,' he roared, 'come out here and tell me how we're doing.'

Campaign headquarters had been set up in Aubrey's flat, Matt using the living room and Aube the bedroom.

Aubrey came into the living room now, a pencil behind his ear. 'Doing? You can't begin to imagine.'

He strode up to Matt, a man transformed. He seemed taller and broader than when Matt had first met him, his hair thicker, his eyes brighter. 'It's approaching countdown, isn't it, Matt, and everything is going fine. I've got stewards, ten of them for crowd control. That wasn't easy but I've got them and I've got the best uileann pipe player in Ireland – you remember, you said you wanted a piper to lead in the bull. But listen to this, what do you think of this – I've persuaded Fintan McManus to sell us his bull. And don't worry about the expense, it's on me, Matt.' He had noticed Matt's change of expression. 'You remember when we were talking about paying McManus a fee for the use of the bull? Well, I started thinking and it seemed a really shabby gesture – empty. So I thought, why not really give them the bull? Why not buy it for them? Let them keep it. So that's what I've done.'

Matt stared at him in disbelief, his little eyes growing pink with anger. 'And what exactly, Aube, could you just tell me, what exactly are they going to do with a fucking bull in the housing estates of West Belfast?'

'Oh.' Matt watched Aubrey begin to deflate like a pricked balloon. 'I hadn't thought about that.'

'No, I don't suppose you had.' A nice guy, but sometimes . . .

'I know – they could eat it.'

'Yeah, sure. And open up a chain of Queen Maeve hamburger joints.'

'That's a great idea. And the profits could go to the wives and children of the political prisoners.'

'Aube. It was supposed to be a joke.'

'Oh.'

'C'mon fella.' Matt took pity on him, and putting a fatherly arm round his shoulder began to guide him towards the door. 'Let's go and have a pint, we could do with a break. Maybe something will have come to us by the time we get back.'

Huffily, Aubrey allowed himself to be led out. He didn't see why the bull couldn't be used for meat; after all, they weren't bloody Hindus up on the Falls Road.

Canice O'Keeffe stood in front of a mirror, staring at his reflection and making awful faces at himself as he tried to get his porcelain teeth round the syllables of classical Greek.

Never an accomplished scholar he had been grateful over the years, nevertheless, to the priests who had beaten into him the rudiments of Latin and Greek. As Minister for the Arts, his classical education had stood him in good stead.

The first time it had come to his aid, he had been a young Minister. Confronted at an art exhibition by an angry sculptor who had thrust what looked to Canice like two pieces of twisted wire at him and demanded menacingly, 'What do you think of that then, Minister, ha?', from the depths of Canice's unconscious had swum up the opening lines of the Odyssey.

ἄνδρα μοι ἔννεπε, Μοῦσα, πολύτροπον, ὃς μάλα πολλὰ
πλάγχθη, ἐπεὶ Τροίης ἱερὸν πτολίεθρον ἔπερσε
πολλῶν δ'ανθρώπων ἴδεν αστεα, καὶ νόον ἔγνω.

he intoned, adding, 'Homer has expressed my feelings exactly.'

The angry sculptor had fallen back. 'Homer? By God. Is that what Homer said?'

His giant chest expanded further, the pectoral muscles expanding in pride. 'Well, thank you, thank you indeed. Homer. By God.'

From that initial occasion Canice had begun to pepper, if judiciously, his speeches with Greek quotations. He had gone back to the original texts the better to refresh his memory, and eventually could quote large chunks of the Odyssey, not merely the first three lines. The artists among whom he moved, being younger than he, had for the most part not had the benefit of a classical education and so did not recognize classical Greek. Some thought he quoted Latin, others Irish. While this lack of recognition on their part upset Canice at first, it was eventually to lead to one of his most dazzling epiphanies: he came to see that artistic communication lay in realms beyond the rational. The artists did not understand what he said, he did not understand what they painted or composed or wrote, and yet between them there flowed a wonderful warm current, an enlightenment, superverbal, superrational, supernatural. True spirituality – he had found the font of true spirituality. And it went way beyond mere intelligence.

However, there were occasions when Canice felt that something less visionary was in order. When something struck Canice in the gizzard, he reverted to the simple. And he had been moved, deeply moved by what Aubrey had told him. It had seemed so right that the great brown bull should be returned to Ulster.

He would eschew all Greek tags and speak from the heart. This is always a dangerous thing for a politican to do but Canice was prepared to throw caution to the winds.

The Chief had not wanted the pageant to have any political overtones, but what was the returning of the bull but a political act? And a generous one at that. It would demonstrate to the

Unionists how prepared were those in the South to make a place for them, to take them to their hearts.

A nation once again, sang Canice O'Keeffe under his breath, knowing that he would conduct himself with non-political propriety but moved none the less, all aquiver at this foretaste of Irish unity.

Not for nothing had he been born and nurtured in County Cavan, where Gaelic blood coursed vigorously. He might have sojourned in a foreign town – what else was Dublin? – but he could still be moved by the ancient dream.

Unlike some, who had no interest in ever reclaiming the Fourth Green Field. Even the Chief –

But here Canice stopped himself.

The Chief was preoccupied with affairs of nationhood (part nationhood), complex, weighty matters. The Chief was a Great Man, and great men were not easy to understand, their motives and methods often obscure to ordinary eyes.

With a flourish Canice took up a silk tie and laid it against his cheek. It suited him, Nuala had been right, and it was suitable too for the occasion: a soberly abstract design with a hint of green.

With a sigh of satisfaction Canice returned to his speech and to the trying on of different facial expressions. This proved more difficult than choosing a tie, but he persisted and eventually arrived at an arrangement of features which pleased him: a raised chin, a smiling mouth but eyes that looked out severely on the world, all twinkles banished.

Canice knew that he was walking into history.

16

The field was in good nick. It was level and free from cowpats and other rural disfigurements. Its hedges were trimmed low and its two gates had been painted brown – a neutral colour.

Like Bill O'Reilly, Matt Savino knew how important it was to get everything looking right. Spend time, money and energy on appearances and you were half-way home.

Matt had spent all three on the field. For ten days local lads had been out with shovels and buckets, rollers, paint brushes and hedge trimmers. Only the weather had been beyond Matt's control.

He glared at the sky, a sullen, dirty grey. A fine drizzle had been falling since dawn and a nasty wind had begun to whip up off the lake. All week the sun had shone and today it had decided to take a holiday. At least the ground, baked by the sun, stood a good chance of remaining firm. Matt gave thanks for small mercies.

Although it was not much after ten, people had already begun to gather. The stewards, with Aubrey, were pacing the field. The oppressed from West Belfast had arrived ten minutes ago and sheltered now behind their bus, smoking peevishly, cold and hating the country. In this benign landscape they felt vulnerable, their lungs unable to cope with the pure air, their eyes blinking at the featureless aspect stretching all around. They longed for the security of city streets and huddled together for comfort.

The media boys and girls were busy assembling their hardware; hysterical and noisy, they were watched with amusement by local children who tried to augment their fun by baiting the various crews – hiding bits of equipment, getting under their feet and answering topographical questions with downright lies.

Along one edge of the field, in the Republic's jurisdiction, local traders had begun to set up their stalls. Matt had thought hard about this, fearing that the transaction of commerce might take from the dignity of the great day. However, being a New Yorker he had decided what the heck, people had to enjoy themselves too. So eventually chocolate, fruit, crisps and buns, together with a selection of soft drinks and fruit juices would be on sale.

The dignitaries would arrive at twelve noon and Maguire's pub had supplied twenty well-padded lounge chairs to receive the distinguished bottoms. These chairs were now disposed in a semi-circle around the dais, ten in the Republic and ten in Northern Ireland. Matt had arranged the place names so that His Grace would smile benevolently from the South across at Father Fagan seated in the North. Symbolism everywhere, the day would be carried on symbolism.

Aubrey approached now, with Hugh Sherwin striding along beside him. Sherwin surveyed his field with pride, tipping the ash from his cigar into a sweet wrapper, careful of his level, green grass.

'Congressman – what a triumph!'

He would have embraced Matt except that Matt, putting up a hand, stepped backwards, an expression of alarm on his face. 'What was that?'

'What?'

'Listen. There it is again.'

They listened.

From somewhere near at hand came the swell of voices. There was something familiar about the rhythm of those voices, the way they rose and fell, and it was only the incongruity of their echo across the field that prevented the listeners from immediately identifying what they heard. Incredulously they stared at one another. Praying – a group at prayer – a prayer meeting?

They turned, circling their gaze around the field to see where it was coming from. Was it a recording perhaps?

It was unlikely that the cameramen and sound engineers had broken into prayer, desperate though the expressions on their faces were, and the Belfast contingent was too busy smoking. Then Aubrey saw something. He pointed. 'Look.'

At the far end of the field, on the other side of the boundary hedge, a placard had been raised. 'Jesus Saves' it proclaimed in letters big enough to be read at this distance.

'Will you looka that!' The cigar fell from Hugh Sherwin's mouth and viciously he stamped it into the grass. 'I knew it. I knew that hoor couldn't be trusted.'

'Whose field is that?'

'Ivan Lister – isn't that what I'm telling you?'

'What's he doing holding a prayer meeting in his field?' Aubrey was beginning to look worried. 'It's not Sunday. Matt, I don't think this is a coincidence, I think this is a deliberate attempt at sabotage.'

'Of course it's sabotage,' Sherwin was dancing with rage. 'Amn't I telling you if you'll only listen? That fellow is nothing but a black Orangeman.'

Aubrey explained to Matt that this did not mean that Ivan Lister was a member of the negroid races, merely a bigoted member of an Orange Lodge.

Two more banners had now joined the original one. They read 'The Beast of the Apocalypse' and 'You Never Know the Hour'. They bobbed about for a bit before settling as the faithful began a hymn.

On this side of the hedge all activity had ceased. Television crews, traders, children, even an apologetic-looking sheepdog all stood motionless, staring towards the spot whence the singing had now begun to soar. If the notes were uncertain, the enunciation was perfect.

> O for a closer walk with God
> A calm and heavenly frame
> A light to shine upon the road
> That leads me to the lamb.
> Return, O heavenly Dove, return
> I hate the sins that made Thee mourn
> And drove Thee from my breast.

The silence swelled as the last of the singing trailed off raggedly.

'It's kinda neat,' said Matt, who had a weakness for hymn singing.

'Neat, I can think of another expression.' Aubrey pointed towards the banners. 'How the hell are we going to stop them? Do you realize, Matt, with that racket going on, nothing on this side of the hedge will be heard. What are we going to do?'

184

But Matt, despite his fellowship with the Irish Republican Army, was a man of peace. 'Then we'll invite them over. I mean – Aube – isn't that what this whole goddamn shenaningans is supposed to be about?'

Sherwin laughed bitterly at this display of American naïveté. 'And you think they'd come? They'll have nothing to do with you, they're a bunch of religious maniacs to a man.'

'Well, we've got an archbishop, one of theirs.'

Aubrey shook his head. 'He's not one of theirs. They consider the Church of Ireland to be almost as heretical as the Church of Rome. That lot are evangelical, saved, they're far worse than the political variety.'

Matt Savino never ran away from a challenge, and besides, he had seen a line of television personnel making its way towards the banners.

'I'll see what I can do,' he said, and surprised Aubrey by the velocity with which he crossed the field.

He got a leg up from one of the cameramen and, grasping a sapling, steadied himself on the stump of a tree.

They were a harmless-looking bunch, about twenty of them, little old ladies in squashed hats and tweed costumes, big country men with broad, weathered faces, and a sprinkling of anxious-looking teenagers. Their leader appeared to be the man with receding blond curls and a reddish-brown complexion. He wore a brown suit and a mild expression.

'Hi,' said Matt, extending a hand through the hedge. 'I'm Matt Savino, United States Congress.'

The leader stared at him and one of the little old ladies shook her banner in his face.

'It's him,' she squeaked. 'It's him. Praise the Lord, we've smoked him out.'

'Do you want to be saved, brother?' the leader inquired in a deep, rich voice.

'Sure I want to be saved,' Matt's reply was equable, conscious as he was of the TV cameras and wanting to offend no one, particularly no one back home. 'Sure I want to be saved, brother, but this isn't a religious festival we're holding. It's a symbolic bringing together of the divided peoples of this tragic and beautiful island. It's a re-enactment of – '

'It's a re-enactment of pagan rituals. Oh yes! We know all

about you, brother. The spies of Jesus are in every hedgerow and every byre and Jesus will not be mocked.' The man's appearance had changed. His eyes blazed and he looked feverish, his lips drawn back to display long, jagged teeth. 'You are bringing to life the memory of the fornicators, Maeve and Cuchulainn.'

'Not Cuchulainn.' Matt wasn't too clear about the charge of fornication but he was goddamn sure that Cuchulainn had no part in this pageant. 'You're wrong there, brother, no Cuchulainn.'

'Lie down with the Lamb, brother.' The leader was not troubled by details of minor inaccuracy. 'Do not build temples to the Mammons of Iniquity. God will not be mocked.'

'Look fella – I told you. What we're trying to do is no way religious. This pageant is secular and non-sectarian. We respect your right to attend any church or temple anywhere you want and we're inviting you to join us, but if you won't could you just tone things down, so's we can be heard over here?'

'Tone it down? Tone down the message of the Lord Jesus? Yeah, rather will we raise our voices aloft and praise His Holy Name. We will drown out all sounds of sin. We will bury you in the Fleece of the Lamb.'

The leader paused, raised his bible aloft and spread his arms. His eyes blazed directly into Matt's. 'Pray with me, brother,' he besought. 'Let us seek out God together.' He stretched out a hand and grasped one of Matt's, but in his enthusiasm he pulled too hard, causing Matt to overbalance on to the thorny foliage of the hedge.

'Jesus Christ,' said Matt in unprayerful tones as something sharp prickled his cheek.

'He blasphemes,' shouted the leader.

'See his horns,' screeched the enthusiastic little old lady, the one who had previously brandished her placard at him.

Matt saw the glee on a television man's face.

This was too much. He had been insulted before but never, neither in Calabria nor Manhattan, in Dublin or Belfast, not even in the columns of the British tabloids, had he been called the Devil Incarnate.

Gathering his dignity he got down from the tree trunk and walked away.

186

Hugh Sherwin was vindicated. 'What did I tell you, Congressman? Didn't I say that you couldn't talk to that crowd? They don't want peaceful co-existence. All they want is holy war.'

'A jihad.'

'A what?'

'Oh never mind.' Matt's tolerance for every variety of Irishman was diminishing rapidly. He looked at Aubrey. 'So what are we going to do now?'

Sherwin answered. 'Smoke the buggers out,' he said with glee.

'Have sense.' Aubrey could feel his irritation rise. 'We won't be able to use the piper. We'll have to rig up some sort of sound system. We'll have to have loudspeakers round the field, not just that one microphone up on the platform.'

'And I've got an idea,' Matt beamed, his good humour restored. 'Why don't I welcome them in my opening speech? Kinda disarm them.'

Hugh Sherwin spat and Aubrey shook his head. 'If you think it'll make any difference. Anyway, I think we should ignore them and they might just shut up.'

Since the arrival of the evangelicals nobody had paid any attention to the busload from West Belfast, who had been here now some forty minutes, growing colder and more anxious as time passed. They looked around them at the blank green fields, the small hostile hills, feeling danger lurking in this alien landscape. They didn't even know where they were, except that they must be bang on the border.

When the first notes of the hymn singing reached them, panic swept the little group. Had they been set up? Were they going to be massacred by a crowd of Orangemen? There were no IRA members among this group, just small people taken from their narrow friendly streets and dumped in a field where the only familiar thing they found was the sound of the enemy in ritual preparation for war.

They were toughies however, street fighters who had grown up, most of them, throwing stones at the British army, and when they heard that thick, ignorant Orangeman describing their church as the Whore of Babylon and holding his bible aloft, they knew it was time to make a stand. Cigarettes were thrown away, two of the women unfurled small tricolours, and forming themselves into a warlike group they marched forward from the shelter of the bus. Without consultation they broke into their religious anthem.

> Fai-ith of our fa-ather living still
> In spite of dungeon fire and sword.

'Jesus-H-Christ,' said Matt Savino, though he couldn't help noticing what fine voices all these shits had.

Aubrey, who had been surprising himself with his powers of organization all morning, now gathered the stewards and within seconds they had surrounded the Catholic hymn singers. At least they could keep the two groups apart.

Matt, bemused, sat down on one of the VIPs' padded chairs. He shook his head. He knew that the Troubles had nothing to do with religion, everybody he spoke to, politician and cleric alike, had always assured him of that. Not religious. Political. Colonial.

It was just that sometimes, like today for example, it was hard to remember that.

Aubrey was addressing the Catholic hymn singers, some of whom were still humming and all of whom stared at him suspiciously.

'I've a suggestion,' said Aubrey. 'Why don't we go down to Maguire's and all have a drink. It's early and you look frozen. Come on, it'll warm us all up, into the bus with you.'

17

God's in His heaven, all's right with the world.

Matt Savino surveyed Sherwin's field as Wellington might have done the field of battle on the eve of Waterloo.

The grass was green and level, the wind had dropped. The very sun had come out and hung now steady in the sky.

Matt Savino gave thanks.

Like lambs the dignitaries sat, gazing upwards in expectation. They had arrived late, delayed because of the police escort, and this delay had proved providential. There had been time to soothe the fears of the Belfast contingent, to calm them with liquor and reassuring words. There had been time to rejig the amplification system and to gather some Honey Fitz tapes. Honey's voice, it had been decided, would be a fitting antidote to the evangelicals. There had been time too to improvise a banner proclaiming Peace and Friendship.

The execution of this banner – black paint sloshed on several white sheets – had been less than perfect; the slogan had been plucked from the air but the whole thing served its purpose, which was to hide the placards of the evangelicals. The watching dignitaries may have seen a resemblance between the banner and Birnam Wood, for it kept moving, changing position, keeping pace with the agile placard holders on the other side of the hedge. Nobody laughed however, all sat expectant and full of good will.

Matt sighed his contentment. If only the sun shone every day, this island would find its problems solved.

Honey Fitz's voice began to throb in the air. Slightly distorted but retaining its sweetness, it drowned out the evangelical squawking and brought the field to quiet attention. Traders stopped counting their takings, small boys stopped shoving one another. Men and women raised their faces to listen to the voice. Everyone loved Honey, she was one of their own.

As was P.J. McGuckian, who entered the field now, arm in arm with his wife. Refusing a seat with the VIPs he went to stand among the locals. His daughter was to star in the pageant which was about to unfold.

Over Honey's voice a bull was heard to bellow.

O good bull. How thespian, how intelligent!

The stewards opened a gate and Annabel rode in on a tractor disguised as a war chariot. The tractor was driven by Seán, and Annabel stood behind him, resting a hand on his shoulder.

As a spectacle it should have been absurd. The tractor was covered in silver-painted cardboard, bits of which fell off on its progress across the field. Redundant cardboard spears, also painted silver, lay across its back. Annabel was dressed in a sort of ball gown made of some gauzy material and clinched around the waist by a diamanté belt; Seán's costume was simpler, a saffron-coloured shift which stopped at his knees.

The onlookers noticed none of this. What they saw riding across the field was the personification of youth, beauty and happiness. It was a public proclamation of love, of faith in the world and hope for the future.

Nobody in the field was unmoved. Annabel's lovely neck rose from the absurd folds of the dress, her eyes shone with happiness and pride; Seán drove steadily, a careful body servant to his queen. Joy crossed the field under the midday sun and a surge of emotion swelled the crowd.

Noreen thought, Oh she is lovely, and reached out to grasp P.J.'s hand. Aubrey thought, That's my sister. Annabel approached the dais and was handed on by Matt.

Now the bull came into sight, trotting along between two stewards. He looked mildly at the well-behaved crowd, unperturbed, even friendly. They had built a ramp for him and he seemed to know it, for he stepped on sedately, with no hesitation. He snorted slightly as one of the stewards sought to tie him to an iron post, then thinking better of it, settled once more. He was a fine brown bull, a noble bull, just, one imagined, like the ancient bull of Cuailgne.

Annabel smiled at him and all the world was gay.

Matt had decided that the proceedings should be simple and brief. He would make an introductory speech. Annabel would read a speech prepared for her by Matt and Aubrey and polished by Seán. In it she would explain that as she, Maeve, had been responsible for the death of the original bull of Cuailgne, she had come here today to make reparation and to offer this brown bull to the people of Ulster. She would then hand over the bull to the waiting Ulstermen. Canice O'Keeffe would make a speech about unity and forgiveness and past wrongs and hopes for the future. The Protestant archbishop would embrace the Catholic priest and the Miss O'Rafferty School of Dance would round off the proceedings by dancing a selection of Irish and Scottish reels. The inclusion of the Scottish reels had been Matt's idea, for Matt had had his eyes opened since he had embarked on his great project. It seemed a perfect method of showing the goddamn factions that if they were hung up on race, they were all the one race anyway: bad-tempered, intractable, goddamn Celts.

Sitting with the other VIPs Canice O'Keeffe wiped a tear from his eye as he watched Annabel. It had been an emotional day so far, being home again, listening to Honey's voice, being greeted with so much warmth by the men and women amongst whom he had grown up. And the symbolism of it all – oh the symbolism.

Canice had spent the journey down to Cavan sitting in the back of the Mercedes and marvelling at the wisdom of Bill O'Reilly. Canice had felt chastened too, for he had doubted this wisdom, had even for a disloyal moment wished that Bill was a more belligerent type of person who would get a move on and do something about the retrieval of that fourth green field.

In his journey across the Cavan potholes, wisdom, too, had come to Canice; he had seen that inactivity did not necessarily mean indifference, that gestures were important, that we must always make it plain to our Northern brothers that their eventual home was with the South but, like heaven, it might have to be delayed for a decade or two. In the meantime, the symbolism was important: keep our heads down and our hearts open and even the Unionists would come to realize that their destiny lay within a United Ireland.

Canice blew his nose and sat up straight. He closed his eyes and began to rehearse his speech, determined to do his bit for Ireland, determined to make the Chief proud of him.

For the last time Matt surveyed the field. The bull was in place, that wonderful girl looked every inch a queen, the clerics were still awake. He didn't much like the look of Minister O'Keeffe, he hoped the fellow wasn't going to be sick. (Canice had merely assumed his mask of inscrutability but Matt wasn't to know that.)

The Ulstermen were edging forward, their eyes glazed but steady enough on their feet; Matt could even admit that the presence of P.J. McGuckian added to the occasion, giving it an extra dimension, a glamour. On the other side of the hedge the evangelicals had fallen silent, either struck down by God or overcome by what they had witnessed.

Matt smiled, closed his eyes, opened them again. Perfection, he was looking at perfection.

At the best of times Hugh Sherwin was a bad-tempered man. Thin and red-nosed, he viewed the world with suspicion, believing, sometimes quite wrongly, that everyone was out to do him. He didn't like anyone very much but he reserved his bile especially for the Prods.

Now while he was sober Hugh Sherwin confined his misanthropy to the inside of his skull; but once he had drink taken he would roll up his sleeves and go looking for a fight.

Whiskey particularly had this effect on him: after drinking the first half glass, his face would grow fiery; with the second he would begin to grind his teeth. If at this stage he stopped he would do little harm, merely going home and beating his wife around a bit. If he continued to drink, however, he would wake up next morning in the small cage-like room reserved in the local Garda station for cases such as his.

Of late he had been cautiously avoiding getting drunk, at least in public, for he had been warned by the Garda sergeant that he would be charged and sent to gaol, a proper gaol up in Dublin, if he didn't mend his ways. This morning, however, the drink had been forced down his neck, first by the Yank and then by young McGuckian. Then he had had to do the decent thing and buy a round himself. At this stage he had blearily and lovingly focused his attention on his fellow drinkers from Belfast. Noting their innocent enjoyment, their obvious delight to be here at last in the free Ireland, he began to grind his teeth at the thought of those hoors in Ivan Lister's field.

Ivan Lister he particularly loathed. A bigot and a bad neighbour, he was forever complaining, forever blaming him for broken fences and straying, disease-carrying animals. A bloody planter, telling him what to do in his own country, running down his husbandry and his animals. But Hugh Sherwin hadn't thought that even Lister could sink as low as he had today. Those bigots singing of Jesus, their faces contorted in hatred, would stay with him for many a day. Sherwin stood up in the pub, blessed himself at the memory of the sacrilege and saluted the brave people of West Belfast. 'I'm off, lads, I'll see you in the field.'

Arriving home, he told his wife to shut up, slammed through the house and out to a disused piggery at the back. This building had become sacrosanct to him: here he retired for a bit of peace, to smoke and dream and recount his many woes. Now he took down a plastic-wrapped parcel and began to spread its contents on the floor. Fireworks. He had bought them in London last October when they had been on sale for Guy Fawkes Night. He had bought them as an act of defiance, not knowing when he would use them, only sure that they would not be set off to celebrate the death of a Catholic martyr. Talk about the Irish having long memories, what about the Brits?

Carefully he began to arrange the starlights and catherine wheels, and his hands stopped trembling, his colour grew less hectic and a dreamy expression came into his eyes. Today, he would do his bit for Ireland.

P.J. McGuckian felt the grass, spread his jacket and invited his wife to sit down beside him. 'Here, lean against me, you'll be more comfortable.'

He was glad the sun had come out for them; it meant too that he wasn't losing valuable fishing time. You would catch little under those brilliant skies.

He looked across at Annabel, his girl. She seemed to grow more beautiful by the hour and dear and funny and loving. Not given to reflection or self-analysis, P.J. knew just what unalloyed joy he felt when he saw her, heard her step.

She was smiling now, not at him but at that young lad. Fair enough, nothing wrong there. A decent enough young fellow and biddable. He would make a useful plaything for Annabel for the next year or so, after which he could be despatched. They would probably have grown tired of one another in any case by then; if not, well, every man had his price.

P.J. looked across the field at the clean young profile. A handsome lad and a decent lad but not suitable material as a husband for Annabel. He was the intellectual type who would reject the crudeness of a monetary bribe but P.J. knew a hundred and one other ways of choking a cat.

A fellowship in some mid-western university, for example; a handsome edition of his poems. No problem.

The sun was warm on his back. He moved Noreen to a more comfortable position against his shoulder and gave her waist a squeeze. A girl's waist still, slim and vulnerable.

He had to admit it – the Yank hadn't made a bad fist of things at all. He might invite a few of the VIPs back for a drink, poor old Canice looked as if he could do with one. And it might sort of mend fences with Aubrey. The lad seemed to have grown up overnight. P.J. had been watching him organizing things, calm and authoritative. Maybe when all this was over and the Yank had gone home he could be persuaded back into the firm. In the last week or two P.J. had begun to feel an increasing impatience with his business empire. It was time to let go, to spend more time with the girls and romp a bit in the sun. If he knew that Aubrey was there to step into his shoes, he would give it all up in the morning.

By God, Savino was outdoing himself in common sense today. Here he was, stepping down after a speech that had lasted no more than five minutes. P.J. knew from back-aching experience that such ramblings could go on for up to half an hour.

He was beckoning to Annie now, who stepped forward, raising her lovely neck and offering a smile that made the sun seem dim.

Her voice was clear and sweet as she began. 'When Queen Maeve of Connacht – '

She got no further as attention swivelled from her towards a sudden commotion at the edge of the field. Hugh Sherwin had chosen this moment to do his bit for Ireland.

Among the evangelicals the fireworks had begun to go off. They were shooting in all directions, their explosions sounding like machine-gun fire. Smoke rose and with it cries of lamentation and fury.

On the other side of the hedge the television men were the first to move and they began running towards the noise, dragging their equipment with them. Then fear broke out in the vulnerable breasts of the contingent from West Belfast and they too began to run. Within seconds the field was in chaos and the bull, surrounded by heaving, screaming humanity, took fright, kicked up its heels, broke free from its tether and tore down the ramp.

When the first explosions went off Annabel had dropped the sheet of paper on which Seán had written out her speech. It was as she bent to retrieve it that the bull kicked up its heels and in so doing caught Annabel a blow on the temple. She did not rise again to her feet.

It was said by some afterwards that it was a Fenian bull, a Papist bull. Why otherwise would it run straight for the evangelicals, towards the danger instead of away from it?

Whatever the truth of this it did indeed gallop a straight course towards the hedge, jump it and continue to thunder across Ivan Lister's field, a hymnbook impaled upon its left horn. It quietened down quickly however, and ten minutes later was docilely chewing grass when its former owner decided he had better, in the circumstances, take it home. It went without demur.

And P.J. McGuckian turned to his wife and asked, 'What's wrong with Annie?'

'I think she must have slipped,' Noreen replied.

'Let's go and get her out of this madhouse.'

They made their way through the crowd to collect her, calmly, unfearful, for they had seen the bull gallop off and disappear on the other side of the field.

Aubrey, too, was unaware of what had happened, for once the commotion broke out on the edge of the field he had gone in search of stewards to try and restore some order.

She was still smiling though lifeless when her parents found Annabel, gathered in Seán's arms. It had been a glancing kick, but a glancing kick from a half-ton bull was enough to fracture the skull of Annabel McGuckian.

18

Aubrey walked through the ruined city. He had been walking since morning, ranging through suburbs and city streets, through neighbourhoods that had been emptied and razed twenty years ago to make way for motorways which today still remained unbuilt. He had walked past Victorian houses of livid brick, past falling down regency villas, past crude modern buildings and shoddy pastiche terraces; past Meccano housing estates, elaborate vulgar pubs and triumphalist vulgar churches.

P.J. had laid his hand on the city but already time had begun to blur the outline of his fingerprints. Decay was going on apace as was progress. Buildings were being squeezed on to street corners in his absence whilst others were decaying without his will. Two months since P.J. had visited here and already there were new holes in the streets, new contours on the skyline.

Aubrey was back working for P.J., running things, keeping things ticking over until P.J. came back . . . if P.J. came back.

Strange to think of his father and feel only pity. A straw man.

And if P.J. was a straw man, he himself must surely be a hollow man. For years he had been fuelled by hatred and resentment; without them he felt as empty and ugly as a spent condom.

A straw man, a hollow man and a girl –

But he would not think about that.

He forced his eyes to look outwards once more, straightening his back, raising his head.

George's Street seemed derelict, shop after shop deserted, their plate-glass windows thick with dust. Here and there a few little brash, fly-by-night enterprises had opened up, selling cheap watches or doner kebabs. Despite their bright paint they had a fleeing, temporary air, a suggestion that they were waving good-bye even as they made their stand.

He turned into Dame Street and stopped before one of his own buildings. He crossed the road for a better view, shading his eyes from the sun.

It was one of his better modern buildings, now the headquarters of an international assurance company. It was simple, even spare, self-confident with good, clean lines. Nothing wrong with it in fact until you viewed it as part of the streetscape. Then its offensiveness and incongruity screamed at you.

When compared with the classically proportioned houses on either side, it appeared squat and heavy, although it was a good seven feet higher than any of the other buildings. This and the fact that it had been recessed to make room for a fountain, broke the line of the terrace so that one's eye was forced to return to it again and again, destroying the harmony of the whole and introducing a shrill note into what must have been a tranquil urban scene.

He sat down on a window-sill and stared across at his work. His was a mediocre talent, he knew that now, but that was no reason to sneer; all talent should surely be celebrated and mediocrity was what kept the world afloat. Original minds had always been in short supply and real creativity was a rare occurrence; nevertheless people got on with the job, using their limited talents to paint pictures, write books, compose music, giving pleasure to somebody along the way . . . the artistic world would be an echoing space if only works of genius saw the light of day.

Aubrey realized that this did not give him a licence to continue designing mediocre buildings, at least not with that brash and destructive belief in his own genius which he had indulged heretofore.

Architecture was different; among the arts, architecture was uniquely dangerous and powerful. Nobody forced Aubrey to read books or look at pictures and if he decided today to compose a concerto, no other concerto would have to be destroyed to make room for his.

But an existing building had been torn down to make room for the one which Aubrey had designed and which he was now looking at; people were forced to live in and work in and look at such buildings – they didn't have any choice.

And this important fact surely circumscribed the artistic freedom of the architect? Given that an architect of genius might not emerge in over fifty years, didn't the others, the necessary and important technicians, have a responsibility towards their fellow citizens? Lacking genius, it behoved an architect to cultivate manners. And ditch dogma.

The debate between modernism and traditionalism now seemed as bogus to Aubrey as his own pseudo-classical terraces, both sides carrying on their crusades with blind egotism, determined to force their abstract theories into the lives of their hapless fellow man, indifferent to all the implications which resulted.

Give the people what they wanted. The people at least had an affection for their city, what was left of it, and Aubrey saw this affection as a greater safeguard than unleashed egotism backed by limited talent.

He stood up, turning his back on his building. If only all his mistakes had been wrought in precast concrete.

Reaching the Quays, he turned in at a public house. He took his pint to a corner and stretched out his legs, overcome suddenly by weariness. He took a swallow, closed his eyes.

'Well, if it isn't the McGuckian cub.'

The man in front of him seemed vaguely familiar and very drunk. He swayed towards him, then collapsed on to the seat beside him, beathing into his face. Aubrey edged away.

'What takes you to this part of town, or have you come to join in the celebrations?' The man raised his glass and clashed it against Aubrey's. 'I'm celebrating my retirement – my enforced retirement I should say. Tell your old man that he'll have to deal with someone less civil next time he visits the Planning Offices – '

That was where he'd seen him of course – one of the officials in the Planning Office.

'I got the push. Could you believe it that Cathal fucking Morgan would get the push. Tell that to your old man and see if he believes it. Not that it matters a damn. This country is finished, finished I tell you, cub McGuckian.' He began to search through his pockets, finally producing a packet of cigarettes. He took out one, tore off the filter and stuck the smooth end into his mouth. He kept it there, puffing and screwing up his eyes against the smoke.

'Have you ever been to Vienna?' he asked, with apparent inconsequence. 'Lovely city but very depressing. Hellishly depressing because it's dead. Vienna died with the break-up of the Austro-Hungarian Empire and Dublin died when they passed the Act of Union. No parliament any more, no toffs – it used to be the second city of the Empire, used Dublin.'

He paused to concentrate on stubbing out his cigarette, mashing it viciously into the ashtray.

'I'm a Dub and I used to be proud of this city. But when I see what they've done to it, fucking peasants like your old man – and then they accused me of corruption. Jesus – I could tell you some tales . . .' His chin sank on to his chest.

Aubrey gave him a nudge so that he was resting at a more secure angle against the back of the chair. What would Matt Savino make of him, he wondered.

New Ireland, old Ireland, Ireland unfree, Ireland ugly. Did any of it really matter?

And the Parthenon had been built by slaves and the cathedral at Chartres by serfs.

He would continue to design buildings because that is what he had been trained to do. He would remember his manners and try not to give offence . . . where he did, time would take care of it. He didn't know if his detachment was a sign of a new maturity or a symptom of depression. He only knew that he must go on.

Standing up, he turned and began to make his way once more on to the streets.

In their bungalow in Kerry P.J. and Noreen endured. They had come here after the funeral because it was a house without associations, a house where Annabel had never slept. Because it had been so little lived in, it had a raw feel and a persistent dankness hung upon it, despite the sun which shone so generously in the autumn sky outside.

Noreen kept house, made meals, swept the floors, cycled the two miles to the village for supplies. P.J. got the milk from a neighbouring farmer, went to the well for spring water, brought in the turf from the shed to feed the fire, which they kept going most of the time.

It was very like the sort of life they had led as children and like children their responsibilities extended only to these daily tasks.

Throughout the day and night they talked to one another in snatches – about the weather and the sweetness of the water and whether Noreen needed a better lamp for her bike now that the evenings were beginning to draw in. During the night they took it in turns to rise and make a pot of tea: at two and at four and again at six.

In spite of this mutual civility, however, they had become blind to one another, sealed in their individual sorrow so that kind words and tender gestures had become empty, perfunctory.

If they wept they did not allow the other to see it. They held themselves erect and their faces rigidly bland. They did not switch on the radio and they did not buy newspapers. Instinctively they protected their wounds, careful that nothing would touch them.

Noreen's sight would be restored. She would emerge eventually from her pain and look to her husband and her son and busy what was left of her life in little acts of kindness. She might even learn to smile again. Perhaps one day there would be grandchildren.

P.J. had only his courage, a redundant virtue now that the worst had happened. Courage suggests life and life suggests hope, but P.J. seemed to have travelled some distance beyond this point.

Mortally wounded, he blundered and bumped into gates and walls and trees, deserted by grace as he had been so cruelly by luck.

Like the great brown bull of Cuailgne who had carried its death wound, who had ranged around Ireland unable or unwilling to die, P.J. wandered the Kerry hills, his blind eyes showing not so much pain as puzzlement.

Like the great bull of Cuailgne he bellowed at the empty hills, so that now local children scattered when they saw him coming and their parents warned them against the poor madman who had come to live amongst them.

P.J. felt his pain through every inch of his huge body. His eyes smarted, his head ached, his legs, when he moved them, felt as if the bones had been crushed. At night when he lay wakeful it seemed as if his body was in a fire; sometimes he imagined he could even get a whiff of charred flesh as he lay in the darkness.

He doesn't think, he feels. When the pain subsides a little, anger rushes in. He has stood on the Kerry hills and cursed out loud – his son, Matt Savino, God. Sometimes he is brought to a halt in his rambling and stops as his darling appears before his eyes. When he stretches out to touch her she is gone and then the pain is even worse. Once after such a visitation, he has found vomit coming from his mouth, falling on the ground in a bitter stream of bile, falling on the very spot where her little feet had stood.

The bull of Cuailgne, carrying its death wound, found it hard to die and P.J. McGuckian will find it hard also . . . only with P.J. it will take longer.

It will take P.J. many years to die.

In more northerly parts of Ireland it has not been a good autumn. In Cavan it has been raining practically every day for a month. The farmers don't mind for the harvest is saved and the fishermen who still sport on the lakes are delighted. Everyone is agreed that in this part of the country it has been a record year for tourism . . . despite some bad publicity in the middle of the summer.

It is raining again over Lough Eannach and a nasty wind is whipping up. The boards of P.J. McGuckian's house have whitened, like the bones of some animal, and already there is an air of dereliction about the place. The only one who ever goes anywhere near it is a young fellow from the village. He can be found there at some time every day. From the other side of the lake people have watched him, circling the house, coming out to stand at the struts of the boathouse, to touch the yellow swimsuit that hangs from the struts. Although it has been hanging there for more than two months, its manmade fibres have kept their elasticity and vivid colour.

And sometimes when the wind fills it out and lifts it, it looks for all the world like a young girl's body, dancing in the breeze.

A NOTE ON THE AUTHOR

All Fall Down is Ita Daly's fourth novel.
She lives in Dublin.